A shadow moved on the balcony

Josy didn't hesitate. She ran, stumbling, to the connecting door.

"Adam!" she cried. The balcony door slid open with a grating sound.

Her scream choked to a sob of relief as the entering shadow called her name. "Josy?" Adam crossed the room and pulled her against him.

She swallowed, struggling for words, fighting the unexpected sensation of being held so protectively. "I thought...someone was...I didn't realize it was you. On the balcony."

"It's okay. You're safe here. No one can get to you now." He stroked her back in a gentle caress.

Josy's pulse beat a ragged tattoo in her throat. He was incredibly strong—yet his hands were gentle. She knew she was safe in his arms.

He released her, and she stepped away. "You should be asleep. We'll...talk in the morning, when we're both able to think clearly, okay?"

Josy knew he was right. It was too late for her questions, and she wasn't sure she wanted to hear the answers. Except for one.

How had she lived for weeks with this man, as his wife, and remained a virgin?

Dear Reader,

You've told us that you love amnesia stories—and in response we've created a program just for these incredibly romantic, emotional reads. *A Memory Away*—from danger, from passion... from love!

An older sister to six brothers and a mother of two sons, Dani Sinclair came up with the idea for THE MAN SHE MARRIED when she began wondering how a man would cope in the minority role in the household. She gave her hero three goddaughters to protect, and a missing wife to track down—a wife who doesn't remember him. Adam lived up to all her expectations!

We hope you enjoy this and all the special amnesia books in the *A Memory Away* program.

Sincerely,

Debra Matteucci
Senior Editor & Editorial Coordinator
Harlequin Books
300 East 42nd St.
New York, NY 10017

The Man She Married
Dani Sinclair

TORONTO • NEW YORK • LONDON
AMSTERDAM • PARIS • SYDNEY • HAMBURG
STOCKHOLM • ATHENS • TOKYO • MILAN • MADRID
PRAGUE • WARSAW • BUDAPEST • AUCKLAND

In memory of my father, Edward J. Shaughnessy,
who encouraged my love of a good mystery.
Wish you could see me now, Dad.
And always, for Roger, Chip, Dan and Barb, with many
thanks to Natashya Wilson, Robyn Amos
and Mary McGowan.

ISBN 0-373-22507-5

THE MAN SHE MARRIED

Copyright © 1999 by Patricia A. Gagne

Printed in U.S.A.

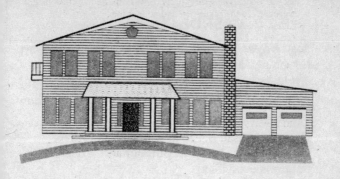

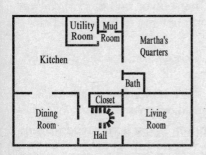

Main Floor

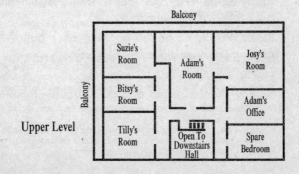

Upper Level

CAST OF CHARACTERS

Josy Hayes—A killer from her past doesn't believe her amnesia is permanent.

Adam Ryser—To keep his three goddaughters, he married Josy. Could the five of them be more than a temporary family?

Eleanor Claussen—She's determined to get custody of her three granddaughters—because image is everything.

Hank Claussen—The senator isn't fond of children or dogs, but will do anything to please his rich wife.

Martha Karp—The housekeeper won't go out of her way to help Josy.

Brug Matthews—The flirtatious foreman is *always* on hand when something goes wrong.

Enrique Pandergarten—Why is a Nevada casino owner involved in Wyoming politics?

Kathy Smith—No one's heard from Josy's mother since Josy's disappearance.

Mark Wilson—Is he just another ranch hand?

Bitsy, Suzie and Tilly—The three girls crave a mother's touch.

Killer—Where Suzie's dog goes, trouble follows.

Prologue

"Dolly! My dolly!"

Adam and Josy shared an exasperated look over the heads of the three children. Josy shook her head in amusement.

"You finish getting them settled in the car," she told him. "I'll go back inside the restaurant for the doll."

"Dolly," Bitsy said, nodding for emphasis.

"Okay, sweetie, I'll get her." She ruffled the child's pale blond hair lovingly and turned back toward the hotel restaurant.

Adam watched the gentle sway of her hips for a moment before he bent over to supervise the belting in of the three little girls in the back seat of the rental car. Children should come with instruction manuals—and fidget controls. He grinned as he climbed behind the steering wheel, feeling truly at ease for the first time since he'd learned that his best friend, Chad, and his wife had died.

Everything was working out far better than he'd ever imagined when he impulsively asked Josy to marry him and become surrogate mother to the three orphans.

His pulse tripped a little faster as he thought about last night and what would have happened if Bitsy hadn't come stumbling into their room, frightened by the storm over-head.

Adam shifted as his body reacted to the memory of the way Josy had molded against him. He tried to concentrate on the promise of her words this morning instead of the promise of her body last night.

He was amazed that he'd exposed his heart to the mercy of another woman. Yet here he sat, daring to believe in happily-ever-after once again. Adam smiled.

He'd never expected all of them to forge such strong bonds so quickly. He knew children were resilient, but it still surprised him how fast the girls had warmed to Josy. Especially three-year-old Bitsy. The little girl had become Josy's shadow, hardly letting her out of sight. Josy was a natural with the kids.

She was pretty good with him, too, he thought wryly. He hadn't anticipated liking her at all when he'd proposed this marriage of convenience. It hadn't mattered then. It mattered a whole lot now.

"Would you consider making this a real marriage, Josy?" he'd asked her this morning as they'd been packing to leave.

Her features had softened as she gazed at him.

"This is a real marriage, Adam."

Words of love had gone unspoken when Tilly inter-rupted.

Taking his new family on this combination honeymoon and business trip had been a good decision, he concluded. The girls were coming to terms with the deaths of their parents while finding security in this new alliance. Hope-fully, that would get them through the troubles he knew lay just ahead.

"Where's Aunt Josy?" Tilly asked, her grave six-year-old eyes looking worried.

"Yeah? What's taking her so long?" Suzie squirmed in her seat, straining to see the door of the restaurant.

Adam frowned and glanced at his watch. The girls were right. Josy should have been back by now. He curbed his annoyance, knowing he was just impatient to get going even though the park was only a ten-minute drive away. The girls were looking forward to spending the day at Sea World. So was he.

"Maybe she stopped to go to the bathroom," he suggested.

"No, Uncle Adam, she already went," Tilly protested.

"Well, she'll be back any second," he assured them. But the seconds ticked away, turning to minutes. The girls went from fidgeting to fussing irritably with each other inside the warm car. Adam felt irritated, as well, and vaguely uneasy. Watching the boats in the busy harbor across the street was no longer entertaining for any of them.

Where was Josy?

"Stop touching me!" Tilly demanded of her younger sister.

"I didn't touch you," Suzie protested, giving her sister a slight shove.

"I want Dolly!" Bitsy whined fretfully.

"When's Aunt Josy coming back?" Tilly asked, giving Suzie a reciprocal shove.

Thoroughly exasperated now, Adam unfastened his seat belt. He felt every bit as edgy as the girls. Josy had been gone long enough to create an entirely new doll from scratch. What was she doing in there? He scanned the busy parking lot, looking for her distinctive honey blond ponytail.

"Maybe she can't find it," Suzie said.

Bitsy immediately began to whine. "I want Dolly."

Adam's annoyance faded as a building sense of unease

took its place. Josy should have been back by now. Maybe something she ate this morning hadn't agreed with her.

He studied the busy parking lot. Anxiety churned his breakfast into an uncomfortable knot in the pit of his stomach. He watched a hotel shuttle bus pull into the turnaround, momentarily blocking his view of the restaurant.

Josy *would* have been back by now unless something was wrong.

"I want Josy," Suzie announced, her lower lip trembling as she rubbed at the arm her sister had hit.

Adam bit back a *Me, too* and opened the car door. "Come on. Let's go inside and find her. Maybe Dolly got dirty and Josy had to clean her off."

He only hoped that was true.

As if picking up on his growing concern, the girls were oddly subdued when he urged them from the car and into the warm sunshine. Bitsy clung to his hand, seeking security.

Had it only been minutes ago that he'd been basking in contentment?

The restaurant was even busier than before, but the hostess smiled in recognition as they entered.

"Missing something?" she asked. "I thought you'd be back for this." She held out Bitsy's stuffed rag doll. The little girl accepted it shyly, hugging it tight against her body.

"The waitress spotted it right after you left and brought it over to me. I was pretty sure you'd miss it and come back."

"Where's Aunt Josy?" Tilly asked.

Adam's gut tightened as his gaze swept the lobby and the breakfast bar to the left. Josy was nowhere in sight. The first real traces of fear gnawed at his stomach. "Have you seen my wife?"

Josy must have taken sick after all.

"Your wife? Uh, no, sir."

Suzie broke away and darted down the three steps into the dining area. "Aunt Josy?"

Her fearful call wasn't lost on her younger sister. Bitsy began to whimper. "I want Aunt Josy."

"Suzie, get back here! Tilly, hold on to Bitsy while I grab your sister." But Bitsy clung to his pant leg and wouldn't let go. Her whimpers became tears.

"I want Aunt Josy!"

The pretty young hostess appeared flustered. "Uh, sir?"

"Suzie, get back here!"

Suzie ignored him. While the restaurant was busy, it wasn't all that large. Adam uncurled Bitsy's fingers and handed her to Tilly. He stepped forward to rake the dining room with a glance. Another family now sat in the rounded booth where they'd eaten breakfast. Suzie was berating the startled group, demanding to know what they'd done with her aunt Josy.

Adam hurried forward to claim his feisty goddaughter. "I'm sorry. We had breakfast at this table, and our youngest left her doll here." He was babbling, but he couldn't stem the flow of words. "My wife came in to get the doll and now she seems to have disappeared."

Disappeared.

The word echoed with icy hollowness in his head.

Is that what she had done? Had Josy disappeared?

No. There had to be an explanation. Adam tamped down his growing alarm. Josy wouldn't walk off and leave them without an explanation. Not after last night.

He spoke as he continued to scan the room. "Did you see a blond woman come in here a few minutes ago? Her hair was in a long ponytail. She's about this tall." He indicated the top of his chin, trying desperately to remember what Josy had been wearing this morning. He hadn't been looking at her clothing. "I think she had on white pants with a navy shirt. There was some sort of stripe down one side."

"White and green," Tilly said at his elbow.

His gaze dropped to find all three children crowded beside him. Fear hovered in Tilly's eyes. Bitsy had stopped crying, but she appeared ready to resume her efforts at the least provocation. The hostess stood a few paces behind them, looking seriously alarmed while their waitress came forward curiously.

"My wife came in after the doll several minutes ago," Adam said tightly. Anxiety gnawed at his gut. "Would someone mind checking the ladies' room for me? She might have taken ill or something."

She must be ill. She wouldn't just disappear. Where would she go?

Why would she go?

"Of course, sir. If you and the children will just come back out to the lobby…?"

Adam realized that the occupants of the restaurant were taking in the scene with avid curiosity. If anyone had seen Josy, they weren't jumping up to say so.

She had to be in the rest room. She had to be!

Tilly edged closer to his side. In fact, all three girls gathered tightly around him as they stood in the lobby waiting for the waitress to return from the ladies' room. Bitsy squeezed the doll against her small chest, her expression wide and frightened.

He mustn't scare the kids. Josy had to be here someplace. They'd turned in their key cards before breakfast, so she couldn't have gone back up to the room. There must be a reasonable explanation. Her clothes were in the car. She wouldn't walk off and leave them.

But as soon as he saw the expression on the waitress's round face, he knew Josy wasn't inside the ladies' room.

"Sir, there's no one in there. Maybe your wife's waiting for you outside."

The suspended fear exploded in his chest. All too vividly, he pictured Josy as he'd first seen her, pressed against a dirty brick wall, two toughs confronting her with harsh words and eager fists.

No!

He'd paid off her mother's gambling debts. There was no reason for those Reno hoods to come after her now. No reason at all for them to track Josy down the coast to San Diego.

Unless her mother had gotten into more trouble.

Unless Josy hadn't told him everything.

Adam tried to shake off that last thought, but what did he really know about the woman who was his wife? Nothing beyond what she had told him.

What if she'd lied?

Icy shards of uncertainty chilled his blood. Could he have misjudged her as badly as he had his first wife?

No. He wouldn't think that way. Even if he'd misread her this morning, Josy was nothing like Alyssa. Josy wouldn't walk away. She wouldn't do that to the girls. She was genuinely fond of the children.

One of them made a fretful sound. He rested his hand on a silky head. "I think we'd better call the police."

The words forced their way past his lips. The hostess stared at him in shock.

"Let me get my manager, sir."

Anger suddenly added to the mix of feelings consuming him. How could Josy disappear like this?

"Do that," he snapped at the hostess, more harshly than he'd intended.

If Josy thought she could walk out on them, she'd better think again. They had a deal. If she didn't want to stay with him forever, fine. But she knew how important this marriage was to him right now.

"Uncle Adam?"

He looked into Tilly's earnest, upturned face.

"Did Aunt Josy go away like Mommy and Daddy?"

His chest felt unbearably tight as he looked into those sad, frightened eyes. He dropped to his knee. The burning sensation behind his own eyes made it hard to see for a minute. He drew all three girls against him, trying to think past his fear.

Three small faces stared at him expectantly, waiting for him to make their world right again. Adam tried to swallow and found his throat achingly tight.

"It's okay." His voice sounded scratchy even to him. "Everything's going to be okay."

"But where is she, Uncle Adam?"

"I don't know, Suze," he found himself responding. "I just don't know."

He'd thought he'd learned a lot about the sort of person Josy was, living with her for the past two weeks. She seemed fiercely loyal to those she cared about. Look how she'd stepped in to take care of her mother's trouble in Reno.

Or had that story been a lie?

Adam didn't want to believe Josy had lied to him about anything. But reluctantly, he realized how little she had actually told him. He didn't even know where she was from. If she had decided to take off, he was going to have a heck of a job tracking her down.

No. He refused to believe she'd run off. She hadn't given him any personal information because he hadn't bothered to ask for any. She was a listener, not a talker.

Why hadn't he asked more questions?

He lifted Bitsy in his arms and stood. She nestled her tear-streaked face against his neck, hiccuping softly.

Josy cared about the girls. She cared about him. They'd nearly made love last night. If it hadn't been for Bitsy...

Was that why she'd disappeared? Had Josy reconsidered their relationship over breakfast and decided he was demanding too much? Was it better to believe she'd left involuntarily, or that she walked away because he nearly broke his promise to keep the relationship platonic?

"Uncle Adam?"

He looked into Suzie's small, frightened face. Bitsy gave in to another bout of crying. Tilly stared at him through eyes that were much too old for her six-year-old face.

"Maybe she got run over by a car," Suzie suggested.

Bitsy began to wail in earnest.

"Excuse me, sir. I'm Matt Consegra with hotel security. What seems to be the problem?"

Bewildered, angry and nearly as scared as the girls, Adam looked into the face of the serious young man and took a firm grip on his emotions. He drew in a deep, steadying breath. Wherever Josy was, he had three small children to think about. It was up to him to stay calm and in control despite every instinct that urged him to storm through the hotel searching until he found her.

He tried to fasten on the anger to keep his sense of betrayal and fear at bay.

"I think we need to call the police. My wife seems to have disappeared."

Chapter One

So she *had* walked out on them.

Adam's emotions writhed in the cauldron of his mind. He felt betrayed. For the past year and a half, he'd had men combing California, Nevada, even Mexico. And all this time, Josy had been only three hours away. Anger bubbled to the surface as he stared at the sheriff's pleated face.

"You're telling me this woman you call Josy Hayes really has amnesia?"

"Nope." The sheriff leaned back in his creaking chair observing Adam with eyes that missed little. "I'm telling you that a whole bunch of doctors told me that the woman we *named* Josy Hayes has amnesia. That fall she took left all kinds of damage behind. The amnesia's the least of it."

Not to Adam. If Josy didn't remember the past, he could go into court on Thursday and lose his best friend's children. And the sheriff expected him to buy into this crazy tale?

"If this is the Josy I'm looking for, how'd she get here?"

"I was sorta hopin' you could tell me," the sheriff stated calmly.

But despite his calm, Adam knew the sheriff was considering possibilities. He'd looked at the wedding picture, then looked hard at Adam. Did he think Josy had run because he'd abused her?

Adam tensed. How could he explain that he'd simply picked badly again and Josy had run off—just like his first wife. If Josy had been kidnapped, as he'd half wanted to believe, then she wouldn't have been found hiking on some mountain, three states and hundreds of miles away from where she'd disappeared.

"And this missing memory…it isn't coming back?"

The sheriff shrugged. "From what I understand, she gets flashes of things every now and again, but that's about it. The doctors say she suffered enormous trauma to the head. It's a miracle she's alive at all. They don't hold out much hope that she'll ever remember much more than she does right now."

A deputy gave a sharp rap on the office door and stepped inside bearing a sheaf of papers. The sheriff picked up the top one and studied it a moment, looking from it to Adam.

"Looks like you're exactly who you say you are, Mr. Ryser." He set down the faxed picture of Adam and scanned the text on the following sheet.

Adam wasn't concerned about information on himself. What he wanted—what he needed—was information on the woman calling herself Josy Hayes.

"Well, now," the sheriff said finally, "you've got impeccable references and a decent reputation. Looks like everything is in order." He tapped the desk with a gnarled finger, then stood abruptly. "Come on. I'll take you over to the shop and introduce you to your wife."

"JOSY HAYES?"

Josy lifted her head to stare at the imposing stranger standing before the counter. There was no way this large, solid man had come here to do ceramics. From his cowboy hat and heavy parka to his dark jeans tucked into working boots, the man was as out of place as any man could be.

His features were too harsh for handsome, but his body was too masculine to be anything else. A chill drifted up her spine as she met his penetrating stare. The shop was isolated at this time of night.

"Who wants to know?" she demanded, unintentionally belligerent to offset her sudden trepidation. Who was this man? How did he know her name? The shop was nearly empty. Only young Seth was in back.

The stranger studied her. Josy tried not to squirm beneath that stare. He made her all too aware that her sweater was too snug and the slacks molded a bit too closely to her skinny frame. Well, it wasn't like she had a lot of choice in the matter. Until now, no one had ever seemed to notice the fit of her secondhand clothes. Including her.

"You gonna pretend you've never seen me before?"

She frowned under the lash of his angry words and planted her hands on her hips, desperately trying to remember being introduced to him. Her short-term memory was far from reliable, but everyone in town understood. Why was he so angry?

Well, she wasn't about to let him intimidate her.

"I don't have to pretend," she told him. "You got a name, mister?"

"Adam," he snapped, waiting for a response, his dark brown eyes missing nothing.

Her hands left her hips under that penetrating stare. She brushed at a spot of dust on her forehead. His eyes followed that gesture, no doubt noticing the fine tremor of her hand. Heck, she could feel it shake. Her entire body wanted to shake as he stared at her. She wasn't afraid, exactly. Maybe she should be, but mostly she felt confused by his anger and by the odd tingle of awareness that jangled her nerve endings. Who was this disturbing man?

"Can I help you fi—?" she began, but he cut her short.

"Adam Ryser?" he said, as if he questioned her memory and her sanity, as well.

Well, everyone else questioned those things—herself included. Being an amnesia victim was a trial.

Abruptly, excitement stole over her. Could this stranger possibly be from her past? Was that why he was looking at her like that? She stared hard, searching for anything the least bit familiar about his stony features. Surely she'd remember a striking man like this one.

"How do you know me?" she asked.

He rocked back on his heels. "I'm your husband."

Ice dredged her mind, followed by a searing heat that covered her entire body.

"No!"

The doctor's words echoed in her head. *I'm sorry to say that one of the necessary procedures we performed destroyed your hymen.*

Whoever this man was, he could not have been her husband. At least, not in the biblical sense.

"Hey, Josy! Did you see the cool...?" Seth's words trailed away as he came to stand a few feet from her. His pimply face went from her to the stranger and back again. All his youthful exuberance disappeared.

"Everything okay?" he asked. His reedy thin voice broke, to his shame, she knew. Josy tried to smile in reassurance but couldn't make her lips obey.

"Go on in back, Seth," she said.

He hesitated, filled with indecision.

The man gave an abrupt jerk of his head toward the pouring room as if to spur the youth into obeying.

"Oh, jeez. You aren't gonna rob us, are you? Oh, jeez. My ma'll never let me work after school again."

Josy reached out to touch Seth's arm. He'd managed to cover it in muddy slip again. "He's not going to rob us, Seth." And then, fighting the excess of adrenaline pounding through her, she tipped her head back in the stranger's direction. "Isn't that right?"

"Yes."

"There, see?"

"We need to go somewhere and talk," the stranger demanded.

Flustered, Josy stared at him. Go with him? She wasn't going anywhere with this demanding stranger, no matter how attracted she was. Who was he? Not her husband—that's for sure. So why was he here? Questions threatened to spill past her lips, but Seth's nervous presence kept them at bay.

"I don't think so."

The man calling himself Adam Ryser pushed back his hat with a flick of his thumb. It was a large thumb on a large hand, in keeping with the rest of his size. All of his parts were large, she decided, but she couldn't help noticing that they were packaged to make a woman remember why it was so exciting to be a female.

"Oh, jeez," Seth whispered again. His fists opened and closed impotently at his sides.

Looking up at the imposing man made her neck stiff, but looking away was impossible. He filled the cluttered store, reducing the shelves of green-ware and bisque to insignificant background. She needed to curb her straying thoughts and start thinking rationally again.

"Seth, I think you'd better call the sheriff."

"Do that, Seth," the stranger drawled. "I just came from

talking with Sheriff Malcolm. He was on his way over here with me when he got an emergency call.''

He'd talked with the sheriff? She stared at his face, trying desperately to remember something—anything—about this man. But nothing filled the aching gaps. He continued to regard her with impassive detachment.

Well, heck. No matter who he was, he didn't have to come in here all big and threatening, making her feel all sorts of things she had no business feeling.

''I find it real hard to believe I married someone who enjoys scaring women and children,'' she stated with a calm she didn't possess.

For a moment, he looked nonplussed. Then he glanced at Seth, who was practically wringing his hands in helpless agitation. A little of the hardness seeped from his expression.

''I apologize,'' he said grudgingly. ''I didn't mean to come on so strong. I don't have much time, and we need to talk right away.''

Fear and longing blended. This intimidating stranger might actually have answers to the millions of questions that plagued her dreams night after night. Only, why had he appeared now, after all this time? And why pretend to be her husband?

But what really rankled was his statement that he didn't have much time. His audacity kept her tongue sharp while her mind cried for answers.

''Too bad you didn't feel that way eighteen months ago.''

Her acerbic statement seemed to shock him. Good. Her memory might be faulty, but she hadn't forgotten how to stand her ground, even though she wanted nothing more than to send Seth home, lock the door and question Adam Ryser until she was completely satisfied.

"Go over to the diner down the street and I'll meet you there after I close," she told him.

"I'm not going anywhere," he said softly.

"Oh, jeez," Seth repeated.

Josy rounded on the boy. "Go finish cleaning up back there. We're leaving on time tonight. Are all the molds open?"

Seth gulped and nodded.

"Okay. Put the tools away and get washed up." She sent Seth a glare that started him moving, and turned back to Adam. "I can't talk to you right now. I have work to do. I can either meet you at the diner or the sheriff's office just as soon as I close."

"I'll wait."

Josy debated her options, then, seeing no way to enforce her request, she turned back to the paint shelf and the inventory list. No matter what answers Adam Ryser had for her, she must remember that he'd already lied. He was *not* her husband.

Unless she'd been a virgin bride.

No way. Not with that man for a husband. She ignored the tingle low in her belly and put that thought from her firmly.

But she was totally aware when Adam Ryser—or whoever he really was—stepped away from the counter. Josy nearly surrendered to the urge to take a deep breath. Part of her clamored to ask questions and demand answers. The other part was scared spitless on a visceral level she didn't want to examine.

Ten minutes later, Seth crept out front, his arms clean and damp, the slip gone from his cheek and forehead as well.

"Is he—" his eyes darted around the room, coming to

land squarely on the stranger sitting silently at one of the worktables ''—gone?'' he finished weakly.

''No.''

Adam merely inclined his head.

''What are we going to do?'' Seth whispered.

A simmering anger at the stranger's presumptuousness warred with the host of questions she had for him.

''We're going to lock up,'' she told Seth firmly. ''If Mr. Ryser wants to spend the night sitting in here by himself, I'm certainly not going to argue. But once the heat is turned off, he'll get pretty cold despite his heavy coat.''

Brave words, but she couldn't control the pounding of her heart or the way her fingers trembled. And she didn't dare look at the man to see what effect her words had.

Josy limped to the office to snatch up her worn coat and snow boots. Like the coat, the boots were a size and a half too large, but at least they were warm, and at the moment, she needed all the warmth she could get.

Husband. The mere word rocked her precarious world on its head. Why had he made such a claim?

His sexy low voice rumbled over her shoulder. ''What happened to your leg?''

She spun and nearly fell as the leg in question buckled. He caught her with those large hands. Hands that could crush and hurt, but only gently steadied her instead. Her body came alive beneath that touch with a riot of disturbing sensations. She should be terrified—and she was—but not for the right reason.

''It broke,'' she told him succinctly. She gazed down at the hand that still held her. Almost reluctantly, he let her go. His eyes were troubled.

''Can't they fix it?''

''They did. I still have it, don't I?'' She'd come terrifyingly close to losing that leg.

Shocked, he stared at her face, examining the healing scars that traced faint lines across her once smooth skin.

At least, the doctors assured her that the skin had once been smooth and blemish free. She didn't remember, and frankly, she no longer worried about a past she couldn't envision. She was alive when she should have been dead. The past was just that. And maybe just as well if it held a man as devastating to her senses as this one.

"Uh, Josy?"

She looked past Adam Ryser to see Seth hovering in the doorway. His coat and boots were on, and he was tugging at a pair of gloves.

"Everything's okay, Seth."

"But, uh, I mean—"

"Don't worry, kid. The last thing I would do is hurt her," Adam promised. His voice was gentle, a low, mellow rumble that soothed now, rather than frightened. "The sheriff knows I'm here. Josy and I have some talking to do."

"Are you really her husband?"

"Yeah. I am."

"Oh. Well. That's good." Seth smiled in relief. "I mean...nobody claimed her and...it's been hard for her, you know? She's a terrific lady." He beamed at Josy, who managed a weak smile in response.

Adam simply tipped his head.

"Good night, Seth," she said firmly.

"Oh...yeah. Good night. Will I...see you tomorrow?"

"Of course," she replied.

At the same time, Adam shook his head. "No."

They glared at one another. Seth shifted uncomfortably. "Uh, well..."

"Good night, Seth," she said again.

"Nice meetin' you kid. Thanks for looking after my wife for me."

"Sure. Okay. Good night." He practically flew out the door.

"I am not your wife," she stated.

"You are according to the state of Nevada."

She swallowed her protest. "Is that where I'm from?"

He tipped his head, regarding her. "You really don't remember? The amnesia's real?" He sounded as if he'd just come to grips with a foreign concept.

Anger washed through her. "You think this is some sort of game? Try it." She aimed a finger at his chest. "Try not remembering more than bits and pieces of your life. Try laying in some hospital bed wondering if you're going to die all alone without the slightest idea what you've done to deserve such a fate. Try thinking you are so unimportant in the eyes of the world that no one even cares enough to come looking for you."

She had to swallow hard to keep the bitterness in check. "If you're really my husband, then where have you been this past year and a half?"

Pain came and went in his dark eyes. "I've been taking care of the children."

AS ADAM WAITED for her to lock up, he peered around at the darkness uneasily. Nothing moved on the deserted streets. Still, he couldn't shake the feeling that they were being watched.

When Josy started down the street, his attention was caught by her limping gait. He couldn't take it in. If it weren't for her spunky attitude and the husky contralto of a voice he'd heard over and over in his dreams, he would have sworn this was not the woman he'd married.

Oh, her size was right, and her hair color; even the general shape of her face was the same. And who could forget those stormy gray eyes? But her features were subtly altered, and the crisscross lines of scars bore testament to the restoration work of a skilled surgeon. Never a large woman, Josy was nothing but skin and bones now.

"Don't you ever eat?" he asked irritably.

She paused to glare up at him. "When I can afford to."

Her words punched the air from his lungs. Pain, raw and wrenching, tore at his gut. She was his wife and she'd been going hungry.

There was no trace of self-pity in her words or on her face. Only the fierce independence he'd admired from the moment he'd fished her out of that back alley and away from the two toughs who'd been sent to scare her.

"Tell me what you remember," he said kindly, trying to control the staggering guilt that battered his mind.

Josy started walking again. "How many days in a week, the names for everyday items, how to—"

"Josy—"

"You think I'm kidding? You think all the experts for miles around haven't tried pulling memories from me? They're gone, Mr. Ryser." She threw up her hands. "Poof. Just like that. The doctors don't think they'll come back either. So if you're going to claim to be my husband, the burden of proof is all on you. And so are the bills."

She peered up at him. "I've got lots of bills. Thousands of them. And not a prayer of paying them all back if I live to be eighty."

She stopped walking as they came abreast of the diner's small parking lot. Her gray eyes fastened on him, demanding answers.

"I work days at the hospital to reduce some of the debt and nights at the Britchers' ceramic store for food and rent. Believe me, the health-care industry in the state of Colorado will be delighted to learn I have a husband. Particularly if you have money and insurance. Do you?"

Déjà vu. He nearly smiled at her belligerence. This was his Josy, all right. She'd stand toe-to-toe with the devil himself. She'd probably win, too. If she hoped to drive him off with threats of large debts, then she really didn't remember her past. And he no longer doubted the truth of her amnesia.

She'd been through so much. The knowledge tore at him, and that irrefutable fact softened his next words.

"I'm sorry, Josy."

And he was. For so many things. He'd come to town, desperate, but afraid to hope. When he first saw her looking so at ease inside that store, anger had settled like a mole in his gut. All he could think about was the way she'd left him and the girls to the mercy of the courts. Now his selfish thoughts haunted him, and he grimaced.

She tilted her head to one side. "No money?"

His lips twitched. "Your bills will be taken care of." More seriously, he added, "I'm sorry you suffered alone."

Josy straightened in obvious disbelief. "Really?"

"Yes."

Stormy eyes focused on his face. "Okay. Tell me something—who's taking care of my children?"

Her words lashed out at him, making him blink in surprise. "You don't have any children."

"Well, finally. The man says something I know to be true."

He stared at her intently. "How?"

"The doctors. There isn't a single part of this body they haven't inspected and dissected. I've never borne a child, never even had intercourse with a man. I know good and well I'm nobody's mother."

Her words left him stunned. She'd never been with a man? He vividly remembered their last night together. The hauntingly sweet way she'd trembled as she came into his arms. She'd been a virgin?

A blush stole across her fair skin while her eyes stubbornly remained fixed on his face.

"Maybe not in the biblical sense," he agreed softly, "but you're my wife, Josy. And when the adoption goes through on Thursday, you'll be the mother of three daughters. We had a deal, you and I. A marriage of convenience. I paid off your mother's gambling debts, and you married me to help me gain custody of the girls."

He could almost hear the conflicting thoughts tumbling about in her head.

"I have a mother?" she said, finally.

"Most people do."

"Then why didn't my mother come looking for me? What about a father and siblings? Why didn't *you* come looking for me?"

He had to keep himself from shaking her at the unfairness of her accusation. "There's no father listed on your birth certificate, and as far as I know, you don't have any siblings. I *did* report you missing, Josy, and I've been looking for you since you disappeared. I'm here, aren't I?"

"Eighteen months after the fact. How come no one connected my accident to your missing wife?"

He rubbed his jaw, suddenly tired to the bone. "I don't have answers, Josy. Only questions of my own. Questions, apparently, you can't answer."

A prickle of unease suddenly lifted the hairs at the back of his neck. Adam turned, searching the empty street.

"What are you looking for?"

He took her arm. "Let's get inside."

He should have remembered how stubborn she could be.

"Not so fast." She pulled free, staggering slightly as her

leg nearly buckled again. She quickly righted herself, stepping out of his reach.

"I've got so many questions I hardly know where to begin, but let's start with what was I doing on Rock Ridge alone without any identification? And if I'm not their mother, where did *you* get three children?"

Adam counted to ten. He took time to go all the way to twenty-five. It didn't help. How could he have questioned her identity even for an instant? She hadn't changed a bit. She was still a mouthy, independent little cuss when she was riled.

"Josy, can we discuss this inside?"

She glared at him. "That's another thing. What's my real name?"

"Josy. Josy Smith Ryser. When we get inside, I'll show you our marriage license and the wedding picture."

The mention of license and picture silenced the words hovering on her lips. She appeared stunned.

"You have a picture? Of me? Before the accident?"

Her expression ripped another tiny hole in his heart. Only now did Adam begin to realize how difficult every single thing must be for her. She didn't even know what she had looked like.

"Yes," he said softly, "I brought a picture."

A picture he'd committed to memory a long time ago, even as he called himself ten kinds of fool for caring so much. In the picture, the Reno wedding chapel appeared festive instead of garishly junky. The groom appeared fatuously pleased with himself.

Adam had traced his finger over her features a million times as he imagined all the things that could have happened to her. And each time he looked at that picture, he tried to remind himself that her sweet, innocent looks were deceiving, just like the woman herself.

Anyone who studied the picture would see the bride was sporting a bruised cheek and the groom had a swollen lip and a badly scraped hand. Adam could just imagine what Josy was going to make of that.

"Let's go inside."

"Okay."

They started down the sidewalk toward the diner.

Because a part of him had been constantly alert to their surroundings, he heard a car engine rev somewhere in the parking lot. That prickly sixth sense grabbed his full attention as a premonition of danger made him spin about.

Adam whirled just in time to see the large dark truck barreling down on them. He grabbed Josy by the shoulders and threw her to the hard ground, smothering her with his weight.

Chapter Two

Josy felt her bad leg twist painfully as Adam landed on top of her, but she had no air left to cry out with. An interminable second passed before she realized a black pickup truck had roared past the spot where they'd just been standing.

He leaped to his feet and gave chase while Josy sucked air into her lungs. Her leg throbbed like fire. She could feel every pin and screw they'd used to hold the bones together.

"Are you all right?"

She swallowed back a groan and struggled to sit up. Adam had returned to bend over her, his expression fierce. Feet pounded in their direction.

"Did you get his tag number?" a voice called out.

"Bessie's callin' the sheriff," another voice announced.

Adam's arms steadied her. "Josy?"

"I'm fine. Just help me up."

"Let's wait and get you checked out. I knocked you down pretty hard. I'm sorry."

"You saved my life." She reached for his support, determined not to cause any more of a spectacle than she already had.

Reluctantly, he lifted her with gentle strength and held her against his body until her leg would support her weight.

Oddly comforted, she inhaled the subtle fragrance of man and wool.

They'd collected a small crowd. Josy recognized most of the faces, if not the names of all the people standing around. Hayes was a small community where people tended to look out for their own.

"You okay, Josy?" The diner's senior waitress called out. "Sheriff's on his way. Want me to call Doc Blackstone?"

"I'm fine. Really. Just a little shaken." And Adam's firm touch wasn't making that any better.

"Why don't you come inside and sit down?"

"I'd rather go home. It was probably just a ranch hand who'd had too much to drink."

A cold coil of fear made her want to tremble at Adam's suddenly harsh expression. Why did he look like that? It was just an accident. They weren't hurt.

But Sheriff Malcolm arrived with flashing lights before she could question Adam. After asking if she was okay, the sheriff gave Adam a hard look, then began asking questions of the bystanders.

No one had much to tell him. Several people had seen the truck tear out of the night and jump the curb, but no one had seen a license plate or even glimpsed the driver through the darkly tinted windows. The sheriff suggested Adam and Josy come back to his office. His suggestion sounded suspiciously like an order to Josy.

"The car didn't have lights on," Adam stated after they settled in scarred old wooden seats inside the police station. "There weren't any tags, either," he added, "but there was a new car sticker on the side. The driver headed right for us. I don't think this was an accident."

Josy felt sick. "Why would anyone deliberately try to run us down?"

''I suspect the answer to that is buried in that past you can't remember.''

''You're saying I was the target?''

The sheriff interrupted. ''The Britchers called me twenty minutes ago. Don and Alice Britcher are the older couple who rent Josy the garage,'' he added for Adam's benefit. ''Don saw someone coming out of your apartment, Josy. A man. When he called out, the guy took off. Don chased him, but lost him. My first thought was that it had something to do with Ryser here.''

''I went straight to her shop,'' Adam said grimly.

''Yeah, I gathered that. And your credentials check out. But Josy has lived here without a problem for more than a year now. I find it strange that, once you show up, she has a prowler and is nearly run down by a pickup truck all in the same night. Hayes is a quiet town, Ryser.''

Adam held the other man's steady gaze without flinching. ''Until now.''

Josy tried to steady her pounding heart.

''Any idea who would want to hurt you or Josy?''

''Me? No. Josy…?'' Adam paused as if to consider his words carefully. ''When we first met, she told me her mother was a drunk and a gambler who'd gotten in over her head to a casino owner by the name of Enrique Pandergarten in Reno. After asking Josy for help, her mother skipped out and left Josy to face Pandergarten's collection squad alone.''

Bile clogged the back of her throat. Josy wished more desperately than ever that she could remember something of her past.

''I paid Pandergarten off before our wedding, but there's nothing to say her mother hasn't gone and gotten into trouble again.''

The sheriff picked up a pencil and began to tap the eraser

against his front teeth. "Maybe so, but the truck incident is pretty stupid, wouldn't you say? Hurtin' someone to scare them is one thing. Killing them's another. Everyone agrees that truck took aim at you two. If you hadn't been fast and lucky, you'd both be dead. Dead people can't pay off debts."

Adam held his gaze without comment. Finally, the sheriff nodded. "Okay, let's come at this from another angle. Who's mad at *you?*" he demanded, leaning forward and setting the pencil down on a sheaf of papers.

"No one's that kind of mad. I'm involved in a legal matter with the Claussens. They want custody of my goddaughters," Adam replied.

Malcolm opened his mouth in surprise, then closed it again. He leaned back in his seat, his seamed face watchful. "Are we talkin' about Hank Claussen?"

Adam nodded. The sheriff gave a silent whistle. "That's a pretty steep accusation, Ryser."

"No accusation. You asked a question and I answered it. My goddaughters are their grandchildren, and Eleanor isn't happy that I was named their guardian."

The sheriff reached for the pencil again. This time, he tapped it thoughtfully against his lips while the silence in the room thickened.

"You think she'd come after you in a truck?" he finally asked.

"Nope."

The two men stared at one another while Josy fought an urge to cut loose a cry of sheer frustration. She'd had enough of this machismo. None of what they were saying made any sense.

"Who's Hank Claussen?" she demanded.

"State senator across the border in Wyoming where Ryser here is from," the sheriff replied.

''Well, what does he have to do with me?''

''Not a thing,'' Adam assured her. ''The sheriff just wanted to know who has reason not to like me. Hank's the shortlist.''

Malcolm continued to tap his pencil and stare at Adam.

''I'm going to take Josy out of town with me. Now. Tonight,'' Adam stated.

That roused Josy from her tumbling thoughts, even as the sheriff disagreed.

''I'm not sure I like that idea, Ryser.''

''Excuse me,'' she interrupted. ''But I believe I have something to say about these plans.''

Both men stared at her.

''Is he who he says he is?'' she asked the sheriff.

Malcolm nodded. ''Sweetwater County even faxed me his picture. Mr. Ryser is a highly respected member of their community. He runs a sheep ranch, among his other ventures. The marriage license is legal and duly recorded. The birth certificate he showed me is also legitimate, but I'm still running a check on Josy Smith.''

''Thank you.''

''Does that settle the issue?'' Adam asked.

She studied his inscrutable expression, convinced that her question had hurt his feelings. Too bad. She had more than hurt feelings on the line. This was her whole life, and she wanted it back—including the missing pieces.

''I'll go with you.''

Adam relaxed, but the sheriff sat up straighter. ''That may not be wise, Josy.''

''Someone just tried to kill her. Can you protect her twenty-four hours a day?'' Adam asked. ''I can. She'll be safe at my place,'' he added, turning his dark eyes on her.

It was hard not to trust someone who had just saved her life, but events were happening much too quickly for Josy.

"What if that truck was aimed at you and not me?"

"Good point, Ryser. Taking her with you could be placing her in danger." Malcolm's forehead creased with worry. "It's your choice, of course, Josy. As far as I can determine, Ryser here is exactly who he says he is. And it appears you are his wife."

"I'd like to see some proof of that."

Adam reached for his breast coat pocket. He took out a document, carefully unfolded it, and spread it on the desk in front of her. Then he set a picture next to it.

Gingerly, she lifted the photograph. There was no doubting the man in the picture was the same sexy man sitting next to her, despite the fact that she'd never seen that particular look on his face. He appeared relaxed—happy even. His arm spanned the shoulders of a slender young woman with long, honey blond hair.

Josy's fingers went to her short-cropped locks and stopped. While the woman's expression was harder to read, she didn't seem the least bit displeased by Adam's arm around her shoulders.

"I don't look a whole lot different now, do I?"

Adam cleared his throat before answering. "No," he said gently. "Not a whole lot."

She stared hard for another minute. "So, what'd you have to do, beat me into submission to get me to say 'I do'?"

His lips twitched, and a grudging amusement lit his dark eyes. "We'd just come from a run-in with the collection goons. Trust me, they looked a whole lot worse than we did. You're a pretty formidable infighter when you're riled."

Trust me.

That was the issue, wasn't it? Ever since waking in the

hospital, she'd had to trust one person after another. She ought to be used to that by now.

She studied the picture in her hand, wishing she could remember. On some level, she did trust Adam, she realized, and not just because he'd saved her life or claimed they were married. She felt no connection to the people in the picture, but she'd felt drawn to Adam from the moment he stepped into the shop tonight. There was nothing as strong as a memory, but his touch evoked all sorts of things inside her. Things that made her question a purely business deal.

Adam was a hard man—forceful, domineering. But he was also kind. He knew how to apologize when he was wrong, and she liked the way he'd put Seth at ease tonight after he realized he'd scared the boy half to death.

She raised her eyes and found him watching her.

"If I'm right," Adam said, his gaze fixed on her, "and someone from your past is out to hurt you, my house will be a lot safer than your isolated room over a dark garage."

"Why would anyone want to hurt me?"

"And why did they wait until you showed up to try?" the sheriff added darkly.

Adam gave a slight shake of his head, his eyes never leaving her face. "I can't answer either question, but I need you, Josy. The girls need you. The choice is yours."

Josy considered her alternatives. Adam Ryser represented the only connection she had to her past. She couldn't send him away until she learned everything there was to know about the woman she had been a year and a half ago.

"I'll go with you."

The sheriff frowned. "You don't want to wait until morning?"

"No," Adam stated positively.

"Then maybe you two should leave from here," he suggested. "I can pack her things and send them along."

"Good idea."

"No, it isn't," Josy argued immediately. "I want to say goodbye and thank you to the Britchers. They've been very kind to me."

"Call them from the ranch," Adam said firmly.

The sheriff nodded assent. "I'll explain what happened Josy."

"I wish someone would explain it to me," she muttered. This morning, she had been nobody—a woman totally alone. Tonight, she had a husband, three children, a drunken mother and a state senator for an enemy. And the past was still an enormous black void.

An hour later, Josy set her jaw against the silence in the truck, knowing she was coming painfully close to feeling sorry for herself. Pity was something she'd sworn she wouldn't give in to, but some days it was hard to keep that vow. She sneaked a glance at the man beside her.

Adam Ryser was so dominantly male. How had she stayed married to him for two weeks and remained a virgin? She was dangerously attracted to him, even though she didn't want to be.

Sitting beside him in the small cab of his pickup truck, she felt a whole new host of uncertainties. Was she out of her mind for going anyplace with this stranger?

"Tell me something," she said to break the unnerving silence of the long ride. "Is my name really Josy Smith?"

"No. It's Josy Smith Ryser," he said emphatically.

"But I was born Josy Smith?"

He slitted a glance at her before returning his concentration to the dark road that stretched endlessly before them.

"According to my investigator, there *was* a Josy Smith. You're the right age to *be* Josy Smith, but there isn't any way to *prove* you're Josy Smith."

"Why not?"

"The state of California has no record of Josy Smith after her birth."

"I was born in California?"

"Grangeville, California."

She thought about that for a moment. "I want to read that report."

"Okay." He glanced at her again. "How come you don't act more upset over losing your memory?"

"I've had a year and a half to get used to the idea," she told him tartly. "Getting on with the future took precedence over remembering the past, but I'd still like to *know*."

"Fair enough. What can I tell you?"

She stared at his strong profile, illuminated by the faint light from the dashboard, and asked the question that hovered uppermost in her mind. "Why would a man who looks like you ask a perfect stranger to marry him?"

Every trace of humor and sympathy left his face. "I told you, we had a business deal."

The stark words crumbled a ghostly hope that had flickered to life in her mind.

"I know what you told me, but that story has so many holes, even you must have trouble keeping it together. Why didn't you make this 'business arrangement' with someone you already knew?"

An emotion she couldn't quite read glinted in his eyes. "You want the truth? I was desperate the night we met. My best friend and his wife died suddenly when their Cessna went down in a storm over Wyoming."

His eyes stared straight ahead while his fingers squeezed the steering wheel.

"The only thing Chad ever asked of me was to take care of his girls if something happened to him. The afternoon you and I met, I had learned I was in real danger of losing them because I'm not married and I'm not a blood relative.''

The angry words completely severed the slender thread of hope she might have clung to that she'd married him for something other than monetary reasons.

"Why?" she asked hesitantly.

"Why what?"

"Why does it matter if you're married if your friend named you as the children's guardian?"

His lips thinned, and she sensed his frustration. "Because," he said slowly, "when Chad made out the will, I was married to his sister. And that's the point the Claussens plan to drive home to the court. I wasn't single when the will was made. I was part of their family. My divorce is supposed to prove my instability to provide a good family home for the girls."

Anger underscored his words, but she wasn't sure which fact was stirring that anger. Every time he explained something, she had more questions. "Your friend named you, not his sister?"

"That is my single defense. That, and the fact that Alyssa doesn't want any part of the children. She divorced me to marry someone with more money and connections."

Before Josy could respond to his cold, bitter words, he straightened alertly, staring at the rearview mirror.

"What's wrong?"

Adam muttered a low curse and depressed the accelerator. "Someone's following us. He's closing the distance fast, coming up behind us without lights."

Adrenaline sent her craning her neck to peer out the window into the black landscape. The road was twisty and starting to climb steeply. She had no idea what lay on either side of them, but she could guess.

"Do you know how to use a rifle?" Adam asked.

Her mouth went dry. "I don't know."

"Well, we'll soon find out. Take it off the mount in back."

"Isn't that a bit extreme? I mean, it could be anyone back there."

"Yeah. Including the person in the truck that nearly killed us earlier tonight. Get the gun."

Josy unfastened her seat belt and leaned over the back seat. She looked at the gun rack, searching for the release brackets. The truck swerved slightly as they went into a curve too fast. She bumped against Adam's shoulder. He was taut with tension. Awkwardly, she got the rifle down, surprised by its heaviness.

"Adam, I don't think I've ever handled a rifle before. It doesn't feel familiar."

"I hope you're a fast learner."

Moonlight glinted off the grille of the fast-closing truck. Was it the same truck from the parking lot? Josy couldn't tell, but she shivered.

In a calm voice, Adam explained how to remove the safety and arm the chamber. He told her how to position the gun so the recoil wouldn't tear up her arm or shoulder too badly. Then he told her to get in back and open the panel that looked out over the bed of his truck so she could position the rifle barrel out the window.

"Adam, this is crazy. What if this is some innocent person who just forgot to turn on their headlights?"

"Then I'll start believing in Santa Claus and the Easter Bunny. Move it, Josy. We're coming up on the pass. When we start down the other side, he's going to make his move. One good shove in the right direction and we're going to take the express way down this hillside."

Josy set the rifle on the back seat and clambered over to keep it company, her heart thudding, her fingers so stiff with nervousness she was certain she wouldn't be able to fire the blasted thing.

"You realize I'll probably miss him completely."

She saw a flash of white teeth in the darkness. "I'm countin' on it, honey. All we want to do is warn him away. If there's two of 'em, we could be in trouble here. I'm hoping it's just the one guy your landlord saw coming out of your apartment."

He shifted gears as they began to climb steadily. Josy released the catch so she could slide back the heavy Plexiglas pane.

"He's getting closer, Adam."

She could make out the dark shape clearly now, even if the sky wasn't cooperating as much as it could have. Moonlight danced in and out of the clouds overhead. There wasn't another car on the road.

Suddenly, the dark shape behind them seemed to spring forward. Her fingers clutched the rifle.

"Get ready," Adam warned. "Just aim in the general direction of the hood and fire when you think he's close enough to notice."

"I don't have to wait to see the whites of his eyes?"

"If you do, we'll be dead."

As they hit the crest of the hill, the dark truck lunged forward. Josy steadied the rifle against the rim of the window and squeezed the trigger.

Despite Adam's coaching, she felt the shot clear down her body. Her ears rang with the sound, and her nose twitched at the smell.

"Good shootin', Tex," Adam said.

"Oh, my God! Adam, I shot out part of his windshield!"

"Yep, you sure did."

The other car braked sharply, skidding into the oncoming lane before coming to a stop. Adam didn't even slow down.

"What if I killed someone, Adam?"

"The sheriff might give you a reward."

"Adam!"

"Relax, Josy. You didn't hit anyone."

"You can't know that for sure." For a minute, she thought she might be sick. "We don't even know this was the same truck that tried to run us down."

"Yeah, we do. How many dark Chevys do you think are chasing us through the night without headlights or license plates? Put the safety back on, but keep the rifle to hand. I'll report this—" He stopped reaching for his cell phone. "Now do you believe me?"

The truck came ghosting out of the night again like an evil marauder intent on prey. Josy didn't wait for Adam to tell her to reposition the rifle. She aimed and carefully squeezed the trigger. Nothing happened.

"The safety," Adam snapped.

Josy released it with numb fingers. This time, she was better prepared for the noise and the jolt. As far as she could tell, she didn't hit a thing, but the dark truck slowed to another stop on the side of the road.

"That should tell him we weren't kidding."

"What are we going to do?"

"Here." He tossed her the small phone. It landed on the floor of the back seat, and Josy scrambled after it. "Call the emergency number."

"And what am I going to tell them? We need help? We just shot at someone for driving without his headlights?"

She sensed his fleeting amusement. "I keep forgetting what a scrappy little thing you are. Okay, you've got a point. Keep your eyes on the road behind us. Let me know if you spot the truck again."

But Josy saw no further sign of the vehicle. The night folded over the other truck, sealing it from view. And that only made her more jittery. "Adam, what if I did hurt someone?"

"I promise, if you did, I'll take full responsibility."

"Oh, that'll soothe my conscience no end. Tell me why you think someone is trying to kill me?"

Amusement left his voice. "I wish I knew."

"But you said gamblers."

"No, I said that was one possibility."

"And you said Hank Claussen was another."

"No. I never said he was behind the attempts, only that he had a reason to be unhappy with me. Not only is he the girls' grandfather, but he's also my closest neighbor."

Josy turned her back to stare at the empty road behind them.

"Why do you dislike him so much?"

Adam raised his eyes to meet hers in the rearview mirror, his surprise evident.

"I never said—"

"Your tone goes all flat when you mention him."

"Hank and I don't see eye to eye on too many issues. And he wants his grandchildren."

"Well, truthfully, that seems understandable to me."

"Yeah, on the surface, I'm sure it does. My plane had a clogged fuel line the day I had to leave for Reno."

"He clogged your fuel line?"

"Let's just say it wasn't an accident, and Hank's offer of a ride came at an awfully fortuitous moment. Now, we both do business in Nevada and we've often flown there together. Only, this time Hank had more on his mind than convincing me to accept legalized gambling. He told me I didn't have to worry about raising his granddaughters. Eleanor had decided to do her duty and keep them. When I told him it was no duty, that I wanted to raise them, he offered to buy them."

Josy gasped. The harsh, bitter words made her shiver.

"I turned him down flat. That's when he told me he'd have to take them. You see, anything Eleanor Claussen wants, Hank gets for her," Adam explained. "Hank was just a rancher until he married the wealthy, politically connected Eleanor. Now he's a rich man with lots of political influence. Eleanor has a judge and a U.S. congressman in her family. Getting the children is a way to keep Eleanor happy."

"But they're his grandchildren!"

"You think people don't buy people? I bought you."

Numb, she stared out over the empty terrain surrounding them.

"I'm sorry." His apology was a harsh whisper. "There's no call to take my frustration out on you. It's just that I nearly had to go into the final hearing this Thursday without you. I might have lost the girls, and Chad would never forgive me. The last thing he'd want is his parents raising his daughters."

Well, that told her clearly where she stood. It also said some pretty strong things about Hank Claussen and his wife.

"Are the Claussens such monsters, then?"

Adam shook his head. "No, not monsters. Just cold people who should never have had any children. But Eleanor always does what is expected." He sighed, rubbing his chin with the back of a knuckle. "Once you meet them, you'll understand."

"Do they know?" she asked.

"That I found you?"

"That you bought a marriage certificate."

His head whipped around toward her, the startled look quickly deepening to fury. "No one knows! And no one is going to know. I told Hank on the plane that day that I was getting married. He was so mad he could barely bring us in for a landing.''

"But you hadn't even met me yet."

"I know that, and you know that. As far as everyone else is concerned, we had a relationship for years before I married you. I told you, I do a lot of business in Nevada. No one questioned our romance and they won't question it now unless you give them cause. You aren't going do that, are you, Josy?''

Her stomach knotted. The truck drifted over the center lane, and Adam quickly corrected. She studied his hands where they gripped the steering wheel.

"I don't know," she told him honestly. "I guess it depends on what I find when I meet the girls."

His glance met hers again in the rearview mirror. "What does that mean?''

"How do I know what sort of person you are? Maybe the girls would be better off with their grandparents. All you've done is try to bully me since we've met. If you're treating three innocent children this way, you wasted your time and your money.''

His shocked expression would have been comical if he hadn't been such a large, dangerous man.

"It occurs to me that this may all be a fake," she went on boldly. "I only have your word on this preposterous situation. That truck back there could be driven by a friend of yours. You could have set up that scene in the parking lot and had him break into my apartment. If the sheriff hadn't vouched for your identity, I wouldn't even be in this truck with you.''

She waved away his attempt to interrupt. "That wedding picture could belong to any woman who resembles me. I'm in no position to prove it either way. What if the real Josy is dead? Or there never was a Josy to begin with?''

She wound down as soon as the last words were uttered. The silence was profound. Josy became intensely aware of her surroundings, the stretch of mountains at her back, the empty countryside enclosing them, the hum of the powerful engine and the warm air from the heater. In those few minutes, she realized he could kill her and dump her body in the nearest ravine and no one would be any wiser.

Josy had a sudden memory of acute terror, of falling through space, air trapped in her lungs—lungs that wanted to let her scream but couldn't.

Then the image dissolved like so many before it, leaving her trembling in the aftermath.

"Well, now," Adam said softly. "Looks to me like we're right back at square one."

Josy forced her body to relax and twisted back to stare at the road behind them. Still empty.

"What's square one?" she asked. Her voice surprised her by holding steady.

"Our original deal was that you'd marry me and I'd pay off your mother's gambling debts. This time, you need money for your hospital bills and I still need a temporary wife. I want my goddaughters, Josy. I'm going to do whatever it takes to keep them."

"Why?"

"Why what?"

"Why do you want the girls so bad? Are they worth money or something?"

His look was bleaker than the winter landscape around them. "I don't need money, and Hank Claussen owns half of Wyoming and parts of Nevada. Eleanor doesn't care about the girls. She already has boarding schools picked out for them—and Bitsy just turned five!" His hand slammed the steering wheel, startling her. Adam Ryser wasn't fond of Hank, but he hated Eleanor Claussen.

"Are you going to help me, Josy?"

"Then what happens?"

He glanced at her. "What do you mean?"

"You get the children and I just walk out the door—is that it?" Anger rose like bile. "How do you think the children will feel about that, or don't you care? Maybe you just want me to pretend to be their mother in front of strangers?"

"No!" The truck veered sharply as he turned to look at her. Adam corrected quickly. "That isn't how it was," he said more quietly.

"I don't remember how it was, Adam."

His jaw clenched. He stared at the road for several agonizing minutes, then slowly, he relaxed. "I know you don't," he said so quietly that that tiny bubble of hope rose inside her once again. "Can't we just take this one step at a time?"

No, she wanted to shout, but there was something in his expression—something sad that tugged at her heart. *Had* there been more between them than just a bargain?

Did she want there to be?

If only she could remember.

"Is that what we did before?" she asked. "Take things one step at a time?"

"Yeah, Josy. That's what we did before. Will you help?"

She wanted to say yes, if only to remove that poignant look from his features, but she couldn't. Not yet.

"I'll know after I meet the girls."

Chapter Three

Her words gnawed at Adam's mind, but he guessed he should be thankful that he'd gotten her to come this far. Once Josy saw the girls again, she might remember all the fun the five of them had had together. Maybe she'd even remember the way it had been between him and her. The way they'd become friends—and more. Quickly, he shoved that thought aside.

As he drove, Adam kept a close watch on the road behind them. Twice, he thought he caught a glimpse of the truck lurking far behind. The other driver was either unarmed or unprepared to go up against two people with a rifle.

He began talking about the girls to keep his mind from circling the reason behind Josy's initial disappearance and accident. He felt sure there was a connection between those events and what had happened to Josy tonight. Adam didn't make the sort of enemies who would try to run him down.

"I think I just saw the truck coming around the bend back down there," Josy said suddenly.

"Yeah. I saw it."

"What are we going to do? If he follows us all the way to your ranch, he'll know where we live."

Adam didn't miss her choice of pronoun. "It doesn't

matter, Josy. He could find out easily enough if he doesn't already know, but I'm guessing he'll turn off when we hit the next junction.''

Either that, or the truck would follow them all the way to the ranch house itself. Adam almost hoped for that. It would mean the driver didn't know him or this area. If he turned off—well, the road led to other places besides the Claussen ranch.

Adam reached for the radio under the dash.

Brug Matthews, his friend and foreman, answered as if he'd been sitting there waiting for their call instead of sleeping like he should have been at this hour.

''Brug, can you ride out to the south entrance? I'm on my way in and I want to be sure my truck is the only one coming through the gate.''

''Trouble?''

''Yeah.''

''Should I call the house and wake Martha?''

''No. Let's not rouse the household.''

''On my way.''

''We're almost at your ranch?'' Josy asked.

''We're on my land right now,'' he told her as he disconnected. ''It'll take another ten minutes before we reach the gate leading to the main drive and the house.''

''Oh.''

She subsided against the back seat looking thoughtful. He suspected she was remembering her temerity in suggesting he wanted the children for their inheritance. The memory almost made him smile.

He watched their back trail, but he couldn't tell if the truck turned off or not. And as Brug waved them through the back gate, Adam found himself suddenly wondering what Josy would think of the house. The blazingly white building with its pretentious colonnades and second-story balcony was totally incompatible with its setting. The structure squatted in the darkness as if set there by mistake.

He hated that house, but it served as a reminder of his past error and the promise he'd made himself never to trust another woman. A promise he'd kept until he met Josy. Adam gritted his teeth. Was he doomed to always play the fool where women were concerned?

Josy said nothing as the ugly edifice drew closer. A quick glance in the mirror showed the lines of strain on her face. It had been a hard night for both of them.

Adam pulled into the turnaround in front and stepped down from the truck. There were no lights anywhere, nor had he expected any. Josy climbed out with more difficulty. He saw her grimace of pain, though she quickly ducked her head to hide the expression. He should have helped her down, even if touching her still disturbed him.

"We'll have to be quiet so we don't wake the girls," he said softly, unsure whether or not to offer her his arm.

She straightened quickly. "Okay."

Funny how awkward this felt. Adam seldom felt unsure of himself.

"Unless you're hungry or something, I'm going to take you upstairs to your room," he told her. "After you disappeared, Martha stored the clothes you left behind in the bedroom closet and dresser. They may be a little loose on you—" he frowned as he thought about how much weight she had lost "—but you should find something to sleep in. You sure you aren't hungry?" He hated that she had ever gone without food.

"I'm fine." Her expression gave none of her thoughts away. If she was surprised by the house, she didn't say so. She followed him slowly onto the front porch. "What are you going to do?" she asked.

"Talk to Brug. You'll be safe here. Don't worry."

"Right."

Adam shook his head, but didn't bother trying to convince her. "Come on." He led the way inside the dark foyer and up the spiral staircase.

"Be careful," he warned, thinking of her bad leg. "These stairs don't have any back risers."

"Not exactly childproof, are they?"

The observation made him scowl. "No. They aren't."

Adam followed her up the stairs, tensing at each halting step she took as she carefully mounted. Had he caused more injury to her leg when he'd thrown her to the ground, or was she just stiff from sitting in the car for so long? He didn't like to think of her in pain. He should have insisted the local doctor check her out before hauling her out of town like that. On the other hand, they'd been lucky to get clear of Hayes in one piece as it was.

He caught another grimace when she stopped at the top of the stairs.

"Should I call a doctor?"

Josy peered up at him in surprise. "What for?"

"Your leg."

"My leg's just a little stiff. Which way do I go?"

Prickly as usual. Adam suspected she'd crawl before she'd complain. "Turn right."

Darn stubborn woman. She should say something if she was hurting. He wasn't a mind reader. Of course, there wasn't much they could do tonight if she was hurt. He wasn't about to set them up as targets a second time by driving her all the way into town for medical attention. She'd have to wait until morning.

He reached for the doorknob to her bedroom and hesitated, remembering what was on the other side. Well, she hadn't made any comment about the house so far.

"In here."

Josy was surprised by Adam's abrupt tone of voice. What was bothering the man now?

The house was nothing at all like she'd expected. Modern and unappealing, it didn't go with her image of a working sheep ranch. Josy gave a mental shrug. It was none of her business how Adam chose to live. She was a visitor. A paid companion, as it were.

She moved inside passively, the questions throbbing in her head matching the pain in her leg. She couldn't help but think it was no wonder the man needed a wife. His housekeeper probably wanted permanent help to take care of this mini-mansion. Funny, she wouldn't have pictured this as Adam's style.

He opened a door and flicked on a light switch. "Bathroom's through that door. If you need anything, I'll be in the room on this side." He pointed to what must be a connecting door.

Josy stared. The surroundings were white. Stark, Hollywood-cliché white. Thick white carpeting sucked at her booted feet. A round queen-size bed sat in the center of the room, its heavy satin bedspread also white. The silly thing looked like a giant marshmallow. How would she sleep in that?

There were no pictures or paintings to relieve the boredom, only a sliding glass door covered by white satin drapes.

She stared at the bed and looked up at Adam. It was on the tip of her tongue to ask if this was a joke, but the tired, harsh lines etched around his mouth and eyes held her silent. Exhaustion was tugging at her, as well.

"This'll be fine," she lied without meeting his eyes. "Thank you."

"Okay. We'll talk in the morning."

She took an uncertain step forward and faltered. His hand

came to rest on her shoulder, steadying her. Josy quivered beneath that warm touch. Adam watched her with unfathomable eyes.

For just a moment, she felt strongly connected to him, as if they'd played this scene before. She searched his face, looking for some sign of recognition or a sign that he felt something of what she was feeling. He simply looked tired. She fought an urge to smooth away his frown.

"Get some rest," he said gruffly, and gave her shoulder an awkward pat before striding from the room.

Josy shivered, feeling ridiculously abandoned. Chastising herself for such a foolish thought, she headed for the bathroom, prepared to see more white. She wasn't disappointed. Even the mirrored walls came as no great shock. Yet, none of it went with the man she had met tonight.

Her reflection stared back at her, looking pinched and tired. Exactly how she felt.

She wished she had kept the picture Adam had shown her.

She would have liked to compare the two faces. A long time ago, she'd stopped looking in mirrors to find answers in features she didn't recognize. There weren't any answers there now, either, but the enormous raised tub behind her with the whirlpool jets was an irresistible draw.

Josy undressed and folded her clothing neatly, laying them on the counter when she couldn't find a hamper. She soaked away her questions and confusion in the warm, moving water until her eyelids grew too heavy to stay open.

In the dresser, she discovered several nightgowns in bright hues and soft sensual fabrics. There were also daring bras and panties. She fingered the items ruefully, unable to connect them to herself. She may have been a virgin before she was injured, but based on this selection of sexy garments, she hadn't planned to stay that way.

Had she planned to seduce her new husband? The thought made her stomach quiver.

She donned a deep rose gown, enjoying the feel of the satin material against her skin, but wishing it were flannel all the same as she trembled in the cool bedroom. Was all that white color starting to get to her, or was the room simply cold?

Josy flicked off the light, wondering what Adam would think of her choice of nightwear. She started to get into bed when a slight but definite draft swept her arm. She hesitated, then walked across the room to the sliding glass door. Locked, but the draft had come from somewhere. A flicker of motion outside held her still, trapping the air in her lungs.

Someone stood on the balcony.

His very stillness caught her attention. She could barely discern his outline, but he was big, and he stood poised outside what must be Adam's room.

Josy didn't hesitate. She ran, stumbling awkwardly, to the connecting door, finding it ajar. Adam's name was a harsh whisper of sound from deep in her throat.

"Adam!"

His room was a sea of black in which nothing moved.

"Adam!" she called more loudly. And the balcony door slid open with a grating sound.

The primal scream that built within her was choked away as the entering figure called out her name. "Josy?"

Adam's harsh voice changed the scream to a broken sob of relief. He crossed the room on silent feet, pulling her against his large shape.

"What is it? What's wrong?"

"I thought..." She swallowed, struggling for words against the unexpected sensation caused by being held so protectively against this man.

"What?" he demanded.

"I saw someone on the balcony. I didn't realize it was you. I thought someone was…"

His tension ebbed, but his arms continued to hold her against him, stroking her back in an unconscious caress. This felt so natural. So unbelievably right.

"It's okay, Josy. I told you, you're safe here. No one can get to you now."

Her pulse beat a ragged tattoo in her throat. Josy knew she was safe in his arms. Adam was incredibly strong, yet his hands were gentle, comforting. His hair was damp, and he smelled of soap and shampoo. She pictured him standing beneath the cascading water of a shower, lather streaking his solid chest.

Their eyes met. A primal hunger hovered in the air between them. Her heart tripped almost painfully. It would take very little to tip the balance here. A touch. A kiss.

The pulse in his neck beat more rapidly. Josy couldn't seem to draw a breath as his head started to lower.

"You should be asleep," Adam said gruffly, releasing her and taking a step back.

His words and his abrupt action shattered the explosive tension. She wrapped her arms around her quaking frame while Adam rubbed his jaw in a weary gesture.

"Look, we'll talk in the morning when we're both able to think more clearly, okay?"

His features were practically invisible in the darkness, but the depth of his exhaustion was underscored in the tone of his voice. He was right. No more questions. She didn't think she could bear to hear the answers.

How had she lived weeks with this man as his wife and remained a virgin?

She inhaled shakily, and knew that he noticed.

"Good night, Adam. Be prepared to answer a lot of questions in the morning."

She sensed his smile in the darkness as she passed through the connecting door to her room.

THE MAN CALLED BRUG WAS the first person she saw the next morning. When Adam didn't answer her knock, Josy headed down the long hall and the spiral staircase. The house was as silent as it had been the night before, but now, bright sunshine flooded the colorless interior.

The front door gaped open, letting in the cold morning wind. A roguishly handsome dark-haired man stood in the turnaround before the front steps, holding a rope tied around the neck of a young roan horse. The skittish animal's sides heaved from his efforts, lather attesting to his frantic bid for freedom. A saddled horse grazed nearby, looking calm and uninterested in the other animal's plight. The cowboy was making slow inroads in his attempts to soothe the roan.

Drawn by the animal as much as by the man, Josy stepped onto the wide porch.

"What happened now?" Adam called. He appeared from around the corner of the house, moving with long, forceful strides.

"Suzie," the cowboy replied with a ghost of a grin.

Josy started down the steps, relieved to see Adam, and wanting a closer look at the skittish horse.

"And the dog?" Adam guessed.

"Her partner in crime," the man agreed. "Killer got loose, went under the fence and started chasing the yearlings. Suzie left the gate open when she went after him."

Adam muttered something Josy didn't hear as he reached for the horse. He looked incredibly sexy in dark form-fitting jeans and a jacket, a dusty hat pulled low on his forehead.

He ran careful fingers over the nervous horse, talking softly, stroking his muzzle. The action reminded Josy of the way he'd held and stroked her back the night before.

So his actions hadn't been anything personal. The sexual awareness she'd felt had been one-sided after all. She'd have to remember that. But the horse, she noted wryly, calmed in exactly the same way she had under Adam's touch.

"Where is Suzie now?"

"She grabbed Killer and ran back inside." The cowboy angled his head toward Josy and smiled. He had a smile New York advertisers would love. She reached the bottom step and found herself automatically smiling back.

Adam looked up, obviously startled to see her. He frowned before introducing them brusquely.

"So this pretty lady is your wife?" Brug asked.

"Yes. Did that south gate ever get repaired?"

Brug's smile faded, replaced by puzzled concern. "Pete took care of it yesterday."

"Good. Get the horse settled, and I'll be back out to talk to you in a few minutes." He gave the yearling a final pat and reached for Josy's arm. "Come on," he said sharply.

Josy pulled free and glared up at him. "I'm the wife, remember? Wives don't take orders. At least this one doesn't."

Adam dropped her arm and stared at her.

"Good morning, Adam," she said with hearty false cheer. She bestowed another smile on the foreman. "It was nice to meet you, Brug."

The yearling gave a snort and danced sideways. Josy stepped back quickly to avoid him, and her bad leg buckled as she backed into the bottom step. This time, she was thankful for the strong, hard arms that whipped out to support her. She had no wish to fall in the grass and be trampled by the nervous animal.

"Uh, I'll just put Cryin' Shame back inside," Brug said hastily. "Nice meetin' you, too, ma'am."

"Josy," she corrected.

Without warning, Adam scooped her into his arms and headed up the steps.

"Put me down! What do you think you're doing?"

"You don't take orders so I'm savin' my breath. Besides, it's traditional for the groom to carry his bride over the threshold," he explained.

"Stick it in your hat. I'm not a traditionalist."

"Tough."

Still struggling, Josy had only seconds to see the surprised face of a lovely dark-haired young woman and the two sets of small blue eyes staring up at her. Then Adam set her on her feet inside the hall, holding her protectively until her legs accepted her weight. A small bundle of white fur immediately wove its way between them, yipping delightedly.

"Suzie! Grab Killer."

Josy stared at the tiny mixed-breed puppy and nearly laughed out loud. This was Killer, the terror of large horses?

The taller of the two blond children ran forward to fling her arms around the excited dog. The younger one took her thumb from her mouth and eased forward to clutch at Adam's jean-clad leg.

Adam swung Bitsy into his arms while he made the introductions only slightly less brusquely than he had outside. He placed a kiss on Bitsy's cheek, and the little girl curled trustingly against his chest, all the while watching Josy.

Martha smoothed her hands down her own jean-encased legs and regarded Josy critically with unfriendly dark eyes.

So much for his housekeeper being some matronly old woman. Martha wasn't much older than Josy. And she was a whole lot prettier.

Suzie didn't spare Josy a glance. She clutched the wriggling puppy against her thin chest while tears welled in her eyes. "It was an accident," she said.

Adam hunched down to eye level without releasing Bitsy. Killer tried desperately to lick his face.

"I know, Suze. And you won't forget to shut gates tightly in the future."

Fat tears landed on the dog, who settled for licking them away. "Please don't shoot him. Please. I'll lock him in my room, and he'll never get out again and—"

"Hey, now!" Adam drew her against his chest with his free arm as she began to cry in earnest. "Who said anything about shooting Killer?"

"Gr-Grandpa. But Killer didn't mean to bite him."

Adam turned bleak eyes toward Martha. "What happened?"

"He showed up yesterday," the woman said. "I told him you weren't home, and he said he knew. He wanted to take the girls overnight."

Adam's expression was a silent curse.

"Brug helped me convince him to wait until you came home. Killer got a little overexcited during the conversation."

Suzie looked up, tears rushing down her face. "Grandpa kicked him, Uncle Adam. And he said you should shoot him when you got home."

Josy's stomach tightened in anger that surely matched Adam's expression. She bent down, ignoring the protest from her bad leg, and stroked the tangled blond hair, causing the child to turn in her direction.

"Adam would never hurt Killer," Josy told her.

"But Grandpa said! Grandpa doesn't like dogs."

"Your grandfather was just angry. Sometimes adults say things they don't mean when they get angry."

Teary blue eyes searched her face before looking at Adam. "You won't shoot him? Even though he chased the horses today?"

Adam's jaw clenched so tight it must have hurt. "No one's going to shoot Killer."

Killer barked at the sound of his name. Suzie's tears stopped running, but reserves hovered in her eyes. "Brug said someone ought to. I heard him when he told the men to go after the horses."

Josy took the dog from Suzie's grasp and stood carefully, letting the rambunctious pet wriggle in her arms and slurp happily at her cheek.

She held the small dog at arm's length so it faced her. "Know what I think, Killer? I think you and Suzie and I are going to have to start training you properly. You've been a bad dog."

Killer barked cheerfully.

Suzie stepped from Adam's embrace and stared at her. Adam stood, still holding Bitsy in one arm.

"Who are you?" Suzie asked.

"Aunt Josy," Adam told her before Josy could reply.

Aunt sounded so strange. Josy was certain she'd never been anyone's aunt before.

"No, she isn't," Bitsy said abruptly.

"She doesn't look like Aunt Josy," Suzie agreed.

"No, I guess I don't anymore." Josy didn't glance at Adam or the silent Martha. If the children didn't accept her right away, Adam could lose the custody battle. And after watching him with the girls, she knew she'd already chosen her position in this quarrel.

"The doctors had to change my face after I had an accident," she told them. "But it's okay, isn't it? I'm still me."

Under her stroking hand, Killer settled in her arms, but Josy knew she couldn't stand there much longer without her bad leg giving out again.

"What accident?" Suzie demanded.

"Josy was hurt that day she disappeared," Adam answered.

The children stared. "Did you get run over by a car?" Suzie asked.

"No, I—"

"She was injured in a fall," Adam cut in.

Josy shot him a fulminating look, wondering why he felt it necessary to answer for her.

"Oh."

Adam suddenly tugged Josy against his shoulder, throwing her off balance. She recovered quickly, managing to stand without wavering, but was extremely conscious of that arm around her shoulders. Why did his touch disturb her so much?

"She's even prettier now, don't you think, Suze?"

Suzie studied Josy critically.

"She looks different," Bitsy pronounced.

Adam nodded. "That she does, but not too different. Come on, troop. I think we need to get Aunt Josy some breakfast."

"What about Killer?" Suzie immediately wanted to know.

"We need to try real hard to keep Killer inside for the rest of the day except when he's on a leash," Adam said. "Agreed?"

"Okay, Uncle Adam. I'm sorry about the gate."

"I know you are, sweetheart. Promise me you won't forget again."

"I promise."

"Good enough."

He set Bitsy down, but she clung like a barnacle to his leg. "I've got to go talk to Brug, honey. Martha, would you mind showing Josy to the kitchen?"

Josy caught a flash of venom in the woman's expression before Martha turned and led the way toward the back of the house.

ADAM STEPPED OUTSIDE and stood on the porch, rubbing his jaw. How could he have forgotten what her proximity did to him? For the two weeks they'd been together, Josy had driven him nearly mad with her saucy mouth and her lively eyes. He'd vowed their so-called marriage would be platonic, but he hadn't counted on the way she'd climbed right into his heart. If Bitsy hadn't interrupted them the night before she disappeared, Josy would have been his wife in every sense of the word.

Her head might not remember, but her body did. Unfortunately, so did his.

Well, she wouldn't turn his life topsy-turvy this time. He wouldn't allow it to happen again. He'd been able to send her away last night, hadn't he?

Barely.

He pushed that thought aside. Seeing her with Brug had tightened his gut into a knot that wouldn't go away. He hadn't liked the way she'd smiled at his handsome foreman, or the way Brug had smiled back. Of course, he should have expected it from Brug. The man was a natural flirt.

He was *not* going to let another woman twist him up like this. Hadn't Alyssa taught him anything at all? He shouldn't care if Josy flirted with Brug. And he wouldn't care if he didn't need her, he told himself. They had to present a happy, united front on Thursday.

He would just have to keep Brug away from the house.
The ambitious foreman was a complication Adam didn't
need right now. Martha wouldn't be happy, either, if she
saw the two of them together. Martha and Brug had been
seeing a lot of each other recently, and nobody knew better
than Adam that women were unpredictable creatures.

He started down the steps and paused as he saw a vehicle
coming up the long drive. Even from a distance, he recognized Calvin Milton's blue pickup truck. Tilly and her
best friend, Elissa, Calvin's youngest daughter, were back
from soccer practice.

Tilly smiled broadly as she jumped down from the cab,
waving goodbye to her redheaded friend. Adam exchanged
waves with Deborah Milton as Tilly ran up to give him a
hug.

"Did you find her?" Tilly asked.

"Yeah. I found her."

"It was Aunt Josy? For real?" Clear blue eyes stared at
him. "Why'd she leave us?"

He heard the pain beneath Tilly's question and tugged
gently on her ponytail. "Josy can't remember anything before her accident, Till." He wondered how much to tell
her. Tilly had always seemed older than her eight years, so
Adam gave her the truth. "She doesn't remember us. And,
sweetheart, she doesn't look like she used to."

"Why not?"

"She fell down a mountain. They had to do surgery to
restore her face, but they couldn't fix her memory. Give
her a chance, okay? We need her."

The little girl frowned. "I know. Does she—? What's
the matter with Brug?"

Adam turned and saw his foreman running from the barn.

"There's a break in the south pasture," Brug called out.

"We've got sheep on the highway and they've caused at least one accident."

Adam swallowed back fear and an automatic oath, conscious of Tilly at his side. "I thought Pete fixed that gate!"

"He did. I was just down there a few minutes ago. Someone must have cut the fence on purpose."

Chapter Four

Martha made a winter ice storm look warm and inviting, Josy decided. And the girls were taking their cues from her. Bitsy clung to her doll and watched Josy with wary eyes while Suzie sat on the floor playing with Killer, absorbing the reactions of the adults above her. Martha rejected every overture of friendship Josy made as she bustled about *her* kitchen.

Then Tilly bounded into the room with the news about sheep on the highway.

"You actually heard Brug say the fence had been cut?" Josy demanded.

"Yep. Uncle Adam's mad. He drove away real fast."

Josy's heart began to pound. Cut fences and a sheep stampede? The image would have been silly if it wasn't potentially so serious.

"Brug didn't go with him?" Martha asked.

"Nope. He said he'd stay and call the police. Uncle Adam told him to watch the house," Tilly announced.

Sheriff Malcolm had been right after all. The truck had been aimed at Adam, not her. The sheep must be a ploy to draw Adam into the open where the man from the black truck could get at him again.

Frightened, Josy stood abruptly, aware that every eye

was on her. There was no way to warn him even if her suspicions were right, but Adam was no fool.

"Aren't you going to eat your breakfast, Aunt Josy?" Tilly asked. "Are you sick?"

"No, honey, I'm not sick." Scared spitless, but not sick. "I'm just very hungry right now."

Martha sneered. She was doing everything she could to undermine Josy's position with the girls. Why? Was she angry because of Josy's original disappearance, or because of her reappearance? Josy couldn't ask in front of the girls.

"Anyone want to give me a guided tour of the ranch?" Josy asked instead, trying not to think about Adam walking into a trap.

"The girls have chores to do," Martha cut in.

She eyed the other woman steadily. "I'll help."

Martha stared pointedly at her bad leg. Josy felt her temper rise along with the heated color in her face. "The leg makes me slow, not helpless, Martha."

"I'll show you around after I finish, Aunt Josy," Tilly offered quickly. The child's concern was evident in her pinched face. This tension was not good for anyone, but Josy didn't know what to do or say to defuse the situation.

"You want to help? Take this thermos out to Brug," Martha suggested suddenly. "He forgot it this morning. The girls can get their work done and then show you around."

The words were fine. The tone was all wrong. Josy stared at Martha suspiciously.

"Okay."

Martha snatched up the black cylinder from the countertop and thrust it in Josy's direction. "You girls go get your laundry."

"I'll hurry, Aunt Josy," Tilly promised quickly. "My room's not too messy."

Josy gave her a grateful smile. "Where do I find Brug?"

"Try the barn. That big red building down the hill," Martha added spitefully.

Josy swallowed a retort. Martha would get away with it for now, but Josy had no intention of letting this problem continue. She'd take the coffee out to Brug and then she'd find a way to get Martha alone. Like it or not, Josy was here until she fulfilled her promise to Adam.

Josy could see where someone like Martha might find Adam wildly attractive. Martha was young and pretty, and there'd been no mention of a husband. Adam had referred to Martha fondly as his housekeeper. It didn't take a genius to guess she wanted to be a whole lot more. Adam would make a good catch for any woman in the market for a husband—which Josy certainly wasn't, but maybe Martha was.

Why hadn't Adam married her instead of Josy, a stranger he claimed to have met in a Reno alley? There was room to drive a tank through that story. Josy needed a closer look at that picture and the signature on the marriage certificate. She wondered where Adam had put the documents.

She went back upstairs for her coat, marveling anew at the size and decor of Adam's home. It was none of her business, but this house was all wrong for a sheep rancher who wanted to raise three young girls.

The children raced past her up the treacherously open staircase to gather their laundry. Josy had hoped that if she hurried, she could catch the other woman alone for a minute, but the girls were faster than her leg allowed her to be. By the time she got back downstairs, Suzie was in the laundry room off the kitchen sorting clothing with Martha.

Josy decided to avoid another confrontation and left through the front door instead of the back. She opened the door, and Killer darted past her.

"Killer, get back here!"

Killer barked cheerfully and romped at her feet, just out of reach. Someone had better see to the training of this cat-size dog before he got hurt or caused any more problems.

Killer didn't run off, so Josy decided against calling Suzie to come and get him. He gamboled at her side as she made her way down the hill toward the barn. Maybe Brug could grab the dog and help her get him back inside.

Clouds raced to cover the morning sun. A gust of cold air made her shiver despite her heavy jacket. Snow? She shivered again. Definitely cold enough.

Two horses moved about the small corral outside the barn, as if they, too, were testing the wind. She recognized one of them as the nervous colt from this morning and tried again to reach for Killer. He danced just out of range, yipping with glee at this new game. Josy gave up.

"Stay right here with me, Killer."

Killer barked. He barely spared the two horses a glance, but Josy didn't feel safe until she'd opened the barn door with Killer still at her side.

Inside the dark interior, pungent, earthy animal odors assaulted her nostrils. The smells weren't really disagreeable, just different. Whatever else lay hidden in her past, Josy was pretty certain barns hadn't played a big role. There was nothing at all familiar about this setting.

The door slammed shut on a gust of wind without warning. Killer jumped almost as badly as she did. In the sudden gloom, every object loomed with menace.

"It's okay, Killer," she lied. "It's just the wind." The dog looked reassured. She wished she felt the same way. There was something scary about this big open barn. She felt exposed. And watched.

"I'd better hurry. There's definitely rain or snow on the

way," she told the dog. Uninterested, he moved forward to sniff curiously.

Josy wished Adam were there. What if he'd walked into a trap? That's exactly what this barn felt like to her.

Josy peered around, feeling unaccountably edgy. A horse snorted and rustled in his stall while Killer darted about, sniffing madly. Time to get out of here.

"Brug?"

The barn was clean, despite all its odors. Josy wondered where the light switch was. The gloomy sky had turned the place into a dim cavern.

The large brown horse snorted and stamped his feet as she neared. He watched her from dark, malevolent eyes.

"Hello, horse. You don't bother me and I won't bother you, okay? Hey, Brug? I brought your thermos."

The silence was broken only by the sound of the wind outside and the horse moving fretfully. The other stalls appeared empty. She hoped they were empty.

Something big and furry leaped to the top of the gate beside her. Josy let out a startled yelp, then realized it was an enormous barn cat. The animal regarded her haughtily behind reflective eyes.

"You scared me, cat. Better not let Killer see you." Actually, she decided she was worrying over the wrong animal. This cat probably outweighed the dog by a good three pounds. With a flick of the ears, the cat leaped to the next stall and disappeared. The horse whinnied loudly at her back.

"I don't like it in here either, horse. How come you aren't outside with the others?"

The horse snorted, tossing his head. He did not look happy. Her gaze traveled down the line of stalls. Where was Brug? For that matter, where had Killer gotten to? It would be just her luck for the silly dog to go haring off after that monster of a barn cat and get in more trouble.

"Killer?" She started past the horse, giving him a wide berth. He gave another loud whinny, startling her. "Hey, take it easy, horse." He was a big animal, even for a horse. If he decided he wanted out, she suspected that flimsy bit of wood serving as a gate wasn't going to get in his way for long. This was no place for her to be.

"Killer?" There was no sound of the dog. No sound of the cat, either. Uneasy, she cast around peering at shadows. There were a lot of shadows.

"Brug?" The silence worked on her nerves. She wanted to go back outside. The cold wind was preferable. "Killer? Come here, boy. Brug? Are you in here?"

Maybe Brug had followed Adam after all. She'd go back to the house and tell Martha he wasn't here. The woman would probably sneer, but Josy didn't care. Ultimately, Martha was Adam's problem, not hers.

A prolonged gust of wind battered something against the side of the barn. The horse gave a startled squeal and lashed out at the stall door with his hoof.

"You convinced me. This spooky old barn is no place for a city girl." And she was certain that's exactly what she was.

If Brug wanted his coffee, he could walk up to the house and get it himself. Josy had had enough. She turned and started back the way she'd come. A sound made her pause.

"Brug?"

It had come from the stall right behind her. The stupid cat, no doubt. Josy started for the main door, but moved too quickly. Her weak leg made her stumble. She reached for something to keep herself from falling, and the thermos dropped from her hand.

"Drat!"

There was a rapid scuffling sound behind her. Off balance, she attempted to turn. The big brown horse reared up next to her, his hoofs striking the wood of his stall sharply as he trumpeted his unhappiness.

She felt rather than saw the motion behind her. And something slammed into the back of her head.

ADAM PULLED THE TRUCK to the side of the road. Two sheep lay dead. One crumpled car had nosed its way into the ditch while another car was pulled half on and half off the road, the driver's fender crinkled like so much tin foil.

The situation wasn't as bad as it could have been. No one appeared hurt. Traffic wasn't heavy on this road, but several cars and trucks were stopped, the drivers helping Pete and Tim herd the bewildered sheep back to safety.

None of the stopped vehicles was a large black truck, Adam noted.

Seventeen-year-old Jerry Minglie, whose dad owned a spread farther down the road, was talking to the middle-aged woman whose car he'd hit. Both seemed shaken, but otherwise unhurt. Adam was grateful for small favors.

"Sorry about the sheep, Mr. Ryser," Jerry said, spotting his approach. "The accident was partly my fault. I dropped my CD case and looked away from the road for a second. When I looked back, the sheep were all over the road. I tried to miss them—I really did."

"It's okay, Jerry. As long as you and this lady weren't seriously hurt."

The stout woman nodded. "I'm Trudy Gebhert. My husband won't be thrilled with the dent, but no real harm was done. I nearly hit a couple of your sheep myself."

"Anyone injured?"

"No," Jerry assured him. "All these other drivers just

stopped to help. I called your ranch from this lady's car phone. Your men got here real fast."

Faster than the police, Adam noted. A patrol car was just pulling up to the scene.

"Did you see anyone walking around or driving away?" Adam asked. The pair looked confused, but shook their heads.

"Hey, Adam. What happened?"

"Mick," he greeted the young officer.

The sheep had been herded inside, and Pete was already pulling materials from his truck bed to repair the fence. Adam noted they were in for some weather despite today's prediction to the contrary.

"Someone cut the fence," Adam told him.

Mick's gaze narrowed. "On purpose?"

"That's what Brug said. I just got here."

"Anyone hurt?" The two drivers assured him they weren't. "Let's go have a look," Mick said to Adam.

No effort had been made to disguise the fact that the fence had been deliberately cut. Unfortunately, in their efforts to get the sheep back inside, the helpful neighbors had obliterated any other signs that might have been left behind.

No one had seen another car or truck, nor anybody on foot near the scene. Trudy Gebhert was philosophical about the whole event. "Probably a teenage prank. As you said, Mr. Ryser, no one was hurt, except your poor sheep. Your man had to shoot one of them, it was hurt so bad. The situation could have been a lot worse."

Adam knew just how much worse it could have been and sent up mental thanks to whatever angels had worked overtime on this one.

Leaving his men and Mick to finish cleaning up, Adam headed back to his truck and called the barn. The phone rang unanswered. He frowned as he started the engine. An

odd little shiver that had nothing to do with the wind trav
eled up his spine.

Brug was probably outside. Or maybe he was havin
more trouble with Harry's Pride. The mean-tempered sta
lion was more trouble than he was worth. They'd had t
isolate him this morning for the vet to come and check hi
over. He was off his feed and running a fever.

Adam tried the bunkhouse. Still no answer. There wer
many reasons Brug might not be answering the phone
Adam worried one of them was that Brug had been neede
up at the main house.

He tried the house and got a busy signal.

Adam turned the truck around in a spray of gravel an
headed back to the ranch. Probably, he was borrowing trou
ble. If anything had gone wrong, Brug or Martha woul
have called. Still, Adam had left Josy alone for too long
Her introduction to Martha and the girls hadn't gone ver
well this morning. He only hoped Tilly had explained hi
sudden disappearance.

Josy had a right to be ticked at him. She'd filled hi
dreams last night and his thoughts all morning, but he tol
himself it was lust, pure and simple. He was not going t
put his heart on the line for her again. Last night, he'd lai
in bed for hours thinking about their relationship.

Adam hadn't planned to ever marry again. But he hadn
planned on being a father to three young girls, either. H
could handle things while they were this age, but in a fe
years, Tilly would be a teenager. Adam was pretty sure h
wasn't ready for that. The girls needed a mother. A per
manent mother.

Two weeks into his hasty marriage, Adam had wante
Josy to be that person. She'd disappeared the very ne
morning. If she'd left because she didn't want to stay, th
was one thing—but if it hadn't been her choice?

That had kept him tossing for most of the night. Not even Alyssa had hurt him as badly. Josy, with her spunk and her laughter, her loving ways, had made him believe that anything was possible. Even happily-ever-after.

Adam struck the steering wheel with the heel of his hand. He'd been stupid. And if he wasn't careful, he'd make the same mistake all over again. The attraction was still there, no matter how hard he tried to fight it. He liked Josy.

And he still wanted her.

Maybe he should offer her another deal. Since Josy couldn't remember her past, maybe she'd accept a future. And this time, he'd keep his emotions out of the bargain. A straight deal. A mother for the girls, security for Josy.

It would work. He would make it work. If nothing else, the five of them needed to go into that hearing on Thursday united as a family. Adam was going to ensure that it happened.

A strong gust of wind scattered dirt across the windshield. Darn weathermen, couldn't they ever get it right? The sky hid behind leaden gray clouds.

Adam turned into the yard and braked. The first thing he saw was the barn door flopping madly in the wind. Alarm sent him sprinting for the barn.

Killer was yapping crazily inside the dark building. Where were the lights?

And then he saw Josy being held against Brug's lanky body.

"What the…?"

Harry's Pride squealed in anger. He towered in the aisle, ears flat to his skull, eyes rolling dangerously. His sides heaved with exertion, and his coat was lathered in sweat. Killer continued to challenge the stallion, holding the horse at bay while dodging his hoofs.

"Get Harry," Brug shouted.

The horse charged without warning. Brug pulled Josy to safety inside a vacant stall. Adam waved his arms and yelled, distracting and confusing the irrational animal. Killer worked as if he'd been trained from birth to herd crazed stallions. Several long, frustrating minutes later, Adam had the horse back inside his stall.

Harry thrashed around and trumpeted his fury. Brug held Josy, murmuring softly against her hair. His hand stroked her back in a soothing gesture that sent a strange, fierce sense of possessiveness right through Adam. He fought an urge to grab his foreman and put a fist right in the man's face.

"What happened here?"

Josy turned wide, slightly unfocused eyes on him. Even in the dim light, he could see her skin was deathly pale. Brug released her slowly. Reluctantly, it seemed to Adam, but he was distracted when she swayed unsteadily.

"I don't know," Brug replied. "The lights went out right after I called the police about the sheep. I went out back to have a look around. Then I heard Killer barking and Harry screaming. I ran back in and found Josy laying in the aisle outside Harry's stall. That loco horse was trying to kill her. If it hadn't been for Killer, he probably would have succeeded."

"Josy?"

Her color was returning, but she looked confused and in pain.

"My head hurts," she said softly, her hand going to the back of her head.

"Here. Let me see. Did he get you?" He cupped the back of her head gently, and she inhaled sharply.

"Ow."

Beneath the short silky strands was a raised area on the back of her head. "She's got a lump back here."

"Maybe she hit her head when she fell," Brug suggested.

"Josy, what were you doing in here?"

She stared at him blankly.

"A better question," Brug said, "is why she opened Harry's gate. That horse could have killed her."

Harry lashed out at his stall door and snorted. Josy swayed again, and Adam slid an arm around her back for support.

"Get on the phone to Luke. I'm taking her to his place. I want her looked at right away. She could have a concussion."

He led Josy to the door. She stumbled and nearly fell.

"I'm okay," she muttered.

"I can see that." He lifted her into his arms, frowning anew over how lightly she filled them. Her clothing probably weighed as much as she did. She reminded him of Killer, nothing but hair and bones. Fragile, delicate bones at that.

"Put me down. I can walk."

"I know, but I like holding you."

She stared at him, then frowned. "I can't remember," she said with a trace of panic.

"What can't you remember?"

"What am I doing here?"

Her fear communicated itself to him. She'd suffered severe head trauma in her initial fall. What would another injury do to her? "It's okay, Josy. You're okay."

She managed a serious glare. "It is *not* okay. Why am I inside your barn?"

Darn good question, but at least she knew it was his barn. He stepped outside into the icy wind.

"Adam, put me down."

He ignored her, grateful that she remembered his name.

Sleet lashed them as he crossed to the truck. The storm had arrived—in more ways than one. Josy resisted being put in the truck.

"I don't want to go anywhere. Where are you taking me?"

"Josy, if you don't get in, I'm going to drop you." She slid onto the seat. "Luke Hamilton is a friend. He is also the local doctor. I'm going to take you to his office and have him look you over."

"No!"

He shut the door and went around to the other side.

"I hate doctors," she said as he climbed behind the wheel.

"Luke will be crushed."

"I mean it, Adam. I don't want a doctor."

"Sorry, Josy, but you need your head examined. Buckle your seat belt."

"That isn't funny." But she reached for the belt, tugging it across her chest with short choppy motions.

"It wasn't meant to be. That's a nasty bruise on the back of your head. I'm worried you have a concussion." The engine roared to life.

"I do not have a concussion."

"We'll let Luke confirm that diagnosis." He started down the long drive from the house. "Were you looking for me in the barn?" he asked before she could argue any further.

Josy bit her lip. "I don't remember."

Her quiet despair tugged at his heart. He reached for her hand, finding it icy cold. Was she going into shock? He released her to crank up the heater another notch.

"What's the last thing you do remember?"

She touched the back of her head gingerly. "Suzie. She was afraid you were going to shoot her dog."

That had happened more than two hours ago.

"Not a chance," he told her heartily. "That little dog just saved your life. Harry's Pride, the unhappy horse in the barn, is a mean-tempered beast at the best of times, but he's sick right now. The vet's coming out this afternoon to look at him. Stallions can be contrary animals. Especially if you don't know what you're doing around them."

"So what was I doing in the barn? I don't know anything about horses."

He wished he understood the workings of her mind. How could she know that but not remember going into the barn? Had someone lured her out there?

Adam checked his rearview mirror. Sleet pelted the truck, reducing visibility. There was one vehicle behind him on the otherwise empty road, but it looked like one of Hank's red work trucks. Adam couldn't be sure, and frankly he didn't care as long as there was no sign of the big black truck.

He was probably letting his imagination run wild. Josy must have gone to the barn for a reason. Brug knew to watch for trouble. He would have said if someone else had been on the grounds.

"I feel funny," Josy said, breaking into his thoughts.

"Are you sick?" Adam asked quickly.

"No, not sick, just...I feel fragile. Like my head might fall off if I move too fast."

Adam increased his speed. The roads weren't bad yet despite the reduced visibility. Fat white snowflakes began mixing with the sleet. He'd take snow over ice any day.

"Try not to move around. We'll be at Luke's place in a few minutes. He's got an impressive operation in one wing of his house. He even has his own lab and X-ray equipment. We're a good distance from the nearest hospital, so Luke is set up to treat just about anything. He even has a helicopter pad for emergencies. Not that you're an emergency," he hastened to assure her.

"Uh-huh. That's why you bundled me into the car so fast."

"Hey, I just—"

"Don't worry, Adam. I don't need to be placated. My head's harder than it feels at the moment."

"I wasn't trying to placate you. Taking you to see Luke is to placate me."

Josy fell silent. Adam darted periodic glances in her direction to make sure she didn't fall asleep. Josy stared out the window, but she didn't close her eyes. He guessed she was trying to reconstruct the morning's events.

Thankfully, Luke's parking lot was pretty empty. His plump wife, Tracy, led them straight back to an examining room, but then shooed Adam out to the waiting room when he would have stayed with Josy.

"It's okay," Josy offered on his behalf.

"He can wait outside until Luke tells him different," Tracy decided. She leveled Adam with a practiced look guaranteed to inspire obedience.

Instead of pacing the cluttered waiting room, Adam went to the truck and called the house. Martha answered on the first ring.

"Brug told me what happened. Who would have thought she'd be foolish enough to open Harry's stall? I just sent her out with a thermos of coffee while the kids were doing their chores."

Well, that explained Josy's presence in the barn.

"The girls are worried."

"Tell them she'll be fine, Martha. I wanted Luke to check her over as a precaution. We should be back shortly. Is Brug nearby?"

"Underfoot as usual," she groused good-naturedly. "I'll get him for you."

"Adam?" Brug questioned in his ear after a brief pause.

"Yeah. Listen, I want you to go outside and have another look around. Don't spook Martha or the kids, but I want to make sure there was no one else in that barn this morning."

He sensed Brug's surprise, but the other man responded cautiously since Martha, and probably the girls, was right there.

"A fuse went bad, Adam, but I'll have a look around."

"Thanks. We should be back shortly."

Adam clicked off and placed another call to the investigator who'd originally located Josy for him. Ned Pohl and his partner ran their firm out of Cheyenne. They specialized in missing persons. He'd already talked to Ned earlier that morning to ask that they continue the search for Josy's mother.

"Hey, Adam," Ned greeted, "I know we're good, but even we aren't this good. I don't have anything for you yet."

"You're slipping, pal. Listen, Ned, I've got something else. Josy was injured this morning. It isn't serious and it looks like an accident, but I've been thinking. Have someone in Reno run a check on Pandergarten for me, okay?"

Ned's voice raised an octave. "The casino owner?"

"Yeah. I want to know if Josy's mother owes him more money, or if Josy had some other connection to him beside the one through her mother."

A chain-smoker, Ned drew hard on one of his constant cigarettes. Adam could almost see him expel a stream of smoke before he replied. "That'll be tricky, Adam. The owners don't exactly broadcast who owes them, you know. As it happens, I do know a reputable firm there that may be able to give us some information. I'll see what I can do.''

"Good. Can you run another check on that hotel in San Diego? I know you looked for connections to Josy among the employees, but what if she saw something there that morning? See if anything made the papers subsequently that might explain her sudden disappearance.''

"What's going on, Adam?"

He stared out over the dashboard into the blinding snow. "Maybe I'm fooling myself, but I don't think she walked away from us because she wanted to that morning. I think either something from her past caught up with her, or she saw something she shouldn't have in the hotel or the restaurant. Pandergarten and her mother are the only connections to her past that I have.''

"Okay, I'll put someone on it. You know, we don't take on bodyguarding cases, but if you want, I can recommend someone.''

"Thanks, Ned, but you don't know Josy. She can be a pretty stubborn little cuss. I don't think she'd take well to the idea of a bodyguard, but I'll keep it in mind. I'm going to make sure Martha doesn't let Josy out of her sight from now on.''

His gaze drifted to the main road. Was that a vehicle pulled off to one side? The blowing snow made it impossible to see clearly. He finished talking to Ned and stepped from the truck.

Probably a stranded motorist, he told himself as he lowered his head and started across the lawn on an intercept course. He wasn't taking any chances that it was a dark black truck with no plates. Blinking snow from his lashes, he made out the shape. Definitely a truck.

Without warning, the vehicle sprang to life, made a sharp U-turn and took off heading away from him.

Adam ran back to his own truck, intending to give chase. He slid on a patch of loose snow and the keys fell from his fingers, bouncing under the frame of the truck. By the time he retrieved them, he knew trying to follow was useless. The other vehicle would be long gone. He hadn't even been able to clearly see the color or make.

If it *was* the black truck, how was he driving with a shot-up windshield? He'd wreck before he reached the curve near the Winston place unless he knew the road well.

Adam reached under the seat and withdrew the .38-caliber handgun he kept there. After making sure it was fully loaded and the safety was in place, he shoved it into his jacket pocket and headed for the building. Amnesia or no amnesia, Josy was going to have to try to remember her past. Her life depended on it.

Chapter Five

Josy knew something else was wrong as soon as Adam walked back inside. When he said nothing, she waited until they were on their way to his truck to question him.

"Are the girls okay?"

"Just worried about you." He held open the door and swung her up on the seat before she could protest. Josy curbed her annoyance. He was trying to help.

"What's wrong?" she asked as soon as he got inside.

"Nothing." But his eyes swept the empty road with penetrating intensity. The wind had blown itself out. Snow drifted from the sky slowly now, as if tired from its earlier efforts.

"Adam, I have a slight concussion. That doesn't make me stupid. What's happened now?"

He started the engine and glanced at her as he put the truck in gear. "What makes you think anything's happened?"

"Don't ever play poker, Adam. You don't have the face for it."

He appeared stunned by that proclamation, but quickly changed the subject.

"Luke says this bout of amnesia may be temporary."

Josy's annoyance deepened, but she gave a careless

shrug. Then she wished she hadn't when her lightly bruised shoulder protested the motion. Amazingly, she didn't have a headache, just this odd feeling of fragility. Luke had assured her the sensation would go away. She had liked the easygoing doctor and his wife, to her surprise.

"My memory is tricky at the best of times," she reminded Adam. "Now, I want to know why you came back inside looking so upset."

He frowned and shifted in his seat, but she knew she'd won. While he told her about the truck, Josy studied his rugged profile, thinking how dangerous he looked. There was something comforting in the knowledge that he was concerned on her behalf. She had to keep reminding herself that it wasn't personal; she was an investment. A temporary one at that.

"I didn't open the stall door," she said when he finished.

He darted a quick, hard stare in her direction before returning his gaze to the road. "You're remembering?"

"Not exactly. I have an impression of an angry horse. He's big and making a lot of noise, kicking the wall because he wants out. There's no way I would have let him out, Adam. I have a great deal of respect for beasts that much bigger than me."

"Yeah," he said, surprising her. "That would have been my take, too. You're nobody's fool, Josy."

The simple words warmed her. Then he reached for her hand, swallowing it in his much larger one. Her breath jammed in the back of her throat. She told herself not to be stupid. He was just holding her hand to reassure her. She had to remember how he'd stroked the frightened horse this morning. She couldn't afford to be drawn into the magic web he wove. Adam wanted a temporary wife, not a real one.

And then his callused thumb began to slide deliberately,

teasingly, back and forth across her knuckle in a sensual caress. He never took his eyes from the road.

"I think there was someone else in the barn with you," he said quietly. "Probably the same person who cut the fence to draw me away from the house."

She had to clear her throat. "Why?" She wanted to pull her hand back, but at the same time, she didn't want him to stop touching her. Maybe the head injury *had* made her stupid. Was she so desperate she was willing to settle for being a stand-in wife to a man who'd made it clear he didn't love her?

"Why am I a threat to someone now, when I wasn't a threat to them a week ago?" she managed to ask.

"Maybe because no one knew you were still alive until I found you." He gave her fingers a gentle squeeze. "I may have led someone right to you."

"But, Adam, that doesn't make sense." Neither did the way his touch made her feel. This was foolish. She was going to get hurt. He was being kind to achieve his own goals. But she left her hand in his.

"The police advertised my amnesia as much as possible. My picture was even televised."

"I never saw the story, but then I spent a lot of time in California and Nevada last year. Maybe the driver of the black truck never saw the story, either."

"That means someone's been watching you."

Adam sat very still. "Yeah."

"For a year and a half?"

He released her hand to grip the steering wheel. Funny how much she missed that small contact.

"I don't believe it, Adam."

"You got a better explanation?"

No, but she wished she did. Panic nibbled at her mind. If Adam was right, somewhere in her memories was a knowledge that constituted such a serious threat to the man in the black truck, he'd tried to kill them. And that knowledge was buried irretrievably. She might die without even knowing why.

"Sheriff Malcolm implied that your hiking accident could have been something else," Adam went on. "There was nothing substantial, but a few things didn't add up. Your shoes and clothing were all wrong for an experienced hiker. The backpack wasn't on your back—it was lying next to you. You also didn't have the right equipment and weren't found on a marked trail."

She knew. Malcolm had been totally honest with her.

"If only I could remember."

THE SNOW HAD STOPPED by the time they reached the house. Tilly burst from the front door and raced down the four steps before Josy could reach for the door handle. The child's features were tight with worry.

"Everything okay?" Adam asked.

"I just wanted to see if you brought Aunt Josy back with you."

"Where else would I leave her, sprite?"

Where else indeed. He needed her, while she was trying desperately not to fall in love with him. Adam opened her door and reached for her gently. She was in his arms again feeling safe and right.

"I know," he said mockingly, "'put me down.'"

The thought hadn't crossed her mind. It should have.

"The girls," she protested.

"They'll have to get used to seeing me carry you. I like carrying you. You barely weigh more than Killer."

"Adam—"

"She didn't eat her breakfast," Tilly announced. "Is she really okay?"

"I'm fine."

"She's fine," Adam said at the same time. "But," he added, "she has a concussion, so we'll have to pamper her."

"You will not have to pamper me."

Martha stood in the hall restraining a wriggling Killer. Bitsy and Suzie watched silently from her side. The woman didn't look happy to see her, Josy thought, but maybe her expression indicated concern. Then again, she probably figured Josy's pampering would entail more work for her.

Josy had a feeling that was almost a memory. Martha didn't like her for some reason. What had happened this morning? These memory gaps were getting harder and harder to take.

"Adam, put me down. I am perfectly capable of walking."

"Quit yelling." He carried her into the living room and set her on the sofa.

"I am not yelling," she told him quietly but forcefully.

"Could have fooled me. Martha, what have we got to eat? We have to fatten this sassy woman up, and I seemed to have missed lunch."

"I'll get a tray ready right away, Adam."

Martha set Killer on his feet, and the small dog quickly jumped into Josy's lap. Adam started to reach for him, but Josy cuddled the dog to her chest. "Good boy, Killer. You were a real hero today."

"He was?" Suzie asked, coming forward.

"You bet he was," Adam agreed. "I couldn't have handled Harry without him."

"Then you aren't mad?"

"Suzie, Killer saved my life," Josy told her. "He faced down that big horse all by himself. He's a good dog," she added, petting the small wriggling form. "What we've got to do is train him to obey voice commands."

"I could get a book at the library."

"Good idea."

Suzie sat down next to her looking relieved. Bitsy took her usual place as close to Adam's side as she could get, while Tilly observed everything from serious eyes that were much too old for her years.

Martha returned with plates piled high with thick meaty sandwiches in homemade bread, potato chips and pickles. Josy had no hope of eating the enormous portions, but her stomach rumbled, reminding her that she was pretty hungry. Martha disappeared and returned with two large glasses of milk and a plate of caramel brownies.

Josy never got to taste the brownies. Exhaustion stole over her as she ate and relaxed, listening to Adam and the girls talk about schoolwork and friends and upcoming plans. She woke partially when Adam tucked an afghan around her, but she was far too comfortable to protest. Killer barked somewhere inside the house, followed by children laughing. Josy snuggled contentedly into the sofa.

Low, angry voices woke her sometime later. The room lay in darkness, the only light a splash of color near the main hall. Disoriented, Josy pushed aside the afghan and sat up, dismayed by how stiff she felt.

"I have every right—" a raised male voice started.

"I am not disputing your rights, Hank, but the girls need time with Josy." Adam's voice was low and even.

"And where is this paragon you think is going to raise my granddaughters?"

"I'll get her so you two can meet."

Josy finger-combed her hair, wishing she could duck into a bathroom before meeting the girls' grandfather for the

first time. Although it didn't sound like Hank Claussen wa
going to approve of her no matter what she looked like.

"She's here now?" He sounded surprised.

"Where else would she be? Like it or not, Hank, Jos
is my wife. Wait a minute and I'll go get her."

His wife. Adam made it sound so natural. So real instea
of some "deal" he'd created.

"I don't have the time right now," Hank protested.

Josy got to her feet, then had to wait for the world t
right itself as dizziness threatened her balance. Her hea
still felt incredibly fragile.

"It'll just take a moment, Hank, she's—"

"I'll be over tomorrow," he said firmly. "I'll meet yo
woman then. In the meantime, be thinking about that offe
It's good money."

Adam's woman? Only in her dreams.

"Don't you even want to stay and say hello to th
girls?"

Hank's reply faded away, and she heard the front doc
open. What had upset the man? Or did he always act lik
that? If so, Josy wasn't surprised Adam didn't like him
She didn't like him, either.

She started forward and stumbled over the coffee tabl
By the time she reached the hall, the front door stood aja
allowing the cold evening air to sweep inside. Couldn
these people learn how to close doors? she wondered. Jos
pulled it all the way open to find Adam on the porc
watching his ex-father-in-law depart.

Adam looked solid and strong, yet oddly alone. Auto
matically, Josy moved to his side and watched a large burl
man step into an expensive-looking dark car. He never onc
glanced back toward the house. The porch light wasn't o
and there wasn't enough light for Josy to clearly see h
features, but the set of his shoulders proclaimed his ange

A low bank of ominous clouds had moved in overhead once again, cutting off whatever source of light the sky would have provided. It had snowed some more, she realized.

"That was Hank?" she asked.

"Yeah."

"He seems to be in a hurry."

"Yeah." Adam watched the car start up. Josy shivered and Adam drew her against his side as if it were the most natural thing in the world. The gesture was intimate somehow. "Come on, let's get back inside. It's cold out here. How do you feel?"

"Sore, if you want the truth."

"I always want the truth, Josy."

She peered into his hard dark features, but couldn't decide what he was thinking. "I never lie. With my faulty memory, it would be too much work. What was that all about? With Hank, I mean."

"Darned if I know. He said he'd heard we had some trouble and he wanted to take the girls for the night. I don't think he expected me to be home or he wouldn't have bothered. We've had variations of this discussion several times already. He knows I want the girls to stay with me until after the custody issue is settled."

Was Adam worried that Hank would take off with the children? The man was a state senator, for heaven's sake.

"What if the court finds in favor of Hank, Adam?"

He stared into her eyes. "It isn't going to happen."

Josy shivered at the intensity underscoring his words.

Amazingly, the rest of the evening went smoothly. The weekend was over and school would be back in session the following day. The girls went to bed without protest. Adam may not have been a father for very long, but based on the shrieks of childish laughter that trailed down the stairs, he was a natural.

Josy smiled as she listened from the living room. This was the sort of family life she'd always wished for.

The thought started her heart pounding as a memory surfaced. She was sitting in darkness listening to raised voices and wishing her family were like the ones on television. And as quickly as it came, the memory stopped, leaving her struggling in vain to capture more.

"What sort of room? How old was I? Why can't I remember?"

Only the soft hissing from the fireplace answered her desperately whispered questions. In the back of the house the telephone began to ring. When the ringing continued, Josy went in search of the phone.

Martha had stayed conspicuously in the background all evening. She hadn't even eaten with the family. Josy knew Adam hadn't liked that, but even though he talked to her, Martha remained adamant and disappeared into her rooms off the kitchen after cleaning up. She'd refused Josy's offer of help and Adam had added his voice to Martha's, so Josy had spent the evening with Adam and the girls watching television.

The kitchen was spotless and empty when Josy reached for the wall phone.

"Hello?"

Silence filled her ear.

"Hello?"

The line was open, but the person didn't speak. There was something frightening in the deliberate silence on the other end of the line.

"Is someone there?"

The hush stretched, growing more ominous by the sec

ond. Josy swallowed and looked to see if Adam had caller ID. He didn't. The other person hung up with a soft click.

Shaken, she stood unmoving for several long seconds. There was no use telling herself not to be afraid. Josy was very afraid. A wrong number would have said so or hung up right away. Whoever this was had wanted to frighten her—and had succeeded. The knowledge made her angry.

Josy crossed to the window over the kitchen table and stared out at the darkness. Snow fell gently, blanketing the night with a soft white cover.

"Who was on the phone?"

Adam's voice startled her. She turned too quickly, and her left leg buckled. Josy grabbed the nearest chair for support.

"Hey, I didn't mean to scare you." He came forward until he stood only inches away. He had a lithe, solid grace about him that disconcerted her.

"I thought you were still upstairs with the girls."

His chin was shadowed slightly by dark bristles that only added to his sexy, dangerous air.

"All's quiet. With any luck, we won't see them until morning. They tend to be heavy sleepers. Who was on the phone?"

The question pulled her thoughts from where they had no business going. Adam was her husband in name only. She must remember that at all times or she was going to come away from this situation with worse than a broken head.

"No one. At least, no one who wanted to talk to me."

"What does that mean?"

"They wouldn't answer. Finally, they just hung up."

"Maybe it was a bad connection."

The telephone rang again.

"I'll get it," he said. "Hello? Oh, hello, Eleanor."
Adam rolled his eyes.

Tension drained from her. Maybe Adam had been right.
Maybe the caller had had a problem on the other end of
the line. Maybe she was growing paranoid.

She wandered back to the living room to give Adam
some privacy. The fire burned low as she curled onto the
love seat. When Adam finished talking to his ex-mother-
in-law, Josy would insist he talk to her. She wanted answers. And she wanted to see that detective's report.

"We've been invited to dinner," Adam announced a few
minutes later. "It's a command performance. Eleanor won't
take no for an answer. She wants to meet my wife."

"Do you know your voice gets all hard and tight when
you mention her?"

He flopped down on the love seat beside her instead of
taking the larger sofa or one of the chairs. Josy found her
knee touching the side of a hard masculine thigh. He sat
much too close, and there was so much of him that she lost
her train of thought as she gazed at him.

"Does it? I didn't realize that."

Josy was unprepared when he reached out a hand and
drew her closer. She shouldn't let him do that, but it felt
so good. Just for a minute, couldn't she pretend that she
really belonged to this man? She readjusted her position to
fit against his side, entirely too aware of Adam and the way
he held her.

"What are you doing, Adam?"

"I thought we were going to talk."

"We are. I meant holding me like this."

"Relax, Josy. We're married. We have to look and act
married if we're going to convince everyone."

"There's no one here but us, Adam." But she allowed
herself to snuggle closer to his side. Her head came to rest

comfortably against his shoulder. A quiver started low in her belly at this intimate contact.

"You need the practice. You aren't used to being held."

"How do you know?"

"You said you were a virgin."

She was glad he wasn't looking directly at her. Heat sneaked up her face. "I should never have told you that. I was trying to make a point at the time."

"So am I. If we're going to be seeing that carnivorous woman, we need to look the part of a happily reunited loving couple or she'll eat us alive. And after all, on Thursday, we have to pull off the same role in front of the judge."

He began to rub her shoulder. Tingles unraveled all the way down her body to that quivery spot in her stomach. And for some reason, all she could think about was the array of silken undergarments upstairs.

She knew why Adam had married her, but why had she agreed? Not for the money. Even without a memory, she knew she would have stood up to that casino owner and his goons. Josy wasn't afraid of hard work. She would have paid back what her mother owed somehow.

Had she seized on Adam's offer because she'd seen her chance to become part of a real family? This family. With this man. Did she hope to change her temporary status as Adam's wife?

"You're awfully quiet all of a sudden," Adam said softly.

"I was trying to remember." His arm felt so good, cradling her like this. Comforting. Soothing. Distracting. Her body absorbed his warmth, yet part of her still felt strangely chilled and tingly.

"I don't remember my mother," she told him. "It seems

like I should at least remember her, wouldn't you think? I mean, she must have played a big role in my life.''

"No, I got the impression you weren't close at all, though I don't think that was the first time she'd called on you to bail her out.''

"It wasn't. Usually, her rich boyfriend took care of...Adam, she had a rich boyfriend!'' Josy jerked up, straining to pull memories from the void in her mind.

"Easy, honey. Don't try. Let them come if they want.''

She twisted to face him. "But it's so frustrating! There's nothing there! I can't picture her, can't remember anything about her. Yet I know she had a rich boyfriend. It isn't even a memory.''

"But more than you knew a few minutes ago,'' he reminded her.

Slowly, giving her time to pull away if she wanted to, Adam drew her back against his chest. She was petite and vulnerable, yet as tough as anyone he'd ever met. A true survivor.

"The girls are warming up to you,'' he said to distract her.

"Ha. Tilly watches me like some half-tamed kitten who expects the worst, and Bitsy never sees anything beyond you. If Suzie is warming up, that's only because I defended Killer.''

"Do you really think you can train that little mutt?''

"I don't know. I've never trained a dog.'' .

He filed that away and wondered if she'd even noticed yet another memory bit to add to her collection.

"We have to do something with him. You've been letting him run wild,'' she scolded. "He needs to learn to come when he's called. I was so afraid he'd run over to the corral and start chasing the horses.''

"But he didn't.''

"That was luck. I couldn't have stopped him. What are you doing?"

His hand stilled on her hair. He realized he'd been absently stroking the soft layers. "Sorry, does it bother you? I've always been fascinated by your hair."

"My hair?"

"It used to hang down around your shoulders. And it always looked so soft. I was right. It's made for a man's touch." He slid his finger from her hair to stroke the side of her face. "Just like your skin."

Josy tensed. "Are you flirting with me?"

"Do you mind?"

She pulled away from him and sat up straight. He'd never seen her look more vulnerable.

"Why?"

"Do you find it strange that I'm attracted to you?"

"Yes. I look in the mirror, Adam. I see a badly scarred woman with no past and a dubious future. You're rich and sexy and handsome enough to be a leading man and you darn well know it."

She had more defensive layers than the Pentagon.

"So you think I'm sexy?" He tried to look harmlessly flattered. Secretly, he was pleased that she found him attractive.

"Don't play with me, Adam. Please? I'll do my best to help you win the custody suit, but don't mess with my emotions, okay? They're a little too raw and exposed right now."

She went right for the jugular. He was guilty on all counts. He'd planned to deliberately seduce her to achieve his goals. But in return, he'd offer her a better future than working her life away in some tiny ceramic store. Was that so wrong?

Yeah. It was wrong. She deserved better. She deserved

a man who would love her unconditionally, and no matter how much he was attracted, he wasn't going to let any woman get that far under his skin again.

"Sorry," he said brusquely, withdrawing his arm.

"Why didn't you marry Martha?"

"Martha?" The question startled him. "Why would I marry Martha?"

"She's half in love with you."

"Martha?" Adam shook his head, amused by the idea. "Where did you get that impression? She's a friend, Josy. Her husband was my right-hand man for six years. He died of peritonitis three years ago when his appendix ruptured while he was out rounding up stray sheep. They'd been living in the apartment off the kitchen, and Martha stayed on afterward, helping with the house and cooking meals as she'd always done. The arrangement suited both of us."

"But when you needed a wife, why didn't you pick her?" Josy persisted.

"It never crossed my mind," he told her honestly. "Is that what's bothering you?"

"Nothing's *bothering* me," she retorted. "I just don't understand why you'd marry a complete stranger instead of someone you knew well. Someone you could trust."

"I can't trust you?" he said, trying to tease.

"You know what I mean."

"No, actually, I don't."

She rose abruptly and crossed to the fireplace, lifting the poker.

"Planning to bean me?"

"Don't tempt me."

Adam leaned back and allowed himself an inner smile at her spunk. Josy believed she was capable of taking on the world. She turned her back on him and stoked the fire back to snapping life. A log broke in half, scattering sparks.

For all that she was too thin, she was nicely rounded in all the right places. Once she filled out again, she'd set a man on his ear. Disturbed by that thought, Adam walked up behind her, admiring the view.

"Why the question about Martha?" Was it possible she was jealous? The idea shouldn't please him if he didn't want any emotional entanglement on either side. This was supposed to be a straight business deal.

"I'm trying to understand what it is you want from me, Adam."

"I thought we'd covered that." Why did she have to look so defenseless? "I want a wife—"

"You mean a temporary wife," she interjected.

Adam hesitated. "Not necessarily," he said slowly.

He could see the erratic dance of the pulse point in her throat and wished he knew what she was thinking.

"Say what you mean, Adam."

"The girls need a full-time mother, not just a temporary one. They'll be teenagers soon. I'm not sure I'm equipped to handle that." He offered her a smile, but she turned away, looking into the fire.

He had the feeling he had just hurt her somehow. That was the last thing he wanted to do. She'd already suffered enough. But she'd given him an opening, and he didn't know what else to do but finish with his offer.

"I know we made a deal, but I was wondering if you'd think about staying on after I get custody. I'll make it worth your while."

Her whole body stiffened. He'd stated his case badly. He couldn't seem to think straight when he got close to her.

"Did you make me this offer before?"

Her voice was so soft he had to strain to hear the words. "Before?"

She looked at him then. "Before I disappeared."

Adam thought about the offer he'd made to her the night before she vanished. That offer had come from his heart. This time, he was smarter. This time, emotions weren't part of the equation.

"We talked about your staying, yes."

"No wonder you said you bought me."

She set the poker down with stiff, precise movements.

"What are you talking about?" His heart pounded. He'd made a hash of this conversation.

"I'm not for sale anymore, Adam."

Her chin lifted in pride, but hurt lurked in her eyes, knifing him in the gut. He hadn't meant to hurt her, but she didn't give him a chance to tell her so.

"You don't need to seduce me into helping you, Adam. I'll live up to the original deal. I'll do what I can to help you get custody of the girls. Then I'm out of here."

She started to brush past him, but he grabbed her arms and she stumbled. He held her, wanting to take away that awful look in her eyes.

"Look, I said it all wrong. I'm sorry."

Josy gave a slight shake of her head. "You meant the words."

"Yes. I did. I do. But I want you to stay. The girls do need a mother."

"And what about you?"

"Me?"

"What do you need, Adam?"

He couldn't answer. A lump had risen in his throat at her bleak expression, trapping the words inside. He cupped her face gently, rubbing his thumb across her lower lip. She trembled, but she didn't pull away.

"I'm sorry, Josy."

Slowly, deliberately, he lowered his head until his lips touched hers. They parted slightly. Soft. So incredibly soft.

She held perfectly still as he kissed her. He could feel her quivering and he started to pull back. Suddenly, her hands tightened around him and her lips began to move tentatively against his. It was all the encouragement he needed.

Gently, Adam drew her against his body. A low groan of desire swelled in his throat when he felt the tip of her tongue. He parted his lips to allow her to explore while heat built inside him with the intensity of a flash fire. He'd prided himself on being a man of control, but this slip of a woman had destroyed all that with the touch of her lips.

Josy dug her fingers into his arms, clinging with heady passion. Any minute now, he was going to lose all vestiges of control and kiss her the way he needed to.

Abruptly, she drew back, her face mere inches from his. "My leg's about to fold."

A tenuous laugh burst free of his chest. The words were the last thing he'd expected from her. He lifted her into his arms, for once glad that she didn't weigh much more than one of the girls. He felt so shaky he wasn't sure he'd make it to the couch, much less upstairs to the privacy of his room. He'd never wanted a woman more in all his life.

"Josy, you never cease to am—" As he turned, a flash of motion outside caught his eyes. Someone watched them through the living-room window.

With a curse, Adam stood Josy on her feet, shoving her behind him. The half-glimpsed face disappeared, and he heard the running footsteps.

"What is it?"

He half dragged her into the hall, away from windows. "Get upstairs. Call the bunkhouse. Tell Brug we've got an intruder. And stay away from the windows! Don't open your bedroom door until I tell you it's okay."

"Where are you going?"

He pulled open the closet door. The .38 was still in the pocket of his jacket. "Outside."

"Don't be stupid! What if he's armed?"

"Then he'd better hope he's a better shot than I am."

Chapter Six

Passion died an immediate death the moment Adam said there was a prowler. How he'd seen anything in the darkness was beyond her.

Stupid macho male. He'd get himself killed if he wasn't careful.

He slung on his jacket as he went through the front door, not waiting to see that she complied with his orders. Just as well. Josy had no intention of obediently going upstairs like some helpless female.

She hurried to the kitchen phone. One of the instant dial buttons was marked Bnkhs. Hopefully, that stood for *bunkhouse*. The phone rang several times before it was picked up, and the voice didn't belong to Brug.

"Uh, this is Josy, at the main house. Adam wanted me to call Brug and tell him we have a prowler."

"A prowler?"

The man sounded astounded.

"He was outside the living-room window on the porch. Adam went out after him. And he has a gun. Adam does. So tell Brug to be careful—"

But she'd lost her audience. The man on the other end was already calling to Brug and explaining. Brug's voice suddenly filled her ear.

"Josy? What's going on?"

"Adam saw someone looking in through the living-room window. He went out after the person with a gun."

"Okay, darlin', take it easy. Pete and I are on our way."

Darling? "Brug, be careful. Adam won't be able to see clearly in the dark."

"Don't worry. He won't shoot one of us by mistake. Just sit tight." The phone disconnected in her ear.

Easy for him to say. What was it with these stupid males? Josy wasn't about to "sit tight." Did they think she was incapable of taking care of herself? She crossed to Martha's door and rapped sharply. Long seconds passed before the door opened.

Martha was dressed in a red silk wrapper and nothing else, as far as Josy could tell. Her hair and face were ruddy and damp. Had she just gotten out of the shower?

Or had she just come inside?

The thought came out of nowhere, but it paralyzed Josy for a moment, even as Martha snarled, "What do you want?"

"I'm sorry to bother you, Martha, but I thought you should know we have a prowler."

"What?" She ran a hand through her damp hair, and Josy thought her skin darkened another hue.

If only she could touch the other woman's skin to see if it was hot or cold.

"Adam went out after him. I called Brug, and he and someone named Pete are going to meet Adam outside. Adam said we should stay away from the windows."

"Let me get dressed. I'll be right out."

Josy braced the door before the woman could close it. "Martha, do we have any guns in the house?"

Martha looked shocked, then scowled. "What would *you* do with a gun?"

"Whatever I have to. We have three children upstairs."

"Then it's probably a good thing Adam doesn't keep any guns in the house." She pushed Josy backward none too gently. "You'd probably shoot one of them by mistake. I'll be right out."

Josy recovered her balance and stared at the closed door. If Martha wasn't in love with Adam, then why was the woman so hostile? Was Josy being ridiculous to suspect Martha of spying on them?

Josy glanced toward the window over the kitchen sink. Snow obstructed her view of the night. She hoped it would also obstruct the prowler's view of Adam, if there really was anyone out there now.

Josy lifted the phone and hesitated. As far as she knew, Adam hadn't reported what had happened to the police last night. Would he want her to report this?

"What are you doing?" Martha asked sharply. She'd thrown on jeans and a flannel shirt, combed her damp hair and even put on lipstick while Josy was debating what to do. The woman could have posed for a magazine cover. Martha was naturally beautiful. And Adam hadn't thought to marry her?

"I was going to call 911."

"Time for that if Adam catches the guy. This isn't the city, you know. We don't have policemen every four blocks. Out here, we take care of ourselves," she added as she bustled about efficiently. "I'll put water on for hot chocolate. Coffee would keep them up all night."

Josy rubbed her arms to keep from shaking the other woman. "Why are you so antagonistic?"

Martha paused, holding a kettle of water, to regard her with dark intensity. "We don't need you here."

"Adam seems to think otherwise."

Martha set the kettle on a burner and turned on the flame.

"What good's a wife who runs away as soon as she has to take care of a couple of kids?"

"Is that what you think I did?" Josy moved to stand behind a kitchen chair so she'd have something to hold on to if her leg decided to give out.

"That's what I *know* you did. He spent a fortune trying to find you."

Josy didn't know how to defend that statement, so she didn't try.

"Martha, you can condemn me out of hand all you want, but I don't think Adam will thank you for undermining me in front of the children. We need to go into court this week united as a family. Whatever you believe about me, we only have a few days to get the girls ready for that hearing. Your job—"

"Don't go telling me my job!" Martha raked her with a scorn-filled glare. "I'm the one who's been raising these girls since you disappeared. I'm the one who's held things together for Adam."

"And you resent the fact that Adam married me," Josy concluded for her.

"Yes!"

They both whirled as the front door opened.

"Josy?"

Relief flooded her. "In the kitchen, Brug." Josy started toward the hall, anxious to hear that Adam was okay. Brug met her more than halfway.

"I thought Adam said he told you to wait upstairs," he scolded.

"He did."

She was surprised when the good-looking cowboy pulled her against his chest.

"Are you okay?" he asked. His handsome face was

cherry red from the cold, his shoulders and hat flecked with snow.

"I'm fine. I thought I'd better tell Martha what was going on."

The younger woman stood in the opening watching them with a look of pure hatred. Josy tried to step back, but Brug didn't seem to realize what she was doing. His grip tightened fractionally, and he tipped his head to study her.

"You're sure you're okay, darlin'? That was quite a scare in the barn this morning. When I found you lying on that floor, I thought you were dead."

"I'm fine, Brug. Really. I just have a bruise on the back of my head." Again she tried to step back without success. "I don't think I got a chance to thank you for your rescue this morning," she added quickly.

"You don't need to thank me."

And the front door opened, bringing another gust of cold air and Adam.

"I'm so glad that crazy horse didn't hurt you any worse." Brug ruffled her hair and released her then, turning to Adam with a smile. "You were right. She didn't obey. She was here in the kitchen with Martha."

Adam radiated tension.

"I put water on for hot chocolate," Martha stated. "Was anyone out there?"

"Someone was out there, all right," Adam said in a cold, flat voice. "But he disappeared into the snow."

Brug nodded. "It's snowing like crazy. There were prints along the side of the house, but they were already disappearing when Pete and I got there. We probably muddled them looking for Adam."

"Where is Pete?" Martha asked.

"He and Tim are checking the roads to see if the gate's been opened or if there's any sign of a truck." Adam's voice was as frosty as the night. "Go out and have another look around, Brug. Check the barn and the pens. Obviously, everything is secure in here."

"Okay," Brug said cheerfully. He appeared unaware of the undercurrent. "Hey, Martha, how about a thermos of hot chocolate to go for us poor frozen heroes?"

Martha shot Josy a frozen look of her own before turning back to the kitchen. Adam, Josy noted, didn't remove his coat or his gloves.

"Are you going back out?" she asked.

"Yeah. Go upstairs and get some rest. You've had enough excitement for one day."

Josy flushed uncertainly. Did his emphasis on excitement refer to the prowler, or what had happened between them in the living room? Surely he wasn't angry because Brug had hugged her. The man was hugging Martha now, flirting openly and calling her darling, as well. Adam wasn't jealous. Was he?

Of course not. More likely, he was mad she hadn't followed directions. "Do you think it was the person from last night?"

"We don't get a lot of Peeping Toms out here in the middle of nowhere. Go to bed."

Josy stared in mute surprise. Adam was furious. At her!

"You go jump in the lake, Adam Ryser. I'm not some dog you can order about. Oh, I forgot, you don't have much success there, either, do you?"

She pivoted on her heel. It would have made a great exit if her leg hadn't buckled. Adam caught her before she disgraced herself completely by falling at his feet. Even though he wore gloves, his touch sent a current of energy right through her.

"Let me go."

"What's got you all riled up?"

"I said—let...me...go."

Surprised by her tone, he released her. "What's the matter with you?"

Josy summoned up her best glare. "I have a headache." His eyes widened farther. "Just try not to get yourself shot, okay? The girls need you."

As exits went, it wasn't her best, but she limped away to dead silence, aware of the other two observers who stood in the kitchen doorway. Every eye was riveted on her as she mounted the open staircase. In the kitchen, the kettle whistled forlornly.

ADAM CLIMBED THE STAIRS an hour later. Snow had ruined any chance of tracking the intruder. Tim did find a place where a truck-size vehicle had parked a good distance down the drive, but it appeared to have been some time ago.

Because it had been hidden under tall pines, snow hadn't yet covered the oil that had leaked, matting the needles. Adam decided the driver of the black truck had probably switched vehicles. A new truck wouldn't be leaking that much oil.

He went into his office and placed a long-distance call to the sheriff of Hayes, Colorado, but Malcolm was on leave for the next week. In the morning, Adam would have to call Mick and bring him up to date, not that there was much the local police could do.

Adam was puzzled. Why hadn't the prowler shot Josy? She would have been clearly visible from the window, and the guy had to know he stood a real good chance of getting away clean—as he'd done.

What was going on?

Adam paused in the upstairs hall and decided he was too tired to think straight. Too tired and too on edge. Finding Josy in Brug's arms for the second time in one day was playing havoc with feelings he didn't want to be having. But here he was, ready to chew out a good foreman for doing nothing more than comforting his wife.

The word stopped him cold. Josy was his wife. And tonight, he'd come darn close to making it more than words on paper.

What was wrong with him? Was that what he wanted or not?

Adam ran a weary hand through his wet hair where the snowflakes had melted. He was tired and acting like a fool. He knew what a flirt Brug was. The man couldn't help himself. Put a woman in front of him, and he went on automatic. Adam shouldn't have thought a thing of that scene in the hall. But he had, and it had unraveled him. Brug's arms around Josy churned something elemental inside him.

He was losing it; that was all there was to it. Josy had every right to be angry. He *had* ordered her around like he would Killer. And she had obeyed just as badly.

The thought brought a wry smile. Maybe he should see if Suzie could get a second book when she went to the library. One on training wives.

He stopped outside Josy's door. He owed her an apology, but no light shone beneath the crack. After listening hard, he realized there were no sounds inside. Well, she'd had one heck of a day. For that matter, so had he. Better if they talked in the morning after they'd both had some rest.

He went to his own door and entered the room without turning on the light. In the bathroom, he stripped down and took a quick shower, his thoughts still on Josy. They'd come close to establishing a new footing tonight. He still couldn't believe how fast she'd turned him on.

Had he blown everything with his stupid reaction to seeing her in Brug's arms again?

"Face it," he muttered. "You were jealous." Not surprising, considering what Alyssa had put him through.

Alyssa had used sex like a weapon. Right from the start, she'd reduced him to male-animal status with one coy, flirty look. He'd felt territorial whenever another man came near her. And he'd sworn he'd never give a woman that sort of power over him again.

He stared at his face in the mirror. Josy and Brug had brought all sorts of things rushing back. But Josy wasn't Alyssa. And he wasn't supposed to be feeling these strong emotions about Josy.

He would not fall in love with her. Not now, not ever again.

He dropped the towel on the sink and rubbed at the stubble on his chin. Time for bed. But he came to a stop several feet away. Someone already occupied one side of the mattress.

For a moment, he tensed. Then he closed the remaining distance. Josy lay there, completely dressed and curled around his pillow sound asleep.

His first thought was a wild rush of pleasure. *She'd come to him.* Then reality caught up. Her parting shot had told him clearly she had no intention of sleeping with him tonight. So what was she doing in his bed?

Waiting for him, obviously. No doubt she'd planned to chew his ear some more for ordering her around. He deserved it, but it was much too late to wake her and apologize. He should carry her back to her room. Adam hesitated. As he stared at her sleeping form, he knew he wasn't going to do that, either. He went to the closet for an extra blanket.

She sighed softly when he covered her, but otherwise didn't move. He started to look for some pajama bottoms and stopped when he realized what he was doing. What did it matter what he wore or didn't? As soon as Josy woke and realized he was in bed with her, she would leave.

Adam slid beneath the sheets and blanket on the other side of the bed, careful not to jar her, and stared up at the dark ceiling, wondering when he'd lost his mind. Josy made a soft sound in her sleep and turned on her side, her slender body spooned against him. He smelled the clean, fresh scent of her hair, but resisted the urge to touch.

He didn't want to love her. He really didn't. Love made you vulnerable, and it didn't last.

Eighteen months ago, he'd thought it could. And she'd disappeared.

Josy shifted restlessly. With a sigh, he rolled over to snug her more closely against his body. Instantly, she relaxed more deeply into sleep.

This was going to be a long night.

JOSY WOKE SLOWLY, coming out of an electrifying dream to find at least part of it was real. She was curled against a long hard body—emphasis on the hard. But it was the large male hand that pinned her to the bed that caused her to draw in a sharp breath. The broad masculine hand covered her right breast. Her nipple pressed against her bra and sweater, pushing itself boldly into that palm. She felt the contact in every molecule of her body.

Another point of contact pressed boldly into her buttock. Josy held perfectly still. Adam continued to breathe rhythmically, deeply, his breath tickling her hair. If she was careful, she could still get out of his bedroom and salvage her pride.

He must have thought she'd been waiting to take up where they'd left off in the living room. Nothing could be further from the truth. She'd been determined to have a meaningful discussion as soon as Adam came upstairs.

Only, she'd been so tired, she must have fallen asleep while she waited.

She had to get out of here before he woke—before the girls woke up to get ready for school! His room lay shrouded in dark gray morning light. If she moved slowly, maybe she could slip free. She would not think about how wondrous it felt to be held like this by Adam.

Josy pulled back the blanket and gently peeled his hand from her breast. Her hip brushed against his erection. Was he naked under that blanket? Oh, great. He *had* thought she'd come to his room to make love. How was she going to face him over breakfast this morning?

Adam made a muffled sound and rolled onto his back. Instantly, she stilled, but his eyes remained shut. She slipped from the bed as silently as she could.

"Going somewhere?" he asked thickly.

The words froze her in place. "Back to my room." Her heart thundered in her chest.

"It's still early."

"I need a shower," she said quickly.

"We could share."

Hot and cold flames licked her agitated senses. The image was so blatantly sensual she couldn't think. He smiled a tempter's smile. No man should look that sexy first thing in the morning.

Ever.

He shouldn't look at her like that, ever.

Stubble darkened his face. His hair was in wild disarray, but he managed to look like every woman's secret sin. And she knew he was fully aroused.

Part of her wanted to climb back into his obscenely large bed and let him teach her all the magical, wonderful things that look of his promised. Fortunately, sanity prevailed.

Josy started for the door. She was in no condition for a verbal skirmish right now.

"Running?" he called softly.

"Yes." If she gave in and stayed now, it would kill her when she had to leave him in the end.

His chuckle followed her all the way through her room and into her bathroom. There were too many mirrors in here. Everywhere she looked, she saw her scarlet cheeks with her hair standing in spiky tufts and her rumpled clothing.

"Real seductive," she told her image. "He was pulling my leg."

Except, his arousal said otherwise. But all men were supposed to wake up like that, weren't they? She'd read that somewhere. One of those useless facts her memory tended to supply without notice.

The shower didn't help as much as she'd hoped, plus she had to wash her hair with tender care. The bruised area was extremely sore to touch, but even the pain couldn't keep her thoughts from returning to Adam. She wanted him in a very basic way, and it was no good telling herself any man would do. She didn't want any man. She wanted Adam. She didn't want a temporary alliance based on some stupid bargain.

If the prowler hadn't come to the window last night, would she have stopped Adam—and herself?

She was still debating the issue half an hour later when she heard the girls in the hall.

Children equated safety. Adam wouldn't say anything outrageous in front of them.

"Good morning."

They looked startled when she opened the door. Tilly had been chasing Bitsy with a hairbrush and a handful of colored twisties.

"I don't want a ponytail," Bitsy protested.

Tilly looked exasperated. "If you don't let me put it in a ponytail, Uncle Adam's going to try and braid it again."

"No!"

"What about a French braid?" Josy offered.

"What's that?" Suzie demanded.

"Come on in and I'll show you."

"In there? In your room?"

"Sure, why not?"

"We're not allowed in there," Tilly said.

"Why not?"

"Martha said it belonged to Uncle Adam's wife."

"Oh. I guess that's me. Now that I'm here, you're welcome to come inside any time you like. Would you like me to put your hair in a French braid, Bitsy?"

The little girl shook her head quickly.

"You can do mine," Suzie offered.

"Okay. Maybe after Bitsy sees it, she'll want one, too."

The girls crossed the threshold as if it was a church. Josy frowned. Why had Martha kept them out of the room? Josy didn't have any belongings of value stored inside. Was it supposed to be some sort of shrine to Adam's first wife, or was Martha hoping to keep it pristine until she herself could claim it?

Killer dashed past the girls and made a flying leap for the bed. There was a collective gasp of horror.

"What do you think, Killer? Isn't that giant marshmallow funny looking?" Josy asked.

"He's on your bed," Bitsy said.

"Yep. Do you want to join him? Heck, we can all get on. Stupid thing's big enough to hold a party."

The concept held them speechless.

"Can I bounce?" Bitsy asked suddenly.

"If you want, but it's pretty soft for bouncing. You're apt to sink right to the bottom, never to be seen again."

She took the hairbrush from Tilly and motioned Suzie to sit beside her. In minutes, she had put the child's hair in a neat-looking French braid while the other two watched.

"Where'd you learn to do that?" Tilly asked.

Josy frowned, searching the void for an answer. "I don't know, but your Uncle Adam said I used to have long hair. I must have learned how when my hair was long."

"How come it's short now?" Suzie asked, admiring her new look in the mirror.

"Me next," Bitsy demanded.

Josy smiled. "They had to shave my hair off after my accident."

"Did it hurt?"

"The accident? Yes, it did."

"Where did you go that day?" Tilly asked.

"I don't know, sweetie. When I fell, I hurt my head pretty bad. When I woke up, I couldn't remember anything."

"Not even us?" Bitsy demanded, wriggling around to look at her.

"Not even myself. Until your Uncle Adam showed up, I didn't even know who I was."

"But you do now, right?"

"You bet she does, Suze," Adam said behind them. "And we aren't going to let Aunt Josy forget us again."

Tilly stood quickly, apprehension lining her face. "It's okay, Uncle Adam. Aunt Josy said we could come in. She even let Killer on her bed."

Josy met Adam's puzzled gaze. "Martha apparently made this room off-limits, probably because you had stored my stuff in here," she explained.

"I didn't realize."

"Do you like my hair, Uncle Adam? Josy says it's called a French braid."

"Very nice."

"She's doing my hair, too, Uncle Adam."

"You'll have the fanciest hair in school today," he told them as Josy finished the braid.

"Would you like me to do yours, Tilly?"

"No, thank you. I like my ponytail."

"Okay."

"How's your head this morning?" Adam asked Josy.

"A little sore," she answered, but she was ridiculously pleased that he'd thought to ask.

"No dizziness?"

Not from the injury. "No."

"Good. What do you say I escort the four most beautiful women in the world downstairs to breakfast?"

"I'd say you're so full of baloney, you don't need any breakfast," Josy retorted.

Adam clutched his chest. "Pierced by your barb!"

"Watch out for hot air, girls."

Suzie and Bitsy giggled, not sure exactly what she meant, but taking their cue from Adam, who walked over and kissed Josy on the tip of the nose before she could move away. Tilly watched the scene quietly.

"Okay, ladies. Last one down has to eat the rotten egg."

Killer barked, and Suzie and Bitsy giggled all the way downstairs. Martha had set the kitchen table for four.

"Where's Aunt Josy going to sit?" Suzie asked.

Martha quickly masked her annoyance. "I didn't think she'd be up this early."

Josy looked right at her. "I generally had to be at work by 7:00 a.m."

"You worked?"

"At the hospital every morning."

"In the evenings, she worked in a ceramic store," Adam put in. "Here, Josy. Sit here while I get another plate."

"I can do it, Adam," Martha said.

"You just finish cooking. Something smells wonderful."

"It's waffles, Uncle Adam," Bitsy said.

Josy sat beside her and smiled. The little girl smiled back. Breakfast was every bit as chaotic as dinner had been, but it was obvious the girls adored their uncle Adam. Unfortunately, she couldn't blame them.

As before, Martha stayed in the background, serving the meal without comment.

"Aren't you going to join us?" Josy invited.

"Martha doesn't eat breakfast," Tilly said.

"She says her stomach doesn't wake up before ten, right, Martha?" Adam teased.

Martha gave a weak smile and turned away.

"What do you guys say we go to the mall after school and have dinner at Hap's?" Adam asked.

"Yeah."

"Uh, Adam," Josy interrupted. "Aren't we supposed to have dinner with Eleanor and Hank?"

Four faces fell as one. "Do we hafta?" Suzie asked.

"Sorry, gals. I forgot. Your grandmother invited us last night. She wants to meet Aunt Josy."

"Couldn't just the two of you go?" Tilly asked.

"She wants to see you, too."

"No, she doesn't," Suzie said. "She just pretends she likes us."

Adam's expression was bleak.

"Oh, Suzie, honey, I'm sure that isn't true," Josy said. "Your grandparents love you."

Suzie made a face.

"School bus is going to be here in ten minutes," Martha said, ending the discussion.

There was a clatter and a rush as the three girls hurried to collect their books and lunches. Or, in Bitsy's case, her midmorning snack. Adam walked them to the road while Josy watched from the front porch, shivering in the early-morning chill. The snow had stopped sometime last night, and the air was clean and crisp.

They turned left, crossing in front of the two-car garage between a gap in the pine trees, Killer herding them closely. Josy realized a road lay several yards away on that side of the house. She hadn't noticed it yesterday, because she'd been focused on the barn.

A cold blast of air made her shiver again. She decided to wait for Adam inside and discovered Martha waiting for her in the hall.

"What I said last night I shouldn't have," Martha said without preamble. "What's between you and Adam is none of my business."

As a peace offering, this one left out a lot, but Josy didn't quibble. "This is hard on all of us."

"My husband and I knew Adam before he married Alyssa. She was a bitch."

"I'm not Alyssa."

Martha's expression spoke louder than words, but Josy was determined to try to reach past her hostility.

"Alyssa is the girl's real aunt, isn't she?"

"Legally, but you don't have to worry about her. She didn't even come back for her brother's funeral. And she doesn't like children."

"Nice. Was this house her idea?"

Martha nodded tersely. There was no sign that she was mellowing.

"Look, Martha, we have to try and get along, for Adam's sake, as well as the children."

"I'm not going to stand by and see Adam get hurt again."

Just how far would Martha go to prevent Adam from being hurt? "Is that why you were spying on us last night?"

Two spots of color appeared high on her cheeks. "I don't know what you're talking about. But if you try to cause trouble between me and Adam——"

She was lying, but they both heard Killer's bark and Adam's voice calling to Brug outside the front door.

"It's your word against mine," Martha warned. "Guess which one of us Adam is going to believe."

Before Josy could respond, Martha dashed toward the kitchen. A minute later, Adam opened the door, letting in Killer along with a surge of icy air.

"Adam, we need to talk," Josy began, skipping any pleasantries.

But the happy man from breakfast had changed places with the worried man standing in front of her.

"I know. Can it wait until after the vet gets here? Brug says Harry's Pride is worse."

"Is it serious?"

"I don't know yet."

Josy decided her suspicions about Martha could wait. This obviously couldn't. "Is there anything I can do?"

"Keep your fingers crossed. I'll be back as soon as I can. And, Josy, stay inside. Close to Martha. I want to know you're safe."

Adam bent his head, kissed her lips and went back outside before she could find her voice.

"Great. Lock the mouse in with the cat." The last place she intended to stay was close to Martha. Josy headed upstairs, Killer at her heels. She should have asked Adam if she could read her report. She was reluctant to enter his office without asking first. Killer trotted down the left hall, and Josy followed. She was actually a bit curious to see the girls' rooms anyhow.

Tilly's room was up front at the far end. Soft yellow walls and brightly colored pictures made this the most attractive room in the house as far as Josy was concerned. The room was nearly pristine for an eight-year-old girl, but Josy smiled as she saw the rumpled bed. Tilly had pulled the covers up loosely—no doubt her idea of making a bed. Josy hesitated, and then set about smoothing the linens. Tilly's bathroom needed a quick scrub, as well. Josy hoped the girls wouldn't mind a little fussing. At least this would give her something to do while she waited for Adam.

THE HOUSE PHONE RANG about midmorning. Adam ignored the sound until it had rung six times. He was just reaching for the extension when it stopped. The vet left after taking blood samples and assuring Adam he didn't think it was serious.

When the phone rang again a few minutes later, Adam headed for the house in concern. Usually only his office phone rang during the day. He hoped it wasn't the school calling about a problem with one of the children.

Josy was in the kitchen wearing an expression that sent fear right through him.

"What's wrong?" She stood next to the wall phone, her skin pale. "Is it the girls? Who was on the phone?"

"The girls are fine as far as I know." She tried for a smile, but the muscles around her mouth failed to hold it in place. "Whoever keeps calling here doesn't want to talk to me. They never say anything, they just hang up."

"A bad connection?" he asked, not believing it for a moment.

"I bought into that last night, Adam. Not twice again

today. Someone wants to scare me. They're going about it just fine, too.''

Adam muttered an invective and then apologized. ''Where's Martha?''

''I have no idea. Do you think she's the one making the calls?''

The question shocked him. ''Of course not.''

''There's no 'of course' about it. I think she was the one spying on us last night.''

''What?'' The idea of Martha spying on them was even more ludicrous than the image of her making prank calls. ''Come up to my office and we'll talk.'' What had happened to make Josy think Martha would try to scare her?

No sooner had they entered his office than his telephone rang. With an apologetic glance, he waved Josy toward a seat as he reached for the instrument.

''Ryser.''

''Adam, Ned Pohl.'' There was a pause while the man exhaled, likely emptying his lungs of cigarette smoke. ''I just got off the phone with Craig Drecker in Reno. He gave me an initial rundown on Pandergarten. The guy's a beaut. An old-fashioned thug.''

Adam heard the snick of a lighter and waited while Ned lit another cigarette. ''Ned, hang on a second. I'm going to put you on the speakerphone if that's okay. Josy's here, and I think she should hear this report.''

''It's your dollar.''

''This is Ned Pohl,'' he explained to her. ''He's the investigator I hired to find you. Now he's looking for your mother.''

Josy sank into an armchair, her expression startled.

''Okay, Ned, go ahead.''

''Pandergarten won his first casino in a poker game. How this guy made it past the inspection process is anybody's s-guess, but he built himself a tiny little empire. Pandergarten is no fool. He hired savvy boys to run the casinos. All three of 'em make money. Maybe not enough to account for what he flashes around, but there's no proof of anything shady. And believe me, the D.A. out there has tried. There's a lot of people who'd like to see Pandergarten deposed. Then again, he appears to have friends in high places."

Ned drew heavily on his cigarette before continuing. "Twice, some zealous prosecutor has charged him with racketeering. Both times, charges were dropped. Witnesses tend to disappear. Eighteen months ago, he was charged with bribing a member of the gaming commission."

"Don't tell me. The member disappeared."

"Nope. The guy died. Shot on the street in a carjacking. At least, that's the official story. There was another witness who said different, but that person also disappeared."

Adam looked at Josy. "Did you say this happened eighteen months ago—"

"Yeah. Coincidence, huh? The story hit the papers the day you and Josy picked up the kids. Josy's mother did her disappearing act four or five days earlier, am I right?"

Josy stared at Adam. "As far as we know."

"Uh-huh. Well, there hasn't been a smell of Kathy Smith since she went to ground. She hasn't used a credit card or done a thing in the name of Kathy Smith since her daughter appeared in Nevada."

"Are you saying my mother is dead?" Josy asked.

The pause lasted several seconds. "I'm saying I can't find a trace of her. If her only connection to Pandergarten was owing his casino some money, she probably disappeared on her own. A dead gambler can't pay a debt, and casinos like to collect their money. But accidents do happen. Pandergarten is surrounded by guys you don't want to meet in some dark alley."

"Actually, we already did," Adam told him.

Josy didn't smile. Her expression was bleak.

"Look, Ned, maybe your investigator friend better back off."

"My thought, too, but Craig's a bulldog. He wants to keep doing a little quiet digging if you're agreeable."

"I don't want him disappearing."

"Yeah. Me, either."

"Mr. Pohl, my memory doesn't work much anymore, but I believe my mother had a wealthy boyfriend who usually bailed her out of trouble. I don't remember my mother at all, but from what Adam's told me, she had a habit of getting into trouble."

"That's what you implied when you mentioned her," Adam agreed.

Ned exhaled loudly into the telephone. His gravelly voice sounded more worried than ever. "A rich boyfriend, huh? Now, there's an idea I really don't like."

Josy worried the knee of her slacks with a fingernail. "You think Pandergarten was my mother's boyfriend?"

"Mrs. Ryser, you don't want to know the sort of thoughts I'm having right now. But it's a lead I didn't have before. I'll let Craig know, okay?"

"Fine." Adam drummed his fingers against the desk. "You know that other friend of yours, the one who does bodyguarding?"

"No," Josy stated.

"I didn't say it was for you," Adam protested.

"You didn't have to. I watched you chase out into the dark last night after that prowler, remember? While I agree *you* need a keeper, I'm sure you weren't thinking of hiring a bodyguard to protect your own macho self."

The snort of laughter from the telephone stopped her words.

"Now I see why you worked so hard to find her again, Ryser. I like your lady. You two work it out. Meantime, I'll e-mail you his name and number and give him a call and tell him what the story is."

"Don't bother," Josy told Ned. "I'll let Adam get me a bodyguard as soon as he hires one for himself."

Ned snorted some more in amusement. "Anything else? I've got a call waiting."

"No. Thanks, Ned. Keep me informed."

"You got it."

As Ned disconnected, Adam turned to Josy.

"Forget it," she said. "If you truly believe I need a bodyguard, then I should leave."

"Now wait—"

"We've got three children to consider, but it was Martha on the front porch last night, not some hired killer."

"Josy, it couldn't have been. I saw a man's footprints heading away from the house."

"Maybe Martha has big feet."

"Better not let Martha hear you say that," he said, trying to tease.

Josy didn't smile back. "She said you wouldn't believe me."

"You actually accused her? What am I saying—of course you did. But why? What made you think such a thing?"

Josy lifted her chin. "When I went to get her last night, her hair was wet and her skin was red, like she'd been out in the cold."

"Josy, she'd probably just gotten out of the shower."

He could see by the stubborn tilt of her head, she'd made up her mind.

"Why would Martha peep at us through a window?"

"She's in love with you and she wants me gone."

"Josy, you hardly know Martha. If she's in love with anyone—"

"That's what she's counting on. Your loyalty."

"But—"

Josy stood, leaning forward onto his desk. "If it wasn't Martha, if it was someone who wanted me dead, then why didn't he kill me last night?"

Adam stared into her stormy eyes and rubbed his jaw. "Good question."

A very good question.

Chapter Seven

They never did have their meaningful discussion. Adam's phone rang again, and this time it was Hank wanting to discuss the possible sale of the property the girls had inherited.

Bitsy came home from kindergarten while Adam was still on the phone, and the day dissolved in a blur. Martha had gone to visit a friend, so Josy made sandwiches and heated soup for lunch. Conveniently, Martha arrived back at the house right behind the school bus, and Josy knew Adam wouldn't try to talk with her while the girls were around.

Josy avoided her until it was time to go to the Claussens. She dressed with as much care as she could, considering there wasn't an outfit in her closet that didn't hang limply on her scrawny frame. The white blouse and straight black skirt were the most presentable items. She even found a pair of crystal earrings and a gold chain necklace, but no other jewelry among her things. After adding a touch of blush and some lipstick, she decided she was as ready as she'd ever be.

In the hall, Adam soothed her concern with an appreciative smile that not only warmed her, but also boosted her confidence. As he herded them all out the front door, Josy found herself looking around for Martha.

"Martha went to dinner and the movies, with Brug," Adam explained without being asked. His look added an *I told you so.*

Josy simply shook her head. She wasn't going to convince Adam without proof. Maybe Martha did have a thing for Brug, or maybe she was only trying to protect Adam. Maybe she disliked Josy because Brug had come on to her so openly. All Josy knew for sure was Martha had spied on them. But watching through a window was a far cry from running someone down with a truck.

Adam loaded everyone into a white van he pulled from the garage. Josy saw there was a second driveway through the pine trees leading to the road where the kids caught the bus. No gate barred this entrance. Too bad Alyssa hadn't added a moat and castle walls to her estate. Adam could have used them since Josy moved in.

A cold, harsh wind tore at the car as they drove, scattering flakes of snow in their path. The somber mood inside the car matched the weather. The girls were not even trying to mask their unhappiness.

The Claussen house was even bigger and uglier than Adam's house, with the addition of a four-car garage and several large outbuildings.

Inside, the formal decor was tastefully done in yellows and muted greens with stately cherry-wood furniture. Eleanor Claussen swept into the front room, formally dressed in an elegant pastel peach outfit that blended with the room's decor. She could easily pass for a woman in her forties, though she had to be much older. She greeted each of her granddaughters formally—no hugs or warmth. Youngest to oldest, each child received some critical comment along with her welcome.

"Elizabeth, a lady always makes certain her shoes are properly tied."

Josy hadn't even noticed Bitsy's untied lace.

"Suzannah, your animal left hair on your sweater."

The sweater was black. The dog was white. Josy made a mental note to have the child dress in light-colored clothing next time they had an appointment with the queen.

"Matilda, don't slouch, dear, stand up straight."

What did she want, a rod down the child's back? Josy automatically straightened her own posture.

Adam gave each girl a small wink. Only Suzie winked back, though Tilly looked grateful. Josy herself was cataloged and dismissed with a cool, limp handshake and the hint of a frown. "Ms. Smith."

"Mrs. Ryser," Josy corrected firmly. "But you may call me Josy."

Faint color stained Eleanor's carefully applied makeup. For what it was worth, Josy had scored a point.

"Yes, of course. Such an unusual name."

"Thank you. I like it."

"And Adam. You're looking fit, if a bit disheveled this evening."

Adam wasn't wearing a tie beneath his sweater.

"Eleanor," he greeted, "you look impeccable as always. Where's Hank?"

Eleanor's thin lips pursed tightly. "I believe there is some sort of problem in one of the barns. He should be in shortly."

"Maybe I should see if he needs a hand."

Josy decided she'd trip Adam before she let him leave her alone with this woman, but Eleanor made that unnecessary.

"You are hardly dressed for the barns, Adam. Come into the parlor and have a glass of wine...or I suppose there is

some of my husband's whisky available. And I had th
cook make some pâté. I know how much you like it.''

Suzie made a gagging face. Josy nearly laughed out lou
The tone for the evening had clearly been set. Adversari
all the way.

No wonder Adam didn't want these poor children livin
here. The place was a museum. Everywhere Josy looke
sat expensive items waiting to be admired—or knocke
over by a careless hand. She couldn't picture schoolbook
or children's toys having the audacity to lie on any of th
pristine surfaces scattered around the room.

The girls sat stiffly on the yellow sofa and fidgete
through small glasses of cola and a formal appetizer tra
complete with reddish pâté and strange objects on cracker
Since the girls left those strictly alone, Josy followed the
lead. The unpleasantly tart white wine scoured the linin
of her stomach.

When a young woman arrived to announce dinner, Jos
nearly choked on her wine. She and Eleanor's maid wer
dressed almost identically. A glance in Adam's directio
told her the humor hadn't escaped him, either. He grinne
and winked at her. Tilly caught the exchange, and her li
lifted, as well.

''Jacqueline, please have someone find out what is keep
ing Mr. Claussen.''

''Yes, ma'am.''

Jacqueline vanished. Josy looked for smoke vapor.

A strong gust of wind rattled the windows. Please, n
more snow. She would not be trapped inside this depressin
house with her husband's former in-laws, even if she ha
to walk back home.

''This is really quite unpardonable,'' Eleanor told the
by way of apology.

"Not much Hank can do about a sick animal," Adam temporized.

Eleanor sniffed delicately. "We have an excellent staff to deal with such matters, Adam."

And a few minutes later, a member of that excellent staff had the audacity to enter Eleanor's immaculate parlor dressed in normal working attire, including dirty boots and a dark cloth parka to which bits of hay and snowflakes still clung. He looked around and gave a sudden start.

"Pardon me. Mr. Claussen asked me to make his excuses. We have a problem in the main barn. He said to go ahead with dinner and he'll be up to the house as soon as he can."

Eleanor was calmly furious, but that wasn't what sent chills skittering up Josy's back. Something about the man's presence badly frightened her.

The almost memory of falling and falling made her dizzy and weak. It was by no means the first time this memory had surprised her. The vertigo only lasted a short second, but each time was as terrifying as the first.

"Thank you, Mark." Eleanor dismissed the man.

He nodded briefly, then he looked right at Josy. Like a frozen pond, his cold gray eyes held not one trace of human empathy as they stared at her.

"Josy, is something wrong?"

The man called Mark left, and Josy trembled, staring helplessly at Adam. What could she say? Her reaction made no sense. "I'm just a little dizzy. Hungry, I think."

"Josy suffered a head injury the other day," Adam offered by way of explanation for Eleanor's benefit.

Eleanor stood, preventing further discussion.

"Let us go and eat before the meal is totally ruined. I do apologize for Hank."

Josy stood on quivering legs and tried to pull herself

together. "No apology is necessary, Eleanor." The woman flinched when Josy used her given name. "I'm sure your husband will be here when he can."

"Of course."

Another gust of wind rocked the house.

"If this keeps up, we'll lose the electricity before morning," Adam said. He took Josy's arm, and she was darn grateful for the support. It wasn't until she saw Eleanor's expression that she realized the older woman had expected Adam to escort her and not Josy into the dining room. Adam seemed oblivious.

The food may have been delicious, but Josy barely tasted a bite. Something elusive hovered in her mind just out of reach. Mark had nearly tripped a memory, but Josy couldn't bring it into focus. Was it the man, or his eyes? And why did she fear him?

Moments like this brought out all the frustration of not having a memory like everyone else. She wanted to *know!*

Dinner was strained and uncomfortable, made more so when Suzie spilled her entire glass of milk. Jacqueline saw to the matter with swift efficiency, but Eleanor's expressive disapproval rang louder than words.

By the time the éclairs had been served, Josy had had enough of phony smiles and polite conversation designed to point out that she was an outsider. Eleanor was never going to like her, and Josy couldn't care less. She'd do everything in her power to prevent this cold, stuffy woman from raising the girls.

"Adam, I'm afraid I've developed a terrible headache." The lie was only a slight exaggeration. Adam took the cue and extricated them with the speed and precision of an experienced veteran.

Wind hurried their path to the van as the loose snow

stung their cheeks. The girls relaxed as soon as the engine started up. So did Josy.

"Gee," she said softly, "that was fun."

Suzie giggled.

Adam relaxed, as well. "If you ever even think about serving me pâté…"

"Ha! You didn't see me reaching for that stuff, did you?"

He grinned. "Actually, it tastes better than it looks."

"It would have to. It *looks* like cat food."

The girls laughed out loud, something they hadn't done all evening. By the time Adam navigated a path to the garage, they were chattering away about what was really on those tiny crackers.

"Is it snowing, or just blowing?" Josy asked as they stepped from the car.

"Just blowing, but these wind gusts are pretty fierce. Let's go, ladies. Time for bed."

The house was a warm, welcome haven after the blustery outside.

"Aunt Josy," Tilly said as she turned to follow her sisters upstairs, "will you show me how to make that French braid in the morning?"

This was the first overture any of the girls had made, and a wave of accomplishment warmed Josy's heart. "I'd be happy to."

"Yeah," Suzie piped up from the top of the stairs, "Sylvia Jessup can't do her hair like that. All her mom can do is make stupid old braids."

Was Suzie comparing her to someone's mother?

Adam gave her a silent thumbs-up and followed his godchildren upstairs. Smiling, Josy headed for the kitchen to make a pot of coffee. Apparently, Martha had foreseen the need. Not only was coffee ready to be turned on, but half an apple pie sat on the counter. Josy's stomach rumbled. Tiny portions of shrimp linguine in clam sauce might be Eleanor's idea of a family meal, but it wasn't Josy's. She helped herself to two generous slices of pie and went looking for ice cream to top them with.

Adam found her sitting at the table, a fork poised over her share. "I was going to wait for you," she told him, "but I was too hungry."

He smiled hugely. "I don't blame you. Now you know why Martha gave the girls such a big snack when they got home from school today. She knows all about Eleanor's dinner parties and her ladylike portions. We're always starving when we get home. Martha left sugar cookies and lemonade upstairs for the girls."

Adam sat beside her and forked up a bite of ice-cream-covered pie. His leg brushed against hers. Josy raised her eyes to meet his.

"Now do you want to tell me what exactly happened when Mark walked in?"

"What do you mean?" But she knew. The problem was, she didn't know how to explain. "Who is Mark?"

Adam's eyes narrowed. "One of Hank's crew. He's worked there almost two years now."

She reached for her coffee cup. "He has cold eyes."

"Is that why you went as white as your blouse when you saw him?"

Josy set down her cup. "He terrifies me. I have no idea why. As far as I know, I've never seen the man before."

"Maybe he reminds you of someone."

Josy shuddered. "I hope not."

Adam swallowed another bite and frowned. "I'll have Ned check him out."

"For heaven's sake, why? I can't possibly know him."

"Maybe. Maybe not."

"Wouldn't he have said something? Adam, he didn't look at me with a trace of recognition. I think he was just the catalyst for a memory that keeps hovering just out of reach. It's so frustrating."

His hand covered hers, offering warmth and reassurance. The lights flickered and dimmed. Josy jumped.

"Hey, take it easy," he said. "The wind gets high, and we get periodic brownouts. Sometimes, the power goes out completely."

Josy sincerely hoped not. "Sorry."

"You have nothing to be sorry for." He released her hand and picked up his fork again. "You did a nice job handling Eleanor tonight."

The praise steadied her nerves, but she was very aware of Adam's leg so close to her own.

"Strange evening," Adam said thoughtfully.

"No argument here." She picked up her own fork.

"I can't understand why Hank sent Mark up to the house. He must have known Eleanor would have a fit. I wonder what's wrong over there."

"I thought you said a sick animal."

"As Eleanor pointed out, they have people to handle things like that. Hank's a politician, Josy. And he wanted to convince me to sell the ranch the girls own."

"What ranch?"

"Chad owned a good-size spread near the border. He left it to me in trust for the girls. Hank's been leasing the property from me to run some cattle."

"And now Hank wants to buy it?"

"No, that's the funny part. A third party apparently approached him to sell, thinking he owned it. He wanted to talk to me about the deal."

"Are you going to sell?"

"Maybe. I can always invest the money for the girls.

Chad bought the property intending to settle down there, but it proved to be too close to his parents. He sublet the parcel and moved to Nevada instead. Smartest move he ever made.''

Adam took another bite of pie and chewed thoughtfully. ''You know, the more I think about it, the stranger it is that Hank didn't at least come up to the house to meet you.''

''That's okay with me. Eleanor was more than enough.''

The telephone startled both of them. Adam nearly overturned his chair grabbing for it before it could ring a second time. Once again, the lights flickered and dimmed.

''Ryser.''

His face grew grim. The unease Josy had felt since a few moments ago returned.

''Where? Okay. I'll be right there.''

Fear churned the pie and ice cream in her stomach.

''Josy, I know this is probably futile, but would you please go upstairs and lock yourself in a bedroom?''

Her fork clattered, unnoticed to the plate. ''What's wrong?''

''Pete just found a truck on the back road down by the gate. Brand-new. No plates. Sticker's still on it.''

''Black?''

He nodded. ''Half the windshield's taped up with cardboard where the glass is missing on the passenger's side.''

The fear uncurled sending tendrils licking through her. ''Oh.''

''I'm going to wake Martha and call the police. I'd feel a whole lot better if I knew you and the girls were upstairs and safe.''

''I'm not helpless, Adam.'' But in that moment, she felt helpless. The man in the black truck was here, on Adam's ranch.

"I know you aren't, but let's not take chances. Humor me, all right?" He stood.

"You're going out there?"

"Only to secure the house from the outside."

"You could do that from in here."

"Josy, we're wasting valuable time. Please. Will you go upstairs and wait this time?"

Josy didn't want to go upstairs. She wanted to stay right here with Adam—safe in this big open kitchen. The lights flickered again.

"Okay."

"Thank you."

To her complete surprise, Adam bent and kissed her mouth before disappearing into the hall. Josy touched her finger to the spot he'd kissed, then called out to him. "Shall I wake Martha?"

"No," he said, coming back into the kitchen, sliding his arms inside his heavy coat. "I'll tell her. I want you to go upstairs. Don't worry. Nothing's going to happen."

"Right. The superhero's on the job."

"I'll show you my *S* when I come back." He winked and headed for Martha's door.

Josy mounted the steps slowly, fear beating a tattoo inside her chest. Cowering upstairs while Adam chased around outside didn't sit well. On the other hand, she wouldn't be much help to him in that wind.

"Please don't let the lights go out," she whispered.

A scratching sound riveted her on the landing outside Adam's bedroom door. Fear actually deafened her for a moment. She fought down the panic and strained to identify the sound. The noise came from the left-hand corridor. Josy could have fainted in relief when she realized it was Killer, scratching frantically at Suzie's door to get out. The last thing she needed was for the girls to wake up right now.

At least the dog wasn't barking. Josy cracked open the door, and Killer bounded free. He tore past her without a sound.

"Killer, come back here," she whispered. The dog was not getting walked tonight even if he had an accident on the carpeting. But Killer didn't pause. He also didn't tear down the steps as she'd expected. Instead, he ran to the opposite hall. Josy hesitated. This wasn't normal behavior.

She followed quickly, hoping her heart wouldn't pound its way up her throat. Killer came to a stop outside Josy's bedroom door, sniffing madly at the bottom crack.

Cold bathed her from head to toe. There was only one explanation. The man from the truck wasn't outside. He was already inside the house. In her bedroom!

Josy ran for the stairs. She went too fast for her bad leg. The weakened muscles gave out, and she stumbled, nearly falling all the way down the spiral staircase. She caught the banister to keep herself erect as she continued her mad plunge down the steps.

If she screamed for Adam, she'd wake the girls. Besides, Adam was outside. If she could reach Martha, she could send her to find Adam. Josy couldn't protect the children by herself.

The kitchen was empty. She rapped on Martha's door. Without waiting, she turned the handle and entered the softly lit living quarters. Empty.

"Martha?"

But she knew Martha wasn't there. The woman had either gone with Adam or more likely, was still in town with Brug. Wind shook the house. Panic threatened Josy's control. She gripped the kitchen counter and tried to think. Sheer force of will kept her from running outside yelling Adam's name like she wanted to do.

Once again, the lights dimmed, but this time, they didn't come back to full strength. "No! Not now!"

She needed a weapon and a flashlight. But the rifle was locked in his truck, and she had no idea where he'd keep the flashlights.

Think!

Her hand trailed across the kitchen counter, knocking against the handle of the sharp knife she'd used to cut the pie. Better than nothing. She headed back upstairs, praying Adam or even Martha would return soon.

Killer sat on his haunches outside her bedroom door. He looked at her quizzically as if to say, *What are we going to do now?*

The animal had a point. She'd be no match for an intruder, armed or not. Leaving Killer to guard her door, Josy went to check on Tilly. The child slept peacefully. The door leading from her room to the outside balcony was securely locked. In Bitsy's and Suzie's rooms, the scene was the same. Josy paused to cover Bitsy. Killer waited patiently outside Josy's bedroom door.

The prowler couldn't know that they'd found his truck. As long as she stayed in the hall, she was probably safe. And Killer, bless his furry white soul, was a great alarm system. Surely Adam would come back soon.

Minutes dragged by with excruciating slowness. Josy was stiff with tension, and her leg throbbed. She rubbed it absently. The lights flickered again. Abruptly, every light in the house went out.

Josy took several careful steps forward until she touched the wall. The darkness was complete. If she wasn't careful, she'd fall down the stairs or back into the railing that circled the open hall below.

She wanted to call to Killer, but was afraid to alert the intruder. Would the power outage scare him off, or would he take advantage of the situation? Josy was very much afraid it would be the latter.

Cautiously, she moved back a step until Adam's bedroom door was at her back. Should she gather the girls all in one room, or leave them where they were?

Where was Adam?

The house rattled. Something banged against an outside wall. And the door at her back suddenly edged open.

She'd forgotten about the connecting door between the bedrooms.

Josy didn't have time to scream. The startled intruder must have sensed her at once. He ran into her, propelling her forward. Josy came up against the dark wood railing. Before she could regain her balance, the figure grabbed her.

Josy slashed downward. The knife plunged into his heavy winter coat. She brought her bad knee up, barely missing her target.

Suddenly, he loomed over her, driving her back against the railing.

He was going to throw her over!

There was a low sound of fury. The grip on her shoulders loosened as his balance changed. Killer silently attacked his leg. Josy used the distraction to raise the knife, going for his head or neck.

He kicked out, and Killer yelped. Her blow glanced off his gloved hand, striking his bared wrist. He gave a soft grunt of surprise. Then his hand groped for her throat. Josy lowered her head and twisted to one side. She had to get away from the railing.

His hand closed over her wrist. They struggled for possession of the knife, but he was much stronger. Killer growled low in his throat, and the man's attention was once again momentarily diverted by the small dog's attack.

He kicked out viciously. Killer yelped as he hit the wall

The intruder squeezed her wrist, forcing Josy to drop the knife. She heard it bounce on the hall floor below.

Adam shouted her name and the intruder dragged her back toward Adam's bedroom.

ADAM TURNED HIS BACK to the wind and looked at the stocky dark form that was Pete.

"Nothing to indicate where he went?"

"You gotta be kidding, boss. The way this wind is kicking snow around? I'm lucky I can see you. I was just making a perimeter sweep like you told us to do."

"Brug and Martha aren't back yet. My guess is, the intruder will try for the house."

"If he isn't already inside," Pete noted.

The thought hadn't even crossed Adam's mind. How stupid to assume the truck had just driven up. He didn't know that. The man could already be inside the house. It had stood empty all evening. And Adam had left Josy inside!

Panic sent him sprinting for the back door.

The lights went out.

Adam cursed as he fumbled for his keys, nearly dropping them in his frantic hurry. He'd never find them if he lost them now.

Wind wrenched the mudroom door from his hand, banging it loudly against the side of the house. Adam plunged inside.

"Josy?"

He reached for the gun in his pocket and stumbled into a kitchen chair. The chair crashed to the floor.

"Josy?"

He couldn't use the gun. He might shoot the wrong person.

Upstairs, Killer yelped. Adam took the stairs in twos.

"Josy!"

The dog clawed at the door to his bedroom, straining to get inside. Adam twisted the knob. The lock was engaged.

"Adam!"

He heard the sounds of a scuffle and stepped back. He kicked hard at the panel near the door handle. With a splinter of wood, the lock gave way. A figure disappeared through the sliding glass door. Wind sent the drapes whipping inside the room. Adam started forward and fell head-first over Josy.

"Josy!" He scrambled back to gather her by feel. She was shaking, but she was alive.

"Don't let him get away! I'm fine."

Adam leaped to his feet. He tangled with the drapes, nearly pulling them from the wall. Snow blinded him the moment he stepped outside. The man could have gone in either direction.

"Pete!"

Wind snatched away his voice. There was no response. Adam went right past Josy's room, to the far side of the house. He couldn't see a thing. The guy could be hugging the wall, or running down below. This was stupid and dangerous. Adam turned back to check on Josy and nearly knocked her over as he went to enter the house. She stood in the sliding glass door, Killer at her feet.

"Are you okay?"

"Yes."

"Come on, let's get this door closed."

"Uncle Adam?"

They both whirled at the sound of Suzie's voice.

"It's okay, Suzie. Everything—"

"There's someone outside my window, Uncle Adam."

Adam let out an oath and sprinted past the child. If the guy got inside one of the children's rooms, there was no telling what might happen.

"Come here, Suzie," Josy called. "Do you know where Uncle Adam keeps a flashlight?"

"Nightstand," he called as he ran, Killer at his feet.

He entered Suzie's room with his gun drawn. Nothing moved. The room was warm. He was fairly sure the man hadn't gotten inside, but he checked the balcony door to be sure. Locked.

He drew back the bolt, trying to open the door as quietly as he could. Silly. Who could hear above the shriek of the wind? Killer stayed inside, which was probably just as well. The small dog might find himself airborne otherwise.

Adam checked Bitsy's window, then Tilly's. Both were locked. Adam moved to the railing. A rope whipped back and forth. The bastard had gone over the side.

"Tim? Pete?"

They'd never hear him over the wind. Adam fought his instinct to go after the guy. He had to protect Josy and the girls. He went back inside, putting the safety back on and shoving the gun in his pocket.

Killer danced at his feet.

"Let's go find the women, boy."

A flashlight beam pinned him as soon as he stepped into the hall.

"All clear, Josy. He got away over the side."

The beam dropped from his eyes. Adam walked over and handed her his gun.

"What—?"

"Just like the rifle the other night. Flick this before you shoot. Point and fire at the middle of your target."

"I'm not shooting anyone. You are *not* going back out there."

"I have to. Pete and Tim are outside."

"Well, what am I supposed to do?"

"Protect the girls."

"Uncle Adam, I'm scared."

"It'll be all right, Suze. Killer and Josy will protect you. I'll be right back."

"That's what you said last time," Josy muttered.

He took her face in his hands and kissed her hard. "Stay with Aunt Josy," he told Suzie, and headed for the steps.

Relief washed over him as he opened the front door. "Never mind, Josy," he called up to her, "the police have arrived."

Chapter Eight

The search came up empty. Police had the stolen vehicle, but Adam doubted it would tell them a thing.

Brug and Martha had arrived home a short time after the police, stunned by all the commotion. They'd had a flat tire on the way home, but Brug immediately joined the search. Martha and Tim went inside to watch over Josy and the girls.

When Adam finally returned to the house, he discovered Josy, Suzie and Killer curled together on the sofa in the living room, sound asleep. The picture they made created a well of emotions, reminding him of his own childhood.

Quietly, he woke Martha from her doze on a chair, and sent her on to bed. He found Tim in the kitchen half-asleep over a cup of cold coffee. He, too, was happy to return to bed. Adam checked on the other girls to make sure they were covered sufficiently, and then walked around checking locks.

Exhausted, he added wood to the fire in the living room and collapsed in the chair Martha had vacated. Killer blinked sleepily in his direction, decided nothing was needed of him and settled his muzzle back down on Josy's thigh.

Adam decided he must be tired if he was sitting here

feeling envious of a dog. Josy's face lay in shadows, and her arm curled protectively around Suzie. She looked so appealing he couldn't bring himself to disturb the peaceful scene. Was it any wonder he was so drawn to this woman? No matter how much he didn't want to admit it, she was etching herself right back into his life. Into all their lives. If only they knew what secrets lay buried in her mind.

The fact that he hadn't asked her the most basic questions about herself shamed him. When they'd first met, he'd been completely focused on his own goals. Then, when she began to matter a great deal, they were seldom alone. Now they were both paying the price for his selfishness.

Adam leaned his head back and wearily closed his eyes.

When he woke, sun streamed in through the windows and the others were gone.

He couldn't believe he'd slept so soundly that he hadn't heard the girls this morning. He hadn't even heard Killer bark. The idea that he *could* sleep that deeply disturbed him.

Outside, drifted snow had piled against the house, leaving much of the field totally bare. There wasn't a trace of wind this morning, and power had been restored. Where was everybody? The house was eerily silent.

Adam stretched to release the kinks from his back, stiff from sleeping in a chair all night. He was too old for this sort of thing. He headed for his bedroom and a hot shower. The splintered door was a jarring reminder of the evening's events. Adam paused in the act of pulling on a pair of jeans. The kids would have gone to school, of course, but where was Killer? The little dustball was generally underfoot whenever Suzie was away.

The silence became ominous.

Adam finished dressing and called out. No answer. By the time he reached the kitchen, he was seriously concerned. Prominently taped to the refrigerator, Brug had left a note saying he'd taken the women into town. Martha left breakfast in the microwave and coffee in the pot, and Adam needed to be there when Bitsy got home.

Surprise mingled with concern. Josy didn't trust Martha. While he was sure Josy was wrong, there'd been no time to talk with either woman. Why would she go off with someone she didn't trust? Especially after last night.

He crumpled the note. Brug would keep an eye on Josy. Only, that was part of the problem. Adam didn't like the idea that Josy had gone with Brug, either.

Adam poured himself a cup of the strong black brew while he debated his options. He couldn't go after them and be back in time for Bitsy. Yet despite the note and his own personal feelings, he couldn't shake the thought that this felt all wrong. The prowler could easily steal another car and follow them into town.

Adam reached for the telephone. He hated asking Hank or Eleanor for anything, but he'd ask one of them to come over to wait for Bitsy.

"I am sorry, Señor Ryser, Señor Claussen isn't here and the *señora* left for her hair appointment. Do you want to leave a message?"

"No, no message. Thanks."

Edgy, Adam headed for his office. He could call Pete or one of the other hands, but he didn't feel comfortable asking them to stay with Bitsy, so he'd just have to wait for Brug to bring Josy back. As heroes went, he felt like a complete bust.

The light on the answering machine flickered a greeting when he stepped into his office. He hit Play, still mulling over his sense of disquiet. Ned Pohl's husky smoker's voice filled the room.

"Two quick bites of info for you, Adam. The apartment

lease was in Kathy Smith's name, but she had a semiregular male visitor and usually paid her rent in cash. Her visitor stayed anywhere from overnight to a week at a time. A very reclusive man, and our witness says definitely not Pandergarten.''

Ned paused, and Adam could hear him light a cigarette. "Here's the real interesting part—Pandergarten and the mystery man were both at Smith's place the day Josy arrived. All three were seen together near the front door that afternoon. God bless nosy neighbors,'' he added in an aside. "It would sure help if your lady could remember *something*. I'll call you later.''

Adam was so lost in thought he didn't hear the start of the next message, but Hank's voice finally got his attention. "...so I'll come by early this afternoon to discuss it.''

Adam rewound the message, still pondering Ned's information. Josy hadn't mentioned meeting Pandergarten in person. He would have remembered that. And surely she would have told him about the meeting the day they'd gone to the casino to pay off her mother's debt. Or would she?

He'd come to like Josy so much in the days following the wedding that he'd made a lot of assumptions about the sort of woman she was. He knew better. Assumptions were dangerous, often hiding the truth. Had Josy been playing a game of her own? Was he a fool to trust her even now?

Her innocent vulnerability made it easy to believe her. But she could be fooling everyone, including the doctors. Her physical injuries were real enough, but amnesia was impossible to prove or disprove.

The answering machine clicked to a stop, but Adam sat staring at his desk. He pictured Josy as he'd seen her last night, with Suzie and Killer curled trustingly at her side. If she was faking, Hollywood had missed out on a world-class actress.

The bottom line was, he wanted to believe her. If it made him ten kinds of fool, so be it. Sometimes, you had to rely on instinct.

He hit the Fast Forward button until he reached Hank's message.

"I'm calling to apologize for missing dinner. Eleanor flayed several pieces off my hide last night, but we had a major problem in the main barn. Couldn't be helped. Anyhow, I still want to talk about that offer to sell the property with you, so I'll come by early this afternoon to discuss it."

Adam frowned as he picked up the phone and dialed Ned Pohl's number. Ned was out. Adam left a message asking him to run a quick check on Mark Wilson. Josy's reaction to the man still bothered Adam. Despite wanting to believe her, he couldn't help wondering if she'd remembered something yesterday. Something she wasn't sharing with him.

He leaned back in his chair and noticed a paper sticking out of his middle desk drawer. Adam opened the drawer carefully. The paper was part of the packet of documents he'd been going over yesterday. It should still be with the stack on the right-hand side of his desktop.

Adam sat very still. The paper contained information on Chad's property. Only the people making an offer would be interested in this information.

He stood quietly and ran a quick check. The papers were the only things he could be sure had been disturbed.

What did Chad's ranch have to do with Josy?

THE LAST THING Josy wanted to do was go into town with Martha and Brug, but when Martha made the grudging offer, it occurred to Josy that it was a perfect opportunity to observe them together and maybe get a few answers.

Josy planned to be very careful around Martha.

They were well away from the house when Josy noticed the angry red cut on Brug's wrist. Alarm slammed into her.

"What did you do to your wrist, Brug?" Amazingly, her voice revealed nothing of her fear.

Brug held up the appendage and offered her an easygoing smile in the rearview mirror. "Martha and I got a flat tire last night. I had trouble getting the spare loose and scratched it pretty good, didn't I?"

"It looks painful," she agreed while her heart continued to pound.

"I've had worse. We saw a pretty good movie last night, didn't we, Martha?" The woman made a sound Brug took for assent, and he launched into a detailed description of the picture and other movies he'd liked.

Josy didn't know what to think. Brug acted so relaxed and normal she couldn't believe he was the man she'd struggled with last night. He'd made no attempt to hide the cut, and he kept trying to jolly Martha into joining the conversation, while offering Josy apologetic looks in the mirror.

Was she seeing bogeymen in everyone?

Brug dropped them at a shopping center, insisting he'd finish his errands and take them to lunch before running them home again. Josy regretted coming along. Martha made it clear she didn't want to talk and didn't care if Josy followed her or not.

"Did you invite me along just to give me the silent treatment, Martha?" she finally asked as they walked from the bank to the grocery store.

"You know why you were invited. You're just like his other one," Martha snarled.

"What are you talking about?"

"Alyssa screwed anything in pants—including my husband—and she didn't care if I knew, either.'' The bitter words were filled with venom.

"I am not Alyssa," Josy told her firmly, "and I have no designs on Brug at all."

"Then why was he so anxious for you to come with us?" Why indeed. "I don't know, Martha—you tell me."

Martha snorted and strode off more quickly than Josy could manage. Her leg was giving her fits.

Why *had* Brug wanted her along? Martha's jealousy she could understand. Brug had flirted with Josy from the first.

Josy chewed on her lip as she considered Brug.

He was the same general height and build as her assailant, but the man who'd tried to force her over the railing had panicked when she'd stabbed him and he'd heard Adam coming. Brug, on the other hand, hadn't blinked an eye when she'd noticed his wrist. The reactions were inconsistent.

But then, everything was inconsistent unless someone wanted to scare her away. And that brought her right back to Martha—and Brug. She still believed Martha was the one at the window and behind the phone calls, but Adam would never believe her without proof. Josy followed Martha into the grocery store feeling vulnerable.

"Martha, is there a ladies' room?"

For a moment, she thought the other woman wouldn't answer. "Through the double doors next to the meat counter. Go down the hall to your right, second door on the left." Martha spit out the words and turned back to the shelves.

"Thank you," she told the woman's back.

The double doors bore a bright red sign that said No Admittance. Josy hesitated. There were no employees nearby to ask permission, and need overcame her reservations.

The bright, busy store yielded to a dark hall stacked with boxes and crates waiting their turn on the shelves. The sense of being where she didn't belong almost sent Josy back out front where there were bright lights and people.

The bathroom was what you'd expect in a house, not a public rest room. Obviously, this wasn't intended for customer use. Josy turned the lock and hurried to use the facility. She was washing her hands when the doorknob began to twist with excruciating slowness. She started to call out that she'd be right out, but there was something terrifying in the slow slide of that knob as it settled back into place without making a sound. Why hadn't the person knocked or called out?

Heart pounding, Josy stood with one hand in the running water, her eyes riveted on the knob. ''Martha, is that you?'' She tried to sound annoyed instead of scared to death.

A thin plastic card suddenly slid between the door and the jamb. Someone was trying to force the lock!

There was no way out of the tiny bathroom except the way she'd entered. Any minute now, the credit card would pop the lock and whoever was on the other side would enter.

Josy flung her body against the door, sinking to the floor so she could brace her feet against the far wall. The lock gave. Someone pushed hard against the door. Josy prayed her bad leg would hold up as she braced herself against the opposing force. The door opened inward a quarter of an inch against her back. Josy did the only thing left for her to do. She screamed.

The sound reverberated in the small room. The door slammed tightly shut as the pressure on the other side stopped. Surely someone would come to investigate. But minutes ticked past. Her legs quivered with strain as she waited for another attack that never came.

If Martha had just tried to scare her, she'd succeeded beyond her wildest dreams. Josy didn't dare move. Why didn't someone come?

"Josy?" Martha's voice carried clearly. "Josy? Are you in there? Brug, I think something is wrong."

Josy tried to stand and found she couldn't. Her leg refused to support the effort. She scooted forward and waited. Brug came through the door, smashing it into her side with the force of his entrance.

"Josy? Hell. Martha, get a paramedic. Josy's hurt."

At least they weren't going to kill her here and now.

"I'm fine. I just can't stand up. If you could give me your arm."

"Did you fall?" He helped her to her feet, holding her against his chest while she waited for the weak muscles in her leg to support her weight again. Brug was all concern, but Josy couldn't read a thing in Martha's expression.

"I'd like to go home, now," she told them. Her little apartment over the garage was looking better and better by the second.

SOMEONE HAD GONE through his entire office, Adam realized after a more thorough search. He wondered what they'd been looking for—and if they'd found it. Nothing appeared to be missing.

The school called as he concluded his search, wanting permission to send Suzie home on the kindergarten bus with Bitsy. The flu was running rampant, and Suzie wasn't feeling well. Adam figured she was probably just tired, but he agreed to their request.

Inexplicably edgy, Adam cleared off some work, then went downstairs to stare out at the cliffs behind the house. He realized he wasn't going to relax until he saw Josy again, so he was glad for the distraction of walking to the bus stop to meet Suzie and Bitsy. Suzie, he noted, looked tired, but she didn't act or eat like she was sick.

"Where's Killer?" she asked suddenly, a soup spoon halfway to her mouth. "Did somebody let him out?"

Adam hoped not. He set down his sandwich with a mental curse. He'd forgotten all about the little dog.

"I don't know, Suzie. I haven't seen him all morning. He might have sneaked out when Josy left. I'll take a look around outside while you and Bitsy check the house. Be sure he didn't get locked in a closet or something this morning." The silly beast was as curious as a cat.

Adam stepped outside, thinking whatever mischief the animal had found this time, he'd probably forgive him after the way Killer had sprung to Josy's defense again last night.

A horse and rider came around the side of the house. Adam had forgotten all about Hank's plans to stop by, but the horse surprised him. While it wasn't a long ride, Hank generally drove over.

"Offer you some lunch?" Adam asked as the stocky man dismounted.

"No, thanks, I can't stay. Eleanor is in a snit over last night. If your new wife is around, I'll offer my apologies in person."

"Josy went shopping with Martha."

"Oh. Too bad," Hank said casually.

Adam had the strangest impression that Hank wasn't the least bit surprised that Josy wasn't here.

"Have you given any more thought to selling the girls' ranch to that investment group? They're offering more than the property is worth, you know."

How did Hank know what the property was worth? Unless he'd seen the papers on Adam's desk.

"You could do worse," he continued. "Invest the money in something that'll turn a higher profit."

Adam didn't like the turn his thoughts were taking. He found himself staring at Hank's riding gloves and wondering what the man would say if he asked to see his wrist.

"Hank, I can't help but wonder what's in it for you. You're leasing that property. If I sell, you'll have to find new grazing land for your herd."

"Well, I'm not pleased about that, but I want what's best for my granddaughters, and it is their ranch."

Adam ignored the thrust. Hank was a businessman. There had to be a reason behind this sudden interest in Chad's ranch.

"I'll talk to the investors," he temporized. "What are they planning to do with the land?"

"What difference does it make?" Hank asked belligerently.

"I'm curious." And even more curious now.

"You won't get a better offer, you know."

"I don't know, Hank. It's got its own water source, some prime grazing land...."

"Are you tryin' to drive up the price?"

"I'm just trying to decide what your interest is."

Suzie burst through the front door, eyes wide with unshed tears. "Uncle Adam, I can't find him anywhere!"

"Who?" Hank demanded.

"Killer seems to have disappeared," Adam explained.

"Now, there'd be a real loss," Hank muttered.

Adam gave his neighbor a warning frown before squatting down level with his goddaughter, who practically flew off the porch to his arms. "We'll find him, Suzie. He has to be around here some—"

"There he is!" Bitsy called gleefully from the porch behind her sister.

Killer pelted up the driveway, barking for all he was worth. Suzie pulled from Adam's arms and whooped in pleasure. She began calling to the dog, loudly clapping her hands together. The commotion spooked Hank's horse, who nearly stepped on Adam's boot.

Hank tightened his hold on the reins and started to swing into the saddle as Killer came flying forward. Finding the small white dog under his feet was more than the peevish horse was willing to tolerate. Even as Adam grabbed Suzie and thrust her on the porch out of the way, the horse snorted and reared. Hank was only halfway into the saddle. He tried to swing himself the rest of the way over, but lost his grip.

Hank fell to the frozen ground. The frightened horse bolted, clipping Hank with a hoof as he passed. Adam rushed to the older man's side. Hank lay stunned and momentarily breathless, but he found enough oxygen to curse when Adam bumped against his thigh.

"If it's the last damn thing I do, I'll see that mangy little mutt stuffed and mounted," Hank railed.

"Where are you hurt?"

Hank continued cursing the dog, his face a mask of pain. Alyssa had once told Adam her father's dislike of dogs went back to his boyhood. Adam figured this incident pretty much put paid to any chance of Hank coming to terms with Killer. Pete came on the run, while Tim went chasing after the irritable horse.

"Help me up," Hank demanded.

"I think you should wait—" But Hank tried to stand on his own and collapsed with a groan and another stream of curses.

"Damn dog broke my hip."

Adam grimaced, not wanting to argue over which animal was responsible. "Are you sure it's broken?"

"Hurts like hell, and it's all that dog's fault."

Killer came over to investigate, and Adam scooped him

up, handing him to Suzie. "Get Killer inside, Suze. It'll be okay."

Horror masked her face. She took the dog and bolted for the house.

"I'm gonna shoot that animal," Hank vowed.

Adam ignored him. He doubted anything was broken, but they'd have to make sure. "Pete, help me get Hank into the truck. Then call Luke and let him know I'm on my way in with another patient."

Hank cursed soundly as they laid him across the bench in the back of the van.

Brug pulled up as Pete sprinted for the barn to make the call. Tersely, Adam explained the situation as Tim walked up leading Hank's horse.

"I'll take him in," Brug offered. "Tim can ride with me."

Adam was about to protest when he saw Josy's pale face. Remembering last night, he agreed. "Call me as soon as you know anything."

He stuck his head inside the door to let Hank know about the change in plan. Hank groaned acknowledgment without lifting his head.

"Where's the dog now?" Martha demanded.

"Inside with the girls. I'll be in after I stable Hank's horse." Tim handed him the reins and went to move Brug's truck out of the way.

"I'll walk to the barn with you," Josy said.

"Uh, Josy—"

"He's another large, dangerous beast, I know. I'm keeping you between him and me."

Something in her expression canceled his amusement. Josy looked entirely too pale, and her limp was more pronounced than he'd ever seen it as they started across the uneven ground. Adam slowed his stride to the annoyance of the horse, dancing skittishly at his side.

"How did Killer get out?"

Josy's question brought him to an abrupt halt. The horse snorted in protest. "I assumed," he said slowly, "that it happened when you left this morning."

"No, he was inside when we left. I remember worrying that his barking would wake you up."

Cold prickles worked their way up his back. The horse jerked, nearly pulling the reins from his hands.

"Pete, get over here," he yelled.

Pete broke into a run.

"What's wrong?" Josy asked.

"If you and Martha didn't let Killer out, someone else was inside the house this morning."

Her eyes widened.

Adam had assumed his office had been searched last night before Josy stumbled on the intruder. But what if someone had seen the others leave and entered while Adam was dead to the world on that chair in the living room?

"Pete, did you or Tim come up to the main house after Brug left this morning?"

"Nope. We were moving hay this morning. Is something wrong?"

"Yeah. Put him in a stall, and keep Josy at your side. Last night's prowler's may still be on the ranch."

Pete swore.

"Adam, the girls are inside!" Josy said. He could see her thoughts were running with his own. The intruder could still be inside the house.

"Call the sheriff. Pete, keep Josy with you no matter what."

"Where's the phone?" Josy demanded of Pete as Adam raced away.

Pete tethered the horse and grabbed her arm.

"Right inside the barn. Come on."

Josy stood near the entrance while Pete called the police. Surely if someone had been in the house, he was gone by now. But as the seconds ticked away, Josy's apprehension skyrocketed.

"Pete, go help Adam. I'll wait here."

"No, ma'am. Adam said to wait with you, and that's just what I'm going to do." But Pete didn't take his eyes from the house.

Martha appeared on the front porch with Bitsy.

"Where's Suzie?" Josy demanded.

Martha shook her head, her expression more puzzled than frightened. "I don't know. Adam told me to get Bitsy out of the house. What's going on?"

Josy explained.

"That's silly. I was just in there. No one's inside. Killer must have gotten out when I let Brug in this morning."

"No, he barked when we left, remember?"

Martha scowled, and Adam appeared on the porch. "Suzie's gone."

A STIFF BREEZE ROSE as the sun began to descend with alarming speed. The sun had melted most of the snow as the afternoon wore on, and Suzie was nowhere to be found.

They had tracks in abundance since Killer had been running loose most of the day, but his tracks were jumbled with bootprints, hoofprints, tire tracks and others. Wind swept the drifted snow to further muddle the scene. And the temperatures began to drop.

Josy had never seen Adam so grim. While she fought the fear clawing at her own insides, she laid a hand on his arm to offer comfort. He barely registered her touch.

The police arrived, and neighbors were called to help

with the search. Tilly came home from school to find the
house had been turned into a command post. Her wide,
serious eyes grew dark with fear.

Josy wanted to cry. It wasn't fair. The girls were too
young to go through this. She should never have come here.

When the phone rang, everyone tensed, but it was Brug
letting them know Luke would keep Hank overnight for
observation. His hip was bruised, not broken.

Restlessly, Josy paced the kitchen. Never had she hated
her memory loss as intently as she did this minute. If only
she knew for sure who was after her and why. While Martha was still her first choice, Martha wouldn't harm one of
the girls.

Josy stared at the hillside beyond the backyard. Two
horses raced across the fenced enclosure that stretched behind the house. Their tails streamed behind them as they
chased the wind in a game of their own devising.

Josy squeezed her eyes shut to hold her tears at bay. She
wished she never had come here. Wished she'd never heard
of Adam Ryser. Then Suzie would be safe.

Or would she?

From nowhere, a sudden thought sprang fully developed
in her mind. She blinked back the tears and stared hard at
the hills behind the pasture. The thought crystallized until
it became a certainty. Josy hurried back into the living
room, where men were still talking with Adam.

She didn't wait to politely interrupt. Josy burst into their
conversation. "Why would a kidnapper take the dog?"

Everyone turned to stare at her.

"The other night, Killer attacked the prowler," she hurried on. "The man kicked him into a wall, but Killer never
gave up and the dog doesn't know me all that well. Suzie
wouldn't have gone willingly with a stranger. Can you see

Killer letting anyone whisk her away by force? No one could possibly have taken Suzie *and* an angry dog."

Adam stepped in front of her. Hope shimmered in his eyes. "You think she's hiding?"

"She has to be upset over what happened with Killer and her grandfather. You tell me."

Adam nodded. "I think you're right. Hank made some threats this afternoon...."

"I agree," Martha hurried to second. "It would be just like Suzie to take Killer someplace and hide. She was sure Hank was going to make you shoot him the other day. If he made more threats in her hearing—"

"Any idea where she would go?" the officer asked. "It'll be dark in another hour."

They all looked to the living-room window where twilight stained the landscape. The officer picked up his radio and listened to the voice on the other end.

"Are there any caves on those hills behind the house?" Josy asked.

"No. And that's the one place Suzie wouldn't go," Adam stated positively. "The kids know how dangerous those hills are."

"But, Adam, that's exactly why Suzie might head for them. I would in her place."

"Adam," the officer interrupted, "Art Goodwin is bringing over the dogs. We'll need something of Suzie's to give them the scent."

"I'll get something," Martha offered.

"What about Killer?" Adam asked. "Could they trace him from one of his chew toys?"

They weren't going to follow up on her suggestion, Josy realized. At least not right away. And every second they delayed was one more second the child could be lying in the cold somewhere badly hurt.

"I'm going to the kitchen," she told them.

Adam nodded absently and squeezed her shoulder.

While water came to a boil in the kettle, Josy investigated the cupboards until she found a package of cookies
a flashlight and some dog biscuits. Taking her coat from
the mudroom, Josy stuffed her pockets. Her gaze drifted
toward the steep cliffs beyond the pasture.

"Aunt Josy?" Tilly watched from the doorway as Josy
filled Brug's thermos with hot chocolate. "What are you
doing?"

"I'm going to look for your sister."

"Uncle Adam will be mad."

The child knew her uncle Adam. "Very likely."

"I'll come with you."

"I'd rather you stayed and looked after Bitsy for me.
She must be awful scared."

Tilly nodded. "She won't let go of Dolly."

The words tripped a memory of a childish voice demanding Dolly. The image was gone as soon as it came.

"Tilly, has Suzie ever talked about climbing the hills out
back?"

Tilly shook her head. "We aren't allowed to go up there
Uncle Adam says the soil is too loose and it's dangerous."

Serious, obedient Tilly probably heeded her uncle's
words. Josy wasn't so sure about Suzie. Besides, right now
Suzie probably thought she was fighting to save her dog's
life.

"Do you think that's where she went?"

Josy nodded.

"Do you think you can find her?"

"I don't know, Tilly, but I'm going to try. Do me
favor. Don't say anything to your uncle unless he ask
okay?"

Tilly contemplated that for a second. "Okay."

Josy gave the little girl a quick hug and hurried through the mudroom. She'd been a little girl once herself, even if she couldn't remember those years. Instinct told her Suzie had headed for the hills.

Josy contemplated them with growing trepidation the closer she got. Climbing was the last thing Josy wanted to do, but Suzie was here somewhere. Josy was sure of it. She only hoped no one else was waiting out here in the night.

Chapter Nine

"She did what?" Adam stared at his oldest goddaughter and tried to curb a rising sense of panic.

"I wasn't supposed to tell unless you asked."

Adam tried to stay calm, but now Josy was out there alone and unprotected. "Okay, Tilly. I'm asking. Where did Josy go?"

"Out back. She said she was going to find Suzie."

This was his fault. He should have listened to her. Now Josy *and* Suzie were in danger.

"Uncle Adam? Don't be mad. Aunt Josy was real worried about Suzie. She took a thermos of hot chocolate with her."

Adam groaned. He should have known Josy wouldn't sit by passively much longer. No doubt she was finding some way to blame herself for Suzie's disappearance when he was the only one to blame for any of this. He had to stay calm. The panic nearly choking him wouldn't help either of them.

"What else did she say, Til? Did she tell you where she was going?"

"The hills behind the house."

Adam bit back a curse. Falling down one hill wasn't enough for her? With that bad leg of hers and all that loose shale, she was in real danger. Art Goodwin and his dogs were outside. If only she'd stayed put just a little longer, they would have picked up Suzie's scent.

"Are you going after her?"

"Yeah, Til, I am."

"I won't tell anyone until they miss you."

He ruffled her hair. "I want you—"

"To look after Bitsy," she said with a childish patience. "Yeah, I know."

"I love you, Tilly."

"I love you, too, Uncle Adam." She wrapped her arms around him and gave him a quick hug. "Bring them back, okay?"

"I'm going to try."

"That's what Aunt Josy said."

Adam found he could still smile after all. Quickly, he rummaged for a flashlight, draped a coiled length of rope crosswise over his chest, checked his gun and slipped outside.

Cold bit at him. The wind had picked up again, though nothing like last night. Moonlight danced in and out of the fast-moving clouds adding a surreal look to the fields.

Adam moved away from the house, crossing the barren yard to the field beyond. Snow lay feathered against the fence line. Even without turning on his flashlight, he spotted Josy's small bootprint in a patch of snow. She'd gone through the gate into the field.

Two mares lifted their heads, but otherwise didn't seem the least bit interested in his presence inside the enclosure. Adam crossed the field quickly. On the other side, he found the place where Josy had climbed over the fencing. So far, he'd seen no sign that Suzie or Killer had come this way. Wind carried the sounds of eager barks from the front yard.

Adam knew the rescuers wouldn't go up the cliff in the

dark even if Suzie had. It was far too dangerous. There was a path of sorts somewhere off to the right, but Josy and Suzie wouldn't know that. Still, it was the easiest way up, so Adam headed in that direction. The path meandered harmlessly for a while before it came up against an old rock slide. At that point, a hiker would have to climb, not an easy task without the proper equipment.

Suzie would have to carry the dog once the path ran out and she couldn't climb with the animal in her arms. He should have explained that to Josy when she'd tried to talk to him earlier. Why hadn't he paid more attention? Suzie wasn't on this hill.

Loose dirt and soil scattered beneath his feet as he hiked steadily upward. The ground was rocky and uneven. Walking was difficult for him. It would be a lot worse for Josy with her bad leg. When he caught up to her, they were going to talk no matter what. She wasn't a loner anymore— she was part of a family. His family. And she could darn well remember that and consult him before she did foolish things like climbing dangerous hills at night.

Adam tamped down growing panic and stopped as his powerful flashlight beam picked up a small paw print in a drift of snow. He told himself it could belong to any animal. A raccoon, a squirrel—Killer.

He shone the light around. Metal refracted in the light. Close inspection showed a metal flashlight like the one he kept in the kitchen. The metal was badly dented. The top had come off, and the batteries were scattered on the ground. This had obviously been dropped from a height. The beam picked up another object. A familiar black thermos.

Adam raised the flashlight, and dread sucked at his body. "Oh, my God. Josy."

JOSY HAD NEVER MEANT to come this far, but as the temperatures dropped, she kept pushing just a little bit farther...until the path suddenly ended.

"Suzie?"

Wind ripped her voice into the sky. She'd guessed wrong after all. Suzie couldn't have climbed past this barrier with Killer. Josy's leg hurt worse than it had for a long time, and it was all for nothing. She swept her beam over the tumbled dirt and rocks and started to turn away.

"Aunt Josy!"

The tiny frightened voice came from overhead. A sudden shower of rocks backed Josy against the side of the cliff to avoid getting hit. When they stopped, she stepped out and lifted her beam upward. The light wasn't very strong, but enough to pick up the small form huddled on a narrow rock shelf several feet overhead.

"Suzie!"

"Aunt Josy, I'm stuck and the rock keeps breaking."

Terrified, Josy realized the shelf was composed of brittle shale. Suzie was in immediate danger.

"Suzie, can you hear me?"

"Yes."

"You have to get off that ledge!"

"It's too dark. I can't see to get down, Aunt Josy."

Josy sent a silent prayer winging upward with the next gust of cold air. Killer suddenly stuck his head over the side of the ledge. There was an ominous cracking sound, and Josy knew there were few minutes to spare.

"Suzie, keep Killer still."

"I'll put him in my backpack again. Can you hold the light so I can climb down?"

If only Adam were here. "Move very slowly, Suzie."

Seconds passed in agonizing slow motion. Josy searched for a path up to the child, but there wasn't one. She could probably climb to reach Suzie, but then what? She couldn't climb back down carrying the child. How had Suzie gotten so high with the dog in her backpack? Adam should have bought the little girl a Great Dane.

There was another hail of loose rocks and stones as Suzie began to squirm backward. Josy shone the weakening light to give Suzie as much of a path as she could. There was a large boulder just below and to the left of the ledge, half-way between them. Josy tried to keep her voice calm as she began to talk Suzie down to that spot.

"You're doing fine, Suzie. Just a couple more feet. That's it. A little more to your left. Good. There's a big rock right below your left foot. That's it. You've got it. Can you—?"

Suddenly, the ledge the child had vacated gave a horrible, loud cracking sound. The flashlight and thermos fell from her hands as Josy leaped forward to avoid the large hunk of rock that plummeted to the ground where she'd been standing.

"Aunt Josy, where are you?"

Darkness enveloped them completely. The fear in the little girl's voice sent Josy scaling upward while her muscles and the pins in her leg screamed in protest.

"It's okay, Suzie. I dropped the flashlight, but I'm right below you. Can you work your way down to me?"

"I can't see!"

"Okay, honey. I'm coming." Could she? A numbing, paralyzing fear gripped her. For a moment, vertigo overwhelmed her along with the memory of falling and falling.

Josy dug her gloved hands into the dirt and hung on as fear sent nausea racing through her.

"Aunt Josy!"

Suzie's fear forced her eyes open. She had to reach the child before the little girl panicked. Slowly, an inch at a time, she began to climb. Abruptly, a strong beam of light from below pinned her against the hillside.

"Josy!"

Adam's voice barely reached her, but the sound acted like a lifeline. She knew better than to look down. If she slipped now...

Josy took a deep breath and yelled. "Shine the beam on Suzie!"

The wind pulled at her voice, but it must have carried because Adam swept the beam away from her, scanning the hillside until he picked out the child clinging to the boulder.

He yelled, but his words drifted away.

"Suzie! Move your leg down and to your right. There's a big root sticking out. See if you can reach it."

"I'm scared."

"I know you are, but you're doing fine." Josy was beyond scared. "Step back with your right foot. Come on, honey, you can do it."

While she couldn't hear his words, Adam must have heard hers because his beam guided the way. Slowly, Suzie followed Josy's instructions. Josy didn't inhale again until the child was off the rock and clinging to the tangled mass of roots only a few feet above her.

"Good girl. Now you have to go a little to your left. There's a rock on your left side."

"Aunt Josy, I can't. Killer's squirming too much."

Josy could see the frantically bobbing backpack. "Adam, shine the light between me and Suzie."

He yelled a reply, but again, she couldn't make out his words. The light, however, covered the distance between Josy and Suzie. She picked out several stable-looking handholds and began to climb. It wasn't far. Surely she could reach the child. She *had* to reach the child. They couldn't stay where they were. Not all of the ledge had fallen. Any minute now, more shale might break free and come sliding down on their heads.

Josy climbed. Her entire body protested, but she climbed until she reached Suzie and the thick mass of roots.

"Aunt Josy!"

"It's okay, Suzie. I'm right here. Can you take off your backpack?"

Suzie wiggled out of the pack while Killer barked, frantically trying to get loose. Josy clung to a root with one hand and reached inside to calm the excited animal.

"I'm going to take Killer down with me." She slung the pack over her shoulder, feeling the dog fighting his confinement and praying the animal wouldn't cause her to fall. Thankfully, Adam's light remained steady.

"Follow me, all right?" If Suzie slipped, Josy hoped she'd be able to prevent the child from going all the way to the bottom.

"Okay, but I'm really scared."

"I know, kiddo—me, too. But you made it up here, so we can make it back down." Josy prayed that her words would come true as she backed slowly, her feet seeking stable footing.

Killer squirmed and yipped unhappily while Josy kept up a constant stream of words to steady all of them. Every moment, she expected the inevitable slide down the hill to happen. She didn't relax until her foot touched solid ground and Suzie stood at her side, clinging to her waist.

"Are you okay, Suzie?"

"Uh-huh."

Every muscle in Josy's body protested the abuse, but Suzie was safe. That was all that mattered.

"Come on, kiddo. Let's get moving."

The child looked up with tear-filled eyes. "Are you okay, Aunt Josy?"

"Fine." The lie whistled between her gritted teeth. She seriously wondered how she was going to walk the rest of the way down the hill.

Killer squirmed. Josy still couldn't believe the little girl had carried the cat-size furball up to that ledge in a backpack.

"Uncle Adam is going to be mad," Suzie said suddenly as they started down the dark path.

"Yep."

"Are you mad, too, Aunt Josy?"

"Sweetie, I'm too tired to be mad. Let's just go home."

Home. Home should have conjured images of her tiny apartment. Or maybe even Adam's ridiculously formal house. Instead, home was Adam himself. Right this minute, she thought nothing would feel better than to have his strong arms securely wrapped around her.

"Are you sure Uncle Adam won't let Grandpa shoot Killer?" Suzie persisted.

"Positive." She put a smile into her voice.

"I love you, Aunt Josy."

"I love you, too. Now, let's go find your uncle."

They met him halfway down the path. He moved toward them like a bear on a rampage. Suzie had been right. Adam was furious, but she suspected fear was the real motivator.

"Well," she greeted, automatically coming to a stop in what she hoped was a matchingly aggressive stance. "I found her." Prepared for a battle, she was surprised by his first words.

"Are you both okay?"

She was warmed by his concern as he ran the beam of light over them, obviously checking for damage. Josy relaxed.

"We're fine, Adam. Hungry. Tired. Maybe a little the worse for wear, but fine."

Adam looked like a man who'd bitten into a cactus and was trying not to scream. The fact that he wasn't screaming endeared him to her. She knew he was upset, but he wasn't loosing control.

"Let's go call off the search-and-rescue teams," he managed to say.

"Uncle Adam? I'm sorry."

"We'll talk later, Suzie."

Suzie clung more tightly to Josy's hand.

"I know what you're thinking," Josy said softly as she began moving one tired foot in front of the other again. "I shouldn't have come up here without telling you."

"You shouldn't have come up here at all," he gritted.

"Well, actually, I didn't intend to. I only meant to go a short distance to see if Suzie had come this way and then I was going to go and get you."

Adam said nothing. He strode along as though they were on a racetrack. Exhausted, Josy deliberately slowed her pace.

"Go ahead. We'll let you come in first," she said.

Adam stopped. "Sorry. How bad is your leg?"

"Nothing a hot bath won't cure." And a handful of pain pills and about three weeks of complete bed rest, but she wasn't about to tell him that.

"Would you like me to carry you?" he offered.

More than anything in the world. "I can make it."

"I don't doubt you for a second."

Josy couldn't quite read his tone of voice, but Suzie stopped her from pursuing the conversation.

"Is Grandpa hurt real bad, Uncle Adam?"

"No. Nothing's broken, Suzie."

"He was awful mad."

"Yes, he was, but that was no reason to run away."

"I thought you were going to wait until we got home to discuss this," Josy said quietly.

Suzie talked on top of her words, but Josy knew Adam heard her. "Grandpa was going to shoot Killer."

Adam came to a complete stop. He squatted down level with his goddaughter. "Let's get something straight right now, Suzie. No one is going to shoot Killer. Not now, not later, no matter what he does."

"But what if we lose the court case and I have to go live with Grandpa and Grandma?"

"That isn't going to happen," Adam said sharply. Josy felt Suzie clench at her side. Adam continued more softly. "But even if it does, Killer will stay here with me. You can come and visit him anytime you want. No matter what, no one is going to hurt Killer, I promise, Suzie. Do you understand?"

"Yes, sir." And she flung her arms around his neck. After a second, Adam scooped her into his arms and started walking again.

"The next time you get scared or worried, come to me or your uncle and talk about it, okay, Suzie?" Josy asked.

Adam faltered, and Josy wondered if she'd overstepped her bounds. After all, she was supposed to be a temporary mother. Well, she was going to take an active role whether Adam liked it or not.

"Then you're going to stay forever?" Suzie asked her.

Josy looked helplessly at Adam.

"Would you like that, Suzie?" His voice was a low, soothing rumble.

"Yes!"

Adam stopped walking. He looked directly at Josy. "So would I. Think we can work out a new deal?"

The lump in her chest tried to yield to the threatening

tears as the two of them waited for her to respond. "Sounds good to me," she managed to whisper.

"Good," Adam said. "Let's go home."

What had she just done? You didn't make promises to a child unless you meant to honor them. Did Adam understand what he'd just committed to? Did she?

"Am I grounded, Uncle Adam?"

"I think," he said slowly, "we ought to discuss any punishment tomorrow when we aren't so tired. In the morning, you can tell me what sort of punishment you think you deserve."

Suzie looked at Josy, then bit at her lip. "Okay. I really am sorry, Uncle Adam."

"I know you are, Suzie. And I know you won't ever scare us like this again."

"No. I won't. Promise."

The search team met them at the bottom of the hill. Josy had never felt more depleted. Killer wriggled out of the pack and immediately set off to state his dominance over the much larger, leashed bloodhounds. If she hadn't been so exhausted, Josy would have laughed at the sight. As it was, she promptly drowned out the sea of voices surrounding her and concentrated on making it to the house before she collapsed in front of everyone.

They were almost there when she felt someone staring at her. Josy lifted her head to meet the cold, empty eyes of Mark, Hank's ranch hand. His features were expressionless, but a shudder passed right through her. Instantly, Adam slid his arm around her.

"Cold? We'll be home in a second."

The man called Mark faded back into the crowd, and Josy shuddered again. She should tell Adam, but what could she say? The man terrified her, and she had no idea why. Crazily, one thought kept playing in her mind. If she demanded to see his wrist, would she find a knife wound from where she had stabbed her attacker?

Josy leaned heavily on Adam by the time they reached the back door. She remembered Martha putting a dish of something hot in front of her while conversations swirled around her. Even the pain in her leg took a back seat to the exhaustion that sucked her into an endless black void.

JOSY AWOKE to a late-morning sun in the ridiculous marshmallow bed, her body one gigantic ache. The promise she had made last night started pinwheels in her stomach.

Adam must have carried her upstairs and put her to bed. But who had removed her clothing and dressed her in this clinging bit of satin that posed as a nightgown? Josy staggered to the bathroom, fighting leg cramps and stiff muscles. She swallowed aspirins from a bottle in the medicine cabinet while the tub filled with hot steamy water. The Jacuzzi effect soon soothed her screaming muscles.

In the cold light of day, the memories of the night before seemed almost unreal. She must have been out of her mind. Especially when she'd promised Suzie she'd stay. What was she going to do?

A sudden knock on the bathroom door jerked Josy from her thoughts.

"Josy? You okay in there?" Adam called out.

She tried to stand and immediately sank back with a moan. Her muscles were totally flaccid. How long had she been sitting in this tub gradually adding more and more hot water?

Another attempt to stand met with the same results.

"Josy? Answer me or I'm coming in."

Josy reached for the bath towel and quickly wrapped it around herself in the water. "Adam? I'm stuck."

The door opened. Her first thought was that no man

should look so unbelievably good first thing in the morning. Only the finely etched lines around his eyes attested to the strain he'd been under last night.

Her second thought was that she shouldn't be sitting in front of him in the nude thinking the sort of thoughts currently playing havoc with her senses.

Water sloshed as she squirmed beneath his stare. She only had to look at any of the mirrored walls to see what a ridiculous sight she made in the full tub of water with the saturated white towel wrapped around her.

Adam started to smile—one of those slow, devastating smiles of his that sent her pulse racing.

"Stuck?"

"Don't you dare make fun of me."

"Wouldn't dream of it."

He closed the distance without seeming to move at all. His eyes glinted with mirth and something else. Something sensual that started a wanton pinging inside her.

"What are you doing?"

"I'm rescuing you." He bent down and slid his arms beneath her armpits. Josy quivered at the contact and took a firmer grip on the towel.

"Wait, I'll get you all wet."

"Yep." He lifted her easily onto the fluffy white carpeting, then reached for another towel. "You can let go of that one now. I'll wrap you in the dry one."

She was pressed against his body, so close he must be able to hear the wild staccato of her heartbeat. She could smell the clean, light fragrance of his soap, could see the smooth path the razor had taken across his skin that morning.

"Th-that's okay. I can do it."

"Josy…" He looked deeply into her eyes.

Her wicked legs weren't going to hold her up against his

sensual onslaught. She was going to melt right here on the carpet, and the meltdown had nothing to do with over-cooked limbs.

"I'm the one who undressed you last night," he stated.

Heat swept her cheeks while a pulsing fire lit a blaze deep in her belly.

"I was afraid you were going to say that."

His smile was wry this time. "You? You're not afraid of anything."

"Want to bet?"

He terrified her. He irritated her. He stirred wanton desires to flash-fire readiness. She wanted him. She had always wanted him, even the night he came striding into the ceramic store as if he owned the place.

"Drop the towel," he said softly.

"I don't think so." His eyes were so deep she could drown without water.

"Please."

Her traitorous fingers released their death grip on the sopping towel. It landed on their feet with a distressing plop.

"Your boots," she protested weakly.

"Are made to withstand the elements. Any elements. Even wet bath towels. Maybe especially wet bath towels."

He swung the dry towel so it caressed her back, and his gaze feathered down to the place where her nipples were raised against his shirt in hard anticipation. This was madness, but she wanted this seduction with every fiber of her being.

He lowered his head slowly. She could pull away if she wanted to.

Ha. Not in a million years.

His mouth covered hers, gently, sweetly, lovingly. He

cradled the back of her head, fitting it to the cup of his hand.

She should stop this kiss so they could talk.

She'd rather die.

A wave of longing, so intense it was physical, allowed her to fuse against his hard long body. The drugging kiss deepened, demanded more and more of her soul. Josy gave it gladly.

Adam's mouth moved lower, scorching her neck with whisper-soft kisses. Lower still, until he reached the apex of her breast.

"Tell me you want this." His voice was husky with passion.

"I want this."

His eyes glinted with pleasure as his lips closed over one hard swell. Magic sizzled along every nerve ending she possessed. He raised his head, and their tongues and lips mated freely. She leaned into his body, molding herself completely against the hard length of him. They fit together as though they had been fashioned as one unit.

This was right. So gloriously right.

Boldly, Adam pressed himself against her, savoring the feeling of her body against his own. He knew the moment Josy became aware of the intensity of his arousal and was delighted when she didn't pull back, but rubbed into that contact.

Her mouth parted, and his tongue took full advantage to duel with her own. He stroked the sides of each breast, and she shuddered.

"Your skin is so soft." He trailed two fingers along her damp collarbone, dipping them down the path to her breasts.

Josy whimpered softly. The sound seemed to startle her. Her eyes went wide and anxious.

"You're very beautiful," he told her huskily.

Her breathing deepened. Her lips parted slightly, and the tip of her tongue peeked from between them. Adam was on fire.

"Liar."

"Look…" He gestured toward the bank of mirrors where their reflection was clearly visible. "See how pretty you are? Your nipples are hard and pointed for me. So beautiful." They seemed to lift in response to his words.

"Adam, please!"

"I intend to please you—all over."

He forced himself to slow down. He knew she watched as his tongue lightly bathed first one breast and then the other. He brought his fingertip up to toy with her erect nipples, and she shuddered at the contact. With a cry, she drew his face down, pressing it against her breast, arching to give him better access.

His mouth enclosed her, and he sucked hard, nipping gently.

Josy cried out.

"Did I hurt you?"

Her face flamed, but she shook her head. "No. I just…you make me feel…so out of control."

His lips quirked. "I like the sound of that."

Her hands lifted to stroke his jaw gently before moving her fingers down to the top button of his shirt. "I'm glad."

Adam went still, watching while she fumbled with each button until she had his shirt open to the waist. Josy ran her fingers tentatively across the coiled hairs on his chest. He drew in a deep breath as she paused at the nubs of his nipples. Watching him closely, she flicked each one in turn with a nail. He stiffened at the sensation, and she smiled in satisfaction.

"You like that, huh?" he asked. "You like the fact that I respond to you the way you do to me?"

"Yes." And she pressed her lips to one nipple and drew it gently into her mouth.

Adam jumped back, his eyes dilated as he held her at arm's length. A fine tremor moved down his arms as he held her there.

"Careful, Josy. My control isn't what it should be. If you don't stop that, I'm going to take you right here on the bathroom counter," he warned her.

"Okay."

Adam stilled. "Josy, I don't think either of us will be able to walk away once I make you mine."

He was fully, heavily aroused, and the words cost him, but it was true. He wanted Josy in the most basic way, but he realized he wanted more from her than a simple act of sex. Watching her last night, risking everything to save Suzie, he realized how much he cared about this woman. He didn't want just any mother for his goddaughters. He wanted Josy. She belonged in his life—in their lives—not just temporarily, but for always.

"Adam," Josy began a little uncertainly.

"Everything's going to be fine, Josy. I want you very badly—that's all."

Josy shivered, but Adam knew it wasn't fear or cold that besieged her frame. She was all soft, yielding female to his masculinity and she smiled a smile as old as Eve.

"You're greedy," she told him quietly. "You want everything."

"Yes." He had to clear his throat, but he didn't break eye contact. "Everything."

She nodded and slowly stepped back to reveal herself fully to him. Her wary eyes watched him closely. "There was a lot of damage."

Her body was gracefully sculpted, but marred by jagged white scars that made him flinch at the pain they represented. Josy stood perfectly still, letting him look, waiting for his verdict.

"You are very beautiful to me. I want to be inside you."

"I want that, too," she replied shakily. Josy stepped toward him, her hand partially raised to stroke his cheek.

"No," he protested. "Don't touch me." He was on the ragged edge of his control. She stopped instantly.

Adam exhaled forcefully. "Sorry," he explained, his tone wobbly, "but you are testing my control to the maximum. We're going to go slow if it kills both of us."

"How much slower can we go?" she protested. "You're still dressed."

"Believe me, I know." He looked to their reflection and smiled. "Does that frighten you?"

"No. Actually, I find it strangely exciting," she admitted quietly. Her gaze strayed to the hard bulge in his pants that strained against the zipper. A touch of moisture marred the dark charcoal of his slacks.

"I won't hurt you, Josy. Not ever."

"I'm not afraid." Her smile was a woman's smile of possession. "May I touch you now?"

Adam wasn't sure how long his control would survive. He was ready for her right this second. The thought of her hands on him was almost more than he could take.

"Where do you want to touch me?"

"Here," she replied, stroking his cheek, rubbing a tiny patch of stubble he'd missed shaving. Her fingers quickly tugged aside his unbuttoned shirt, and she slid her hands into his lightly colored chest hair.

"And here," she continued, kissing his shoulder.

A shudder passed down the length of him.

"And here," she said, using one nail to provoke the nub of his nipple.

Adam jerked, his breath raspy as her hand quickly trailed downward to stroke the evidence of his arousal.

His hand stilled her questing one. "Keep touching me there, and I won't be able to wait."

"Maybe I don't want you to wait. Maybe I want you now," she demanded impatiently. She reached for his zipper.

"Josy..."

"No, Adam," she charged, "it's my turn. No more teasing. I want you."

Adam scooped her into his arms before she could protest and strode into the bedroom. Her surprise turned to amusement. "I think I like a forceful man," she told him.

"Good. I intend to be very forceful."

He had to sit on the edge of the bed to remove his boots, and that gave Josy a chance to continue to torment him with soft touches and even softer kisses. He shed his clothing in record time and stood.

Josy's eyes widened and then dilated to mere slits as she studied him for a second. If she changed her mind now, he'd go insane. But Josy opened her arms in welcome, and he covered her with kisses as he probed carefully at her soft, exceedingly tight passage.

"Don't stop," she urged when he hesitated.

"I couldn't if I wanted to, but wait just a moment. No. Don't move. Hold very still."

He held still poised above her, while he struggled for more control. She was wet and hot, but so narrow he would hurt her if she wasn't as fully aroused as he was. Her left nipple was only inches from his mouth. He bathed its nub with his tongue and lips. Josy gasped in surprise, but her body automatically allowed him easier access to the responsive peak.

Adam suckled, pulling hard as he began to lower himself over her. Her body parted more easily, welcoming his intrusion. It took all his remaining control not to greedily thrust into that enticing warmth. Adam used his teeth to nip carefully at her nipple, and Josy went rigid. He surged inside her and she cried out in an unexpected climax. Her contractions nearly sent him over the edge, as well.

"Shh. It's okay. You're so beautiful. Shh." Adam pressed her tightly to his chest as her body shuddered in the aftermath.

Tears splashed from her eyes, dampening his collarbone. She lifted her head, blinking them away.

"I'm sorry," he whispered. "Did I hurt you?"

"No. Oh no. It was so...oh, Adam."

Adam smiled, kissing the top of her head. He'd loved watching her face when she climaxed. It was a heady thing, knowing he was the cause of such intense pleasure. The thought caused him to stir helplessly.

Josy's eyes widened, and she looked directly into his. "You didn't...you let me, but you didn't..."

"Don't be embarrassed."

He intended the kiss to be gentle, but Josy had other ideas. Her mouth became greedy and demanding.

Josy drew on his tongue, satisfied when Adam stirred more fully within her.

Smiling wickedly, she let her hands play among the wiry hairs on his chest, then arched against him to rub her breasts on his sweat-slicked skin. Adam groaned. The sensation was highly erotic.

"Josy," Adam warned huskily, "you're playing with fire."

She licked his chest, tasting the musky saltiness and delighting in his shudder. "Then burn me," she whispered, licking at his throat and then sucking gently on the skin near his pulse.

His control finally shattered, Adam began to move. Josy responded instantly, wrapping her legs around him to hold him closer, tighter.

Josy demanded more and more until Adam gave a hoarse cry of satisfaction. He lowered his eyelids, breathing in ragged gasps, and his head sank forward to pillow in the hollow of her shoulder. Tenderly, absently, she stroked his back, even as his fingers feathered through her hair.

"I wanted to go slow, to take you with me this time," he whispered in her ear.

Josy placed a finger over his lips. "Don't you dare apologize. It was...I can't find the right word. I don't think there are any words for that sensation."

Adam smiled and rolled to the side. "We did nearly set the bed on fire, didn't we?" he asked lightly.

"Yes. We most certainly did," she responded smugly. Adam laughed and kissed the tip of her nose.

"And now I suppose you're hungry."

"Starving."

"I'll go downstairs and see what Martha fixed for lunch while you get dressed."

"I have to get dressed?"

"Unless you want to shock Martha."

"Can't have that."

"Besides, Bitsy will be home from school soon."

Josy sat up a bit stiffly, surprised that it felt so natural to be naked in front of Adam.

"I didn't realize it was so late. I'll be down in a couple of minutes."

Adam pulled on his jeans and stopped.

"Are you okay?"

His tenderness reached right into her heart, making it sing with happiness.

"I'm wonderful, Adam. Really."

"Okay." And his smile said it really was okay.

It wasn't until she came out of the bathroom to find him gone that Josy realized neither of them had said the words that would have made the past few minutes perfect. She loved him so much it brought tears to her eyes.

She blinked them back, pulled the sweater over her head and reached for her comb. It wasn't like her to be so emotional. But then, nothing else had ever mattered this much. Did Adam want her to stay because he loved her, or because he wanted a permanent mother for his goddaughters?

She stared at her reflection, realizing she needed to know this answer. It wouldn't change anything. She loved Adam and the girls unconditionally. She just needed to know how much work she had ahead of her before she could convince him to love her back. Even if they lost the court case tomorrow, Josy wasn't walking away from this family unless she was forced at gunpoint.

Chapter Ten

Josy set down her sandwich. ''What do you mean the hearing is postponed?''

''Hank strained his back when he fell yesterday,'' Adam told her. ''Luke can't find anything wrong, but Hank says he's in such pain that walking is impossible. The judge is agreeable to the postponement if we are. I got a call right before lunch.''

Her skin pinkened slightly, and he knew she was remembering what they'd been doing together right before lunch. So was he. Skipping the rest of his lunch and going back upstairs to make a meal of another sort strongly appealed to him. Josy looked incredibly pretty sitting at the kitchen table in that soft blue sweater. Of course, she'd looked even prettier lying in that big round bed with no clothing on at all.

''Are we?''

Adam jerked his thoughts back to the here and now. After all, Martha was helping Bitsy rinse her dishes at the kitchen sink only a few feet away. This was not the time or place to be thinking about Josy in the nude.

''Are we what?'' he asked.

''Agreeable to a postponement.''

Adam frowned. "I want this over with as much as any-one, but a few more days won't hurt."

Josy chewed and swallowed thoughtfully, pushing her plate to one side. "And maybe the judge will think that if Hank can't show for a hearing, he might have trouble car-ing for three small girls."

She was quick on the uptake. "That, too."

"Adam, we need to talk." Josy sent a hesitant look in Martha's direction.

Martha's lips narrowed in a tight line. "Don't mind me. I'm going to take Bitsy upstairs and change her clothing. They painted at school, and I want to get her out of this shirt before the stain sets. Come on, Bitsy."

Adam was stunned by the animosity Martha radiated as she led Bitsy from the room without a backward glance. Until this moment, he hadn't given Josy's suspicions any credence at all. Now he wondered. The last time he'd ig-nored Josy, she'd not only been right, but she'd also nearly killed herself proving her point.

"You still think Martha's responsible for the phone calls and that window episode?" he asked quietly.

Josy hesitated, looking him in the eye. "I think she could be behind my problems, Adam. She...and maybe Brug. And before you argue, let me tell you about a conversation we had and what happened yesterday when I went into town."

Adam listened without interrupting, although it was an effort. He could picture Josy trapped in that bathroom all too clearly. If Martha or Brug had done that to her...

"Why didn't you tell me about this sooner?"

Her expression turned wry. "We've been a little busy since then."

"Okay. I'll take care of it. From now on, you aren't going anywhere without me."

Josy arched her eyebrows, and he recognized battle lines being drawn. "Is that right? When's the coronation?"

"What?"

"Obviously, you've named yourself king—I was just wondering where your crown was. And your scepter. A scepter is good. You can use it to ward off the bad guys."

She had a sassy battle cry, he decided with a wince, but he wasn't giving in on this point. "Josy, you aren't safe outside this house."

"And I'm safe inside? Never mind. That wasn't fair," Josy apologized. "The point is, my being here is dangerous to the children. I think I should leave right away."

"No!" Visions of her walking out on him were more painful than he would have thought possible. "No," he said more calmly. "We have a deal."

"The deal didn't include putting children in danger."

"I agree."

"You do?"

"Yes." He sat back, relieved he had this under control at least. "That's why I called my sister in San Diego this morning. She's agreed to take the children for a week while we try to clear things up here. Hank's request for a postponement couldn't have come at a better time. We have three weeks. During that three weeks, I'm going to stick to you like glue."

Josy shook her head. "Adam, the girls should stay here with you. I'm the one who should go."

His chest tightened, but he tried for humor. "You want to go visit my sister?"

"Don't be funny."

"Where would you go?" he asked, trying to be reasonable. And he was rewarded when Josy bit her lip, obviously not prepared for that question.

"Back to Hayes, I guess."

He tried not to show his vulnerability to that answer. She could just leave after what happened between them upstairs? Hadn't it meant anything to her?

"Sheriff Malcolm—"

"Has already told us there is nothing he can do to protect you," he interrupted. "He doesn't have the manpower. You'll be a sitting duck in that isolated apartment. Is that what you want?"

"Of course not! But if someone is just trying to drive me off, I'll be perfectly safe in Hayes."

"Don't be a fool."

Anger ignited her features. "And what is it you're being? You've got blinders on, Adam! Look at the facts. I was perfectly safe until you walked into my life and that black truck barreled out of the night. Even though we shot at him, he never once fired back."

"He may not have been armed."

"And in the barn? I was an easy target, but no one killed me then, either. The phone calls, the other incidents…even yesterday. If someone really wanted me dead, I wouldn't be sitting here right now and you know it!" Twin spots of color sat high on her cheekbones. More calmly, she said, "Someone wants me to go away, Adam—to get out of your life. And I *will not* take chances with those little girls!"

"Josy…" In the face of her anger, his own subsided. Her words made a horrible sense. Was she right?

Adam pushed back his chair, the need for action clawing at his gut. He walked to the sink, his mind tumbling with questions.

"I'm sorry, Adam. I know you don't want to believe me. I don't blame you. I hope I'm wrong, but it all fits, don't you see?"

Adam turned back to her, wanting to wipe that haunted

look from her features. Features that had become dangerously dear to him.

"If Martha and Brug were behind all your troubles, I
could deal with the situation, but you've left a few things
out of the equation. While they were in town terrorizing
you in that grocery store, who was going through my office? Someone was in here that morning, because whoever
it was let Killer out."

Josy's expression turned thoughtful.

"And if you'll recall, the black truck was *behind* us, so
Brug couldn't have been driving. I called him from the car,
remember? I suppose Martha could have left the girls by
themselves, stolen the truck and gone to Hayes to scare you
by nearly running us both down, but I seriously doubt it."

Josy acknowledged his logic with a shake of her head.
"Okay, maybe it's more complicated than I thought."

She nibbled on her lip, distracting his thoughts once
again. But she quickly brought him back to reality with a
sudden change of topic.

"What do you know about that man who works for
Hank?"

"Mark Wilson?"

"Mark, yes. He was here last night."

"Half the town was here last night."

"But he's the only one who stared right through me. He
scares me, Adam."

And Josy didn't scare easy.

"I know it sounds crazy," she rushed on, gripping the
edge of the table. "I can't explain the crawly way he makes
me feel. All I know is, I kept wondering if we checked his
wrist if we'd find a wound from the cut I inflicted on the
attacker the other night."

"I thought you said Brug—"

She waved off his protest. "Brug might have told the

truth about his injury—I just don't know." She sighed. "I know you think I'm grabbing at straws and maybe I am, but Mark works for Hank and Hank wants you to sell the girls' ranch. He also wants to win the custody suit. What if he sent Mark Wilson to search your office, knowing we'd be having dinner with Eleanor?"

"Mark was at their ranch that night, remember?"

"Before dinner, yes, but he could have left and driven over here after we saw him. We left right after dinner. Maybe he found himself trapped inside the house when we came home early. The balcony doesn't run along the office side of the house. He might have been trying to get back outside when the lights went out."

"Then why didn't he just go? Why come out in the hall and attack you?"

Josy frowned, pondering the question.

Adam had never paid Wilson any attention, but now that he thought back, the man was always hovering in the background whenever Adam went to Hank's place.

"Do you think Wilson could be part of your past?"

"I don't know."

Her features were tight with strain. Adam reminded himself how difficult it must be not to remember even the smallest things.

"Mark's been with Hank almost two years now," he said thoughtfully.

Instantly, Josy perked up. "Did he appear before or after I went missing?"

The question landed with the force of a blow. When *had* Mark Wilson appeared on the scene? Adam couldn't remember. "There's one way to find out." He headed for the mudroom.

"What are you doing?"

Josy got stiffly to her feet, using the table for support.

Her leg must be giving her fits, Adam thought, and no wonder with all that climbing. He hated seeing her in pain.

"I sent Brug over to the vet's before lunch," he told her. "So I can't talk to him right now, but I *can* have a talk with Hank and Wilson."

"Wait, Adam! You can't accuse—"

"Trust me a little here, okay?"

"What about Martha?"

They heard Bitsy coming down the hall, Killer barking at her heels.

"Martha won't hurt you while Bitsy is around," Adam said quietly. "If you stay close to her until I come back, you'll be fine."

"I'll be even better if I go to Hank's with you."

Bitsy rushed in full of chatter, unaware of the tension that filled the kitchen. Josy stopped arguing immediately, but her look told him she'd made up her mind.

So had he, and this was one battle Adam planned to win. If Wilson or Brug had anything to do with harming Josy, Adam was going to find out.

Then he'd tear the men apart with his bare hands.

JOSY WAS FURIOUS. Pete had arrived at the back door, allowing Adam to escape outside. Fifteen minutes later, Adam sent young Tim inside to let Josy know he'd gone to Hank's.

She decided to throttle him as soon as he got home. Hadn't he just told her he wasn't letting her out of his sight? That was precisely the argument she'd planned to use if he'd given her a chance. Now she was stuck with Martha, who appeared more hostile than ever as she set about cleaning the kitchen.

Bitsy clung to her doll, watching the two adults warily. Josy couldn't do anything about Adam right now, but she could have it out with Martha just as soon as she could get Bitsy out of hearing range.

"Bitsy, why don't you go put on *Sesame Street* while I talk with Martha?"

"I don't have time for chatter right now," Martha interrupted. "*I* have a lot of work to do."

Josy faced her grimly. "I'll help while we talk."

The woman raked her with a dismissing frown. "You're supposed to rest."

"Bitsy, let's go in the living room, okay?" Josy asked.

"Martha doesn't like you," Bitsy said. She gripped a rag doll firmly against her chest as if afraid Josy were going to snatch it from her.

Even Martha had the grace to look chagrined. While agreeing with the child's assessment, Josy simply shook her head. "She's just a little upset right now, honey. Come on. It's okay."

Bitsy let herself be led to the living room. "Are you gonna disappear again?"

Josy smoothed back a strand of wispy hair. The girls had had so much upheaval in their short lives. Adam mustn't send them away. And Josy couldn't stay and put them at risk.

"I might have to go away for a little while," she temporized, "but it won't be like the last time. I'll be back."

"Suzie said you were going to stay and be our new mother."

A solid lump blocked her throat. There was such uncertainty in the little girl's eyes.

"Would you like that, Bitsy?"

Bitsy lowered her head and began fiddling with her doll. Josy kissed the top of her head.

"It will all work out somehow, I promise." But she wondered how she was going to keep that promise.

Josy returned to the kitchen. Martha had donned a sweater and gone into the backyard to hang a load of wash on the line that ran between two slim metal poles.

Josy grabbed her parka and stepped onto the deck. "You can run," she challenged Martha, "but eventually you'll have to talk to Adam if not to me."

Martha dropped a child's T-shirt back into the basket and turned. Her pretty features were dark with anger. "I'm not running from *you*," she snapped. "I told you, I have work to do."

"So do I."

"Then go do it."

"I am. You made the phone calls, you watched us through the window and you got Brug to try and scare me away."

"You're crazy."

"Really? Phone calls can be traced, Martha. Which one of us do you think a judge is going to find crazy? The victim or her attacker?"

"I never attacked you!"

But she didn't deny the other, Josy noticed. "No, you had Brug do it for you."

The mention of Brug touched a nerve. Martha suddenly looked uneasy. So Brug *was* involved.

Josy moved onto the grass with care. Her leg was exceptionally sore. She wasn't sure how far she could trust it.

Martha came toward her, her face ugly with anger. "I know all about you. You're nothing but an opportunist, out for what you can get."

The sound of a rifle shot echoed over the hills. There was a pinging clink as a bullet ricocheted off the narrow post that stood between them. Martha stopped moving. A second shot immediately followed, and Martha grabbed her shoulder. Before the third shot rent the air, Josy threw herself at Martha, causing both of them to tumble to the ground hard.

"Roll toward the house!"

Martha made a low sound of assent. Josy was already taking her own advice. She hoped the overhang from the second-story balcony would provide some measure of safety—maybe take them out of the gunman's line of sight.

Adam had been dead wrong. Josy wasn't the least bit safe here at the house.

When she reached the concrete patio, Josy grabbed one of the plastic deck chairs. It was a ludicrous shield, but she hoped it would deflect a shot the way the pole had done. She reached for another chair to toss to Martha, when she saw the trail of blood the dark-haired woman was leaving in the yellow grass. Martha had stopped rolling. She was trying to stand, but her movements were slow and uncoordinated. Blood matted her sweater.

Josy started toward her. The back door suddenly flew open. Bitsy's confused features were all she saw.

"Bitsy! Get back inside!" she yelled at the child. "Someone's shooting."

Bitsy backed up, but Killer slipped between her legs, barking for all he was worth. He ran from Josy to Martha excitedly.

Josy nearly fell over the dog as she grabbed Martha by her uninjured shoulder. Half dragging, half supporting the woman, she staggered for the back door. At any moment, Josy expected to feel the numbing cold of a bullet penetrating her back. But the gunfire had stopped.

They made it as far as the laundry room before Josy's weak leg gave out and they ended in a heap on the cold tile floor.

"Martha's bleeding!" Bitsy said from the doorway. She stood in a direct line with the window.

"Bitsy! Go into the living room. Get behind the couch...."

"No! I want to stay with you!"

Josy couldn't be sure what Bitsy would do if she sent her away. Was it better to keep her nearby?

"Okay, Bitsy. It's okay. Come over here. Sit in front of the clothes dryer." The heavy machine would offer the best protection from a stray shot. Fortunately, the child obeyed, though her eyes remained riveted on Martha.

Martha half leaned, half lay against the washer, her eyes closed, her skin pasty white.

"Is she gonna die?" Bitsy asked.

"No, sweetie. She isn't going to die."

Please, God. Don't let her die. Josy offered up the prayer as she blocked Bitsy's view and tore at Martha's sweater, terrified by the amount of blood that had soaked through her back. Josy fumbled with the buttons on the red flannel shirt beneath the sweater.

Blood soaked her fingers. Too much blood. There was a neat round hole where the bullet had entered, a gaping jagged tear where it had exited lower down on her back.

"Martha?"

Martha's eyes fluttered, but otherwise, she didn't respond. Josy hadn't spent months of convalescence without learning a few things. Martha was going into shock. If Josy didn't act fast, Martha would die.

Pressure and elevation, right? And warmth for the shock. Oh, God, don't let her memory be playing her false. Where was the pressure point for a shoulder? She didn't know. Josy glanced around frantically for something to use to stem the flow of blood.

"Bitsy, I need your help, sweetie. Can you reach a towel from that stack of laundry without standing up?"

Bitsy nodded, her eyes wide with a mixture of fear and curiosity. Josy was amazed the child wasn't hysterical. She was also grateful. She felt a little too close to that edge herself. Maybe the little girl didn't realize how serious things were.

Bitsy tumbled the laundry from its neat pile on the folding table and handed Josy a fluffy white towel. In the process, she dropped the object she'd been holding. Only then did Josy realize it was the cordless phone from the kitchen.

"Good girl, honey! Let me have the phone."

"It's Uncle Adam."

Josy snatched up the instrument, but all she heard was empty static. Immediately, the blood flow increased from Martha's wound. Heart in her throat, Josy dropped the phone and used both hands to press against the wound. The shot must have hit an artery. She had to keep pressure on the wound.

"Bitsy, do you know how to dial 911?"

Bitsy nodded. "We learned in kindergarten." Her voice was shaky.

"Good girl. I'm so glad you're here to help me. Can you grab some more towels and cover Martha's legs?"

"There aren't any more towels," she said fearfully. "Can I use this?"

Josy didn't even look to see what *this* was. "Yes. Anything. We have to keep Martha warm."

"Like they did when the baby sheep got all cut up on the wire?" Bitsy started piling clothing on Martha's legs. "Tilly cried, but I didn't. Uncle Adam says I'm brave." But her lips trembled, and her eyes seemed to dominate her small round face.

"Uncle Adam's right. You *are* brave." And she thanked God for that. Josy was scared enough for both of them.

"Call 911 and tell the operator we need an ambulance. Can you do that?"

"Okay."

As Bitsy dialed, Josy realized she hadn't locked the back door. Fear rippled through her. The shooter might be heading for the house. She had to keep Bitsy safe!

"Aunt Josy, the man wants to talk to you."

"I can't let go of Martha. Can you hold the phone for me?"

Awkwardly, Bitsy brought the phone level with Josy's mouth.

"This is Josy Ryser. I'm pinned down in the laundry room at the back of my husband's home by a sniper. I've got a five-year-old child and a badly injured woman." Josy could hear the panic rising in her voice. She worked to control it. "I think the bullet hit an artery," she said more calmly. "We need medical and police assistance right away."

Josy couldn't hear the man's reply, but unfortunately, her fear had communicated itself to Bitsy. The child looked ready to cry.

"Bitsy, you're a real brave little girl," Josy said as calmly as she could. "Tell the man I can't hear him. I can't let go of Martha."

Bitsy hesitated, then relayed the message. She listened for a second and then looked at Josy. "The man says help's coming. He wants to know if Martha's breathing."

The next several minutes were a nightmare as Bitsy acted as a relay while Josy staved off her fear of further attack and tried to keep Martha from bleeding to death.

Why didn't Adam come?

ADAM WAS ANNOYED. Eleanor refused to allow him to see or talk to Hank. In her most formal voice, she insisted that Hank was resting and couldn't possibly have any more visitors right now.

Adam had passed a white Mercedes with rental tags leaving the ranch on his way in. He couldn't identify the people inside because of the tinted windows, but he thought there'd been at least two. Frankly, Adam didn't care who they were. He wanted to talk with Hank. But no amount of cajoling would get Eleanor to budge.

Frustrated, Adam hesitated. Hank might be unreachable, but Adam could have a little chat with Mark Wilson, maybe wrestle him to the ground for a look at his wrist.

Adam headed for the main barn, but the only person he could find was a young boy mucking stables. The boy didn't know where anyone was. He'd only worked there for two weeks so he wasn't a source of information.

Stymied, Adam headed back to his truck. Hank's red pickup was gone from its normal spot outside the main barn, but a dark black stain marked its spot. Adam bent for a closer look. Lots of vehicles leaked oil. This was far from proof of anything, but he wondered if the pickup truck would also have a collection of pine needles in the bed. There wasn't a pine tree in sight anywhere near the barn.

He spotted the twitch of a curtain in the front bedroom window. Hank's bedroom. So Hank knew he was here.

Anger churned in his belly. He went back to the front door and pounded. No one answered. Eleanor could give stubborn lessons to a mule. The door was locked, so he started around the side of the house when common sense pushed past the anger. Doing something stupid would only give him momentary satisfaction. If Hank knew anything about what had been happening to Josy, the best way to nail the bastard was publicly and legally for all his constituents to see.

Adam strode back to his truck and picked up the cellular phone. Ned Pohl was still out of his office. Bitsy, however, answered on the fourth ring.

"Hi, Uncle Adam."

"Hi, Bits. Where's Aunt Josy?"

"In the backyard with Martha. I'll get her."

What was Josy doing outside with Martha? He tried to calm the trepidation that filled him. Audibly, Adam followed Bitsy's progress to the back door. He heard Josy yell to the child, and his stomach turned to ice.

"Bitsy! Get back inside! Someone's shooting."

Fear, like he'd never experienced before, sent him scrambling into his truck. Grass and dirt churned beneath the tires as he took off. He disconnected and dialed the emergency number with one hand while steering with the other. He gave the dispatcher terse information and hung up so he could concentrate on getting back to his ranch in one piece. The distance seemed to double with every frantic beat of his heart.

He saw Killer, his white fur stained red in several places, as soon as he came to a stop. Adam leaped from the cab and sprinted for the porch just as a medevac helicopter came in over the empty front corral. Brug was running in that direction, a rifle in his hand.

Adam opened the front door yelling Josy's name. Killer burst past him, racing for the kitchen. Bitsy nearly fell over him as she came flying down the hall.

"Uncle Adam! Uncle Adam!" Bitsy launched herself against him. The phone smashed against the arm of his jacket as Adam lifted the child with a grateful prayer of thanks. He heard a man's voice coming from the receiver.

"Where's Aunt Josy?" he asked, bringing the phone to his ear while he cradled the child close to his chest.

"Martha's shot. There's lots of blood just like the baby sheep, Uncle Adam. I called 911 and talked to a man."

"Good girl, Bits!" He kissed her head, then spoke into the phone. "This is Adam Ryser. I just arrived home. The medevac unit is landing, so I'm going to hang up. Thanks for your help."

"Adam!"

Josy's voice led him to the laundry room. He found Josy on the floor, crouched over Martha in a sea of folded laundry. Both women were bloody.

"Josy!"

"I'm fine," she said. "It's Martha. I think the bullet hit an artery, Adam."

Just then, Brug led the paramedics into the room. The next several minutes were a jumble of confusion as the paramedics took over from Josy while Brug tried to crowd in close and Killer danced underfoot in excitement.

Josy insisted she wasn't hurt despite the blood staining her coat. She gathered Killer in her arms to get him out of the way and followed Adam into the kitchen.

"What happened?"

Tersely, she told him, stroking the excited dog.

Brug joined them a few minutes later, his face pasty, his expression devastated. "I went after the guy, Adam. I'd only been back a few minutes. Just long enough to send Pete and Tim to check on a broken fence post out near the back road. When I heard the first shot, I grabbed a rifle from the tack room and ran outside. I didn't know anyone had been hit."

His torment was visible. Brug obviously cared about Martha. Adam drew Josy against his side with his free hand.

"I saw the guy in that cluster of rocks above the west pasture," Brug continued, almost to himself. "I fired a couple of rounds and he took off running, so I went after him, but he had too big a head start. I was going uphill, and there wasn't any cover. When I realized there was no way I could catch him, I decided to come back and see what he'd been firing at. That's when I saw the helicopter and knew someone had been hit. They must have been on a run nearby to get here this fast. The whole thing only happened minutes ago."

"I know," Adam told him. "I called Josy from the Claussen place and heard her shout at Bitsy to get back."

Josy raised her head from his chest and smiled up at the child in his other arm. "Bitsy was superbrave. She helped me help Martha."

Bitsy smiled back shyly. Adam kissed her cheek feeling like the luckiest man alive.

Brug didn't share their smiles. "Martha looks bad, Adam. Real bad."

The anguish in his friend's eyes was something Adam understood all too well. He felt a pang of guilt over his own relief that Josy and Bitsy were safe.

"Did you recognize the guy, Brug?"

Brug hesitated. He cast another anxious look toward the sounds coming from the laundry room. "I never got close enough."

Adam had the distinct impression he was lying, but a police siren screamed its arrival in the front yard. With Bitsy in his arms, this wasn't the time for questions.

"I'll go talk to them," Brug said. "I need to do something."

Adam nodded.

Brug turned away and then turned back again. "I'm going to the hospital with Martha," he announced.

"Good. I can't leave Josy and the girls here alone. You'll call me as soon as they know anything?"

"Yes," Brug promised. "And afterward, I need to talk to you, Adam."

Adam felt Josy straighten in his arm. "You want to talk now, Brug?"

An officer Adam didn't recognize entered the hall.

Brug shook his head. "Later."

By the time the other two girls got home, things had settled down. The media were being kept at bay, and the investigation was centered outside where the shooting had taken place. Josy had given her statement several times, and the strain was taking its toll.

Adam was surprised and grateful when his neighbors Calvin and Deborah Milton arrived. Deborah took over the kitchen while Calvin offered to take the children for a couple of days. Adam had planned to fly them to San Diego, but it was too late now and this seemed like a better solution. He didn't want the girls so far away tonight.

They clustered around Josy on the living-room couch. Bitsy curled trustingly in Josy's lap while the other two sat on either side, and a freshly bathed Killer nuzzled next to Suzie.

Adam knew a moment of peace as he surveyed the scene. He wanted to keep them all right there, safe, content, his. But for tonight, they could stay with the Miltons so he and Josy could talk and plan without interruption.

Tilly was pragmatic about spending the night with her friend's family, but Suzie protested until Killer was included. Only Bitsy cried, making the decision hard on everyone. Josy took her aside and talked with her quietly. Whatever she said made a difference. Dolly and Bitsy went with the others.

Eventually, the house quieted. Deborah left a casserole

warming in the oven. Pete and Tim had cleaned up the dog and all traces of blood from the floor before returning to the bunkhouse. The police stationed a man out front, and suddenly it was just Adam and Josy in the big silent house.

"I'm not hungry right now, Adam. What I'd really like is a bath."

"Okay. Let me check out the room first."

"Do you really think the shooter got inside with all the police around?"

"No, but we aren't taking any more chances." He made her wait in the hall while he checked her room and his and both sets of doors.

"This has to end," she told him quietly.

"It will. They'll find him."

"Platitudes?"

"Truth." He kissed her nose. "I'll be in my office while you bathe. Leave the doors open so I can hear you holler in case you need anything."

"All right."

Her easy acquiescence bothered him. The last time she'd gone quiet like this, she'd taken off after Suzie. Well, she wasn't running anywhere this time.

"Josy, the shooting wasn't your fault."

She gave him a tired nod and entered the bathroom.

Troubled, Adam went into his office to call his sister. When he finally finished reassuring her, he saw there were ten messages on his answering machine. Three were from the man Hank had told him to talk to about selling the girl's property. Adam's jaw clenched tightly. The next six were business related. Adam made notes since it was too late to return those calls. The final message was from Ned Pohl.

"Adam, listen up. You're up to your armpits in alligators, my friend. Mark Wilson doesn't exist."

Adam stopped breathing. A motion from the doorway

caught his attention, and he saw Josy standing there toweling her damp hair, dressed in a loose-fitting pink sweat suit and a pair of thick socks. She stopped moving as soon as she heard Ned's voice.

"But," Ned's voice continued, "Wilson's description fits someone else to a tee. Pandergarten has a cousin, Vincent. The guy's a living, breathing gangster. Arson, murder, assault, you name it. He's got a long rap sheet, and all of it ugly. There are current warrants on him right now, including an arson fire that killed seven. Two were children. This is one mean bastard. You need to alert the locals."

Adam crossed to Josy and slid his arm around her shoulders. She trembled slightly.

"It gets worse," Ned went on. "That holding company that wants your land? It's a front for one of Enrique Pandergarten's companies. Interesting, no? Claussen has another proposal before the legislature on the issue of legalized gambling, and Vincent works for Hank. Now we discover Enrique wants your property on the Wyoming-Colorado border. I just can't figure out how your lady comes into this."

Adam stroked her back while his mind churned with the new information.

"Call me," Pohl requested. "I don't like the way things are shaping up. My Reno contact says Pandergarten left for Wyoming this morning. This is not good, Adam. I think it's all coming to a head. Keep your lady close. Better yet, leave town. Take a second honeymoon. But call me."

Adam turned to Josy. "Hank has a red pickup truck he and his men use for ranch business, Josy. It has an oil leak."

"I still think it was Martha at that window," she said.

"Maybe it was," he agreed reluctantly. "Wilson may have come, saw Martha outside and decided to try again later. If Ned's right, and he usually is, you have every reason to be afraid of Wilson. He's probably the one who shot Martha.''

''I still don't understand. He's had plenty of opportunities to kill me if that's what he wanted.''

''Maybe he doesn't want to kill you. Maybe you were right all along. Maybe he only wants to scare you away. I'd bet my ranch something happened the day you ran into Pandergarten and your mother's boyfriend outside her apartment. Something that made you a threat to one of them.''

''But I don't even remember that meeting.''

''You know that, and I know that, but Pandergarten may not know that. Or maybe he just doesn't care.''

The phone rang, and Adam reached for it as Josy limped over to the guest chair and collapsed in the seat looking exhausted.

''Ryser,'' he answered. ''Brug!... She did? Great! That's real good news. How soon will they know?... How are you holding up?... Yeah, Josy's fine. The girls are spending the night with the Miltons.... No. I'm going to keep her close.... Okay, we'll talk first thing in the morning. Call me if there's any change.... Right. She'll make it, Brug. Martha's tough.''

Josy watched him as he replaced the receiver.

''Martha came through surgery. She isn't out of danger yet, but it looks good thanks to your quick actions.''

''I'm glad.''

''Brug's going to stay in town tonight, but he wants to talk to me in the morning.''

''Adam, I know you don't want to hear this, but Brug could have fired those shots today. He had a rifle.''

''He explained that!''

''I only heard three shots.''

Adam stared at her, his gut churning. Hadn't he had the same fleeting thought when he first saw Brug running toward the helicopter? "Are you absolutely sure there weren't more?"

"No, but I'd like to know for sure that someone else was up on that hill. It's a mistake to discount Brug completely. If he was trying to scare me and hit Martha by mistake…"

"Mark Wilson—"

"Is more likely, I agree. I just think you need to keep an open mind. Either Brug's in love with Martha, or he had a hand in what happened, Adam."

"After tonight, can you doubt Brug has feelings for her?"

"No, but I told you, she wants me gone."

Adam stood up. "The police will test Brug's rifle, but I'll keep an open mind," he promised, wondering if he could. "Let's go downstairs. I want to talk with the officer on duty. The police need to know about Mark Wilson."

"Call the Miltons first, Adam. The girls need to know that Martha is going to be all right."

Dark circles smudged her eyes. She looked frail and done in, yet she was still thinking of everyone else. He'd die before he'd let any more harm come to her.

"Okay, mamma hen," he teased.

He was relieved when she smiled back as he dialed the Miltons' number. That done, he went outside to talk to the policeman on duty while Josy set the kitchen table for dinner. Adam knew the officer slightly because he had a child in Suzie's class. After passing on Ned's information, Adam relaxed for the first time all day. This was a police matter now.

"It's almost over, Josy," he told her as he took the casserole from the oven and sat down. He covered her hand with his own, finding her skin cold.

"I wish I could believe that."

He wished he could, as well.

"I was thinking we might want to go and have a look at the girls' ranch tomorrow," he said as she began to eat. "It's not too far from Hayes. We could drive down, and you could visit with your friends there. Would you like that?"

Her expression lightened. "Yes. Thank you. But what do you hope to gain by looking at the land? Or are you just trying to get me away from here for a few days?"

She was far too astute. "Hey, you can't blame a man for wanting to get a beautiful woman alone for a while."

"Uh-huh. What about the girls?"

"I was going to fly them to my sister's, but I think they're better off at the Miltons'."

"I don't like sending them anywhere, Adam. They need the security of being with you."

"Well, for tonight, it's a done deal. We'll see what tomorrow brings. Finish eating, and I'll rinse the dishes. We'll turn in early. Your eyes are half-closed as it is."

"I'm okay."

"You're a lot better than okay, lady."

Upstairs, Josy headed for her room, but Adam stopped her. "We'll sleep in my room tonight."

"Uh, Adam…I'm not…that is…"

He kissed the top of her head. "Sleep, Josy. Just sleep. I don't think I have the energy to do more than that myself tonight. I just want to hold you so I know you're safe. Is that okay?"

Her smiled enfolded his soul. "Very okay."

Of course, when she came to bed dressed in a long gown of emerald green, he found a reserve of energy that made him wonder if he could keep his promise to just hold her. The cut of the gown was so demure it was provocative in a way she probably hadn't planned. He could clearly see the outline of her small tight nipples through the satiny fabric.

She saw where his gaze had landed, and soft color bathed her features. "It's the plainest gown I could find. There isn't a piece of cotton or flannel in any of those drawers."

Adam grinned. "I'm glad."

"You said we were going to sleep," she admonished with an answering smile.

"And we will." He pulled back the covers and invited her inside.

"What are you wearing?" she asked suspiciously as she sat down on the edge of the bed.

"Same thing I always wear."

She slid beneath the covers and came up against him.

"You're naked!"

Adam grinned. "That's how I sleep. But don't worry." He kissed the tip of her nose. "Nothing's going to happen."

"Well, darn."

"I beg your pardon?"

"I said darn."

Adam came up on one elbow. "I thought you were too tired."

"I thought so, too. Looks like I was wrong."

"Josy—"

"Could you stop talking long enough to kiss me?"

Adam stopped talking.

Chapter Eleven

The shrill scream of the smoke alarm brought them out of sleep. Adam rolled away from Josy's warmth and reached for his pants.

"Adam?"

Smoke tickled the back of his throat.

"Grab your clothes," he yelled. "We're on fire."

Adam fumbled for the light switch. Nothing happened. His sleep-dredged mind slowly accepted that this was all wrong. Beneath the smoke lay another smell. Gasoline. He pulled his jeans on quickly and reached for his boots. Josy appeared hazy in the doorway between their rooms, clutching a bundle of clothing.

Adam moved to the sliding glass door and inched back the drape. The night was lit with an unholy orange light that flickered and danced across the ground. Even as he reached for the lock, a lick of flame shot up over the balcony.

Adam swore.

"What is it?" Josy pulled on her sweatshirt, crossing to join him.

"The balcony's burning."

Josy ran to test the bedroom door while he grabbed the flashlight from the nightstand.

"The door's hot, Adam."

He heard the fear in her voice. It echoed the fear tearing at him. They were trapped. He grabbed for his shirt. "Smell the gasoline?"

"Oh, my God. He got inside, didn't he, Adam?"

"That would be my guess." Adam ran to his bathroom. Josy began to cough. "Where's the sheriff's man?"

Adam didn't want to think about that. He soaked two face towels in the sink. "We'd better assume he's out of the picture and we're on our own."

"Adam, the floor is hot. We'll have to risk the balcony."

He handed Josy one of the wet cloths. "No. If we do the expected, we're going to end up dead. He's probably got a nightscope trained on this side of the house. Where're your shoes?"

Josy coughed and placed the towel over her mouth and nose. "I forgot them. They're in my bathroom."

"Never mind. There's no time." Smoke filled the room at an incredible pace.

"What are we going to do?"

"We're going up."

"Smoke rises," she protested.

"I know." He could hear the crackle of flames over his racing heart quite plainly now. "Come on."

Josy followed him to the walk-in closet where he pulled down the steps leading to the attic.

"Hurry."

Smoke had already begun to filter into the crawl space at the top of the house as they scrambled up under the eaves. The floor up here was unfinished, a sea of naked beams and pink insulation.

"This way."

Josy coughed and clapped the towel back over her mouth. He led her toward the front of the house while smoke thickened the air. The other opening didn't have stairs. It was designed to be pushed upward from below. Adam worked frantically to pry the plywood up, ripping two fingernails below the quick in the process.

"Got it." Smoke billowed in through the opening. The bastard must have doused the entire downstairs to get the fire to spread this fast. "I'll go first and catch you."

Josy gave a strangled cough of assent, and Adam lowered himself through the opening. He reached back up to grab Josy's legs and lowered her to the ground.

"We're in the spare bedroom at the front of the house," he told her through his towel. "We'll go through the window to the front-porch roof. He'll be looking for us to come out the back or the other side of the house. This should buy us some time." Adam paused to cough deeply.

Josy coughed almost continuously now, and his own lungs strained for oxygen. He couldn't see a thing. The flashlight was useless in the smoke. Josy clutched his shirt as he worked his way across the room by touch. In the background, the smoke alarm continued to shrill its warning, a sound that was almost drowned out by the roar of flames.

Adam felt for the window and stopped. He wrapped the towel around his hand and punched out the glass. The sudden inflow of cold air felt wonderful, though it only gave a momentary respite from the dense smoke trying to replace all the oxygen in his lungs.

He cleared the frame of glass and backed out onto the roof over the front porch. A missed shard of glass cut his hand, but then he was on the sloping roof, much too high up for comfort. Josy scrambled out after him.

Dancing flames lit the yard below them. The police car sat in the turnaround like a silent, empty sentinel.

Josy coughed smoke from her lungs as she surveyed the scene.

"Come on," Adam urged. "We're sitting ducks up here." He led her to the far end of the roof with the sound of the fire a dull roar of noise at their back.

"Ever shimmy down a tree?" he asked.

"Not to my knowledge."

"I'll help. There's a column in this corner. You just wrap your legs around that, then inch your way down."

"That's all, huh?"

"That's it."

Josy paused to cough smoke from her lungs. "I've got a better idea. You go down, get a ladder and bring it back."

There was a loud crash. Suddenly, glass shattered on the other side of the roof as flames shot through Tilly's bedroom window.

"I don't think we have that kind of time, Josy."

"Point taken."

Adam suddenly cursed. "I forgot about your leg. Do you think—?"

"Go! We'll worry about my leg after we get out of this. Don't worry, I can make it. I have no desire to become human toast."

"I love you, Josy Ryser."

And Josy was left watching as the infuriating, impossible man disappeared over the edge of the roof.

Carefully, she peered over the edge to watch him shimmy down the post. His words flooded her with hope. Did she dare to believe he meant them? Good sex and a fire at one's back could make a person say just about anything.

She clung to the hope instead of the fire-crazed terror beating at the back of her mind, and tried to do exactly what Adam had done, lowering herself carefully over the edge and swinging her legs until she found the tall round column. Adam yelled something, but she couldn't make out the words.

She started to slip and grabbed the gutter for support. The gutter ripped away from the wall beneath her hands. Josy had managed to get her legs around the column or she would have fallen. Unfortunately, while her legs wrapped just fine, the weak one didn't understand the command to shimmy, nor did it have the strength to hold her where she perched so precariously. Already off balance, she slid painfully down into Adam's waiting arms.

"I told you not to grab the gutter. You really know how to scare a man."

"Keep it in mind," she panted.

"Let's go." Adam ran for the police car but stopped suddenly, motioning her toward the front of the vehicle. "Get down. Behind the car."

Josy glimpsed the shattered side window and the figure slumped inside as she followed him around to the passenger's side.

"Adam—"

"Get down beside the front tire, Josy. I'm going to see if he's still alive."

Adam tried the passenger's door, but it was locked.

"Wait here."

"No! Adam…"

She was talking to empty air. He was determined to play hero. In a crouch, he moved around to the driver's side and reached inside. Josy heard the locks open.

"Is he—?"

"Dead," Adam said tersely. He came back to her side and opened the passenger's door and slipped inside. Josy realized he was reaching for the police radio, but the car's interior light would be a beacon to the killer.

Josy surveyed the area while Adam used the microphone. Something moved on the far side of the burning house. For a moment, she thought it was Killer, then she remembered that Killer was at the Miltons'.

"Adam!"

He came out of the car with the dead officer's weapon in his hand. Josy pointed. Adam reached back inside for the officer's larger flashlight. The beam clearly picked up an arm, moving in the dirt. Someone lay on the ground near the corner of the house.

"Wait here," he ordered.

"Not a chance."

He either didn't hear or didn't want to waste time arguing. Falling timbers from the burning house set the front bushes on fire as she followed Adam to the corner. The body was male, but that's all Josy could see as Adam bent over him.

"Brug," Adam said on a cough.

"But he's supposed to be with Martha." She'd fearfully expected the victim to be Pete or Tim. "Is he alive?"

"Yeah. Here. Hold this." He handed her the gun and flashlight as he began checking the man for injuries.

Josy squatted beside them feeling a helpless sense of déjà vu. Like Martha all over again. Adam couldn't get Brug's coat off, so she set the gun and flashlight down and helped. A bullet had torn through Brug's chest to the right of his heart. There was no exit wound. His eyes suddenly fluttered open.

"Adam."

"Right here, buddy, take it easy. I'm going to roll you over and—"

"No," Brug protested, struggling to breathe. "She wasn't supposed to be hurt." He coughed, a harsh rattle of sound Josy could hear above the roar of the fire. "He

said...keep him informed. He said...scare her...'way.''
Brug coughed harder.

Adam placed a restraining hand on his shoulder. ''Don't
try to talk. We'll get—''

''Listen! Martha...protect...me.'' Brug struggled to get
the words out. ''He said...Josy...oppor...tunist. You married...to get...girls. Didn't know...a lie!''

Flecks of blood stained the spittle he coughed up.

Their eyes locked over Brug's body in horrible compre-
hension. Adam looked grimly devastated. Josy wanted to
cry for all of them.

''We'll talk later, Brug. You're bleeding internally,
buddy. You've got to save your strength.''

''No. He's—''

''Adam!'' Josy had seen the motion from the corner of
her eye. Mark Wilson loomed out of the night like the devil
himself. Dressed in black, he was outlined by orange
flames. He raised the rifle, taking careful aim at her. Adam
lunged across Brug's body. The sound of the shot came as
Adam flung her to the ground.

Josy lay stunned, pinned by Adam's weight. Oh, God,
he'd taken the bullet meant for her! But Adam rolled away,
reaching for the gun she'd set down.

The gun Brug now held a foot from Adam's face.

The world came to another terrifying halt.

''Brug?''

Josy cast a frantic look around. Mark Wilson lay crumpled on the ground, the rifle still clutched in his hand. Two
figures sprinted across the open yard from the direction of
the bunkhouse. One also held a rifle.

The gun fell from Brug's fingers. ''Did I...get...
bastard?''

Josy let out a shaky breath that ended in a series of

coughs. Adam reached for Brug, who fell back onto the grass.

"Yeah, buddy. You got him."

Without warning, the balcony collapsed in a hail of raining sparks. Josy scrambled to her feet, brushing at embers that singed her clothing.

"You and Josy okay?" Pete yelled as he and Tim raced up.

Mark Wilson's coat caught fire, but the man didn't move.

Adam grabbed Brug by one arm. Josy hurried to grab the other as Adam began to drag him away from the intense heat. Pete rolled Mark Wilson in the dirt to douse the flames. Josy suddenly stumbled. Tim pushed her aside and took over while Josy trailed them across the grass.

"Is Brug dead?" Tim asked.

Adam stopped to cough more smoke from his lungs. "No, but he took a slug through the chest. I think it punctured the lung."

"We called for help."

"So did we." Adam stopped near the corral, far enough away from the burning house for safety, though Josy could still feel the heat. Tim ran back to help Pete.

"Holy cow," she heard him exclaim, "that's Mark Wilson!"

BY THE TIME the fire department arrived, there was nothing left to save. Including Mark Wilson. Brug's shot had killed him instantly. Brug himself was in critical condition. Doctors removed a bullet from his collapsed lung, but there was extensive damage.

Hours later, Adam sat in the quiet motel room and alternated between watching Josy sleep and dawn edging across the sky. Josy tossed restlessly and began to moan softly in distress. Adam left the chair by the window and crossed to the bed to stroke her bare shoulder. Instantly, she quieted. He kissed her temple lightly and went back to the chair. Despite his own exhaustion, sleep eluded him. His chest was tight, and the back of his throat ached from all the smoke he'd inhaled.

"Adam?" She sat up drowsily.

"Go back to sleep, Josy."

Her voice was scratchy from the smoke, as well. "Come to bed."

He started to protest, but realized it would be easier to do what she asked until she fell back asleep. He didn't remove his jeans, simply slid into bed alongside her.

She came into his arms naturally, fitting herself along his length. Despite the showers they had both taken, they still smelled of smoke. Or maybe the scent was embedded in his nostrils.

"Go back to sleep," he told her again.

"I can't. I keep dreaming about the fire."

He stroked her hair gently, feeling a crinkly spot where the ends had been singed. He'd come so close to losing her. His throat constricted painfully.

"It's okay. It's all over now."

"I was so afraid, Adam," she admitted softly.

"It's all right. It's all right, Josy." He felt the dampness of her tears on his chest.

His mind told him this emotional roller coaster was perfectly normal. They'd seen a man die tonight. They'd nearly died themselves. All he wanted was to cling to Josy so he could be sure she was really there, safe in his arms.

Her hand caressed his cheek. Her skin felt so soft against the bristles on his unshaved chin.

"Josy?"

She placed feathery kisses along the column of his neck. Adam tried to swallow and couldn't. His emotions were on overload or something. Her touch was like match to kindling. She didn't know what she was doing.

"Josy..." His voice didn't hold entirely steady as she planted another kiss along the side of his neck. Adam felt that kiss in every receptive pore of his body. He was suddenly hard with wanting.

"Hmm?" She nuzzled his neck, while her fingers traced a path down his chest.

He shuddered when she suddenly nipped the soft skin of his neck, then soothed it with the tip of her tongue. Making love to her was becoming as vital as breathing.

"Do you know what you're doing?" he asked, drawing back a fraction to study her face.

"I'm seducing you. Now be quiet."

His chuckle of relief melted into a long hot kiss as Josy sought his mouth. They melded together with an urgency he'd never experienced before. He pushed aside the rough blanket even as she fumbled for the zipper on his pants.

He should slow down, get her ready with foreplay, but she was as demanding as he. She pushed his hands aside and freed him, her mouth closing over his shaft, greedily, making him lose any semblance of control.

"Josy, slow down."

She lifted her head. "I can't."

Adam groaned as she kissed her way up his body. Her mouth closed over his, shutting off his protest. She drew back to gaze at him. "I don't want to slow down. I want you, hard and deep inside me."

Adam groaned, wanting that, too. As soon as he wriggled out of his jeans, she pushed him back against the pillow and straddled him. Surprised, Adam found her mild aggression highly arousing.

Afraid he'd hurt her, he found her wet and as ready as he was. She clung to him tightly, fitting herself around and over him as if she could fuse their bodies into one. The bed rocked with the force of their union, and the climax, when it came, left him drained physically and emotionally. Josy collapsed against his sweat-slick chest and pillowed her head in the crook of his shoulder.

For a long time, they just lay there totally replete. The room gradually brightened with the first rays of morning.

"I was thinking," Josy began.

"Uh-oh."

She swatted his chest lightly, but her expression was no longer that of a passionate woman. "I'm serious."

Reluctantly, Adam allowed her to roll to one side.

"Mark Wilson must have spread gasoline all over the inside of the house."

Adam stared at the ceiling, hating the need for this conversation. "Yeah. That's how I have it figured, too."

She propped herself on an elbow to look at him. "Why didn't he just come up the stairs and shoot us? We were sleeping, Adam. We thought we were safe with the police outside. We would have been easy targets. Why burn the house?"

A discerning question. One among many that had been troubling him for hours while she slept. "Ned said Wilson was wanted for another arson where seven people died, remember? Maybe he liked setting fires."

"Do you think Mark was the 'he' Brug was keeping informed about us?"

Adam released his breath slowly. "Sounded like it to me."

Her hand came to rest comfortingly on his chest. "Brug and Martha thought they were protecting you, Adam. I don't know what he told them, but Martha called me an opportunist right before she was shot. Pandergarten either knew or suspected our marriage was a sham. He had his cousin use Brug's loyalty to drive me off.''

"But why did Brug listen to Wilson?"

"Was Brug a gambler?"

"Not that I know of." But he had started to realize he didn't know Brug or Martha at all if they could have done this sort of thing.

"I'm sorry, Adam, I know Brug was your friend."

"He still is," Adam assured her as he trailed his hand lightly across her shoulder. A tiny ridge of scar tissue met his fingertip. "In the end, he saved our lives."

"It isn't over, is it, Adam?"

"No. It isn't over."

"And we still don't know why."

"Pandergarten obviously sees you as a threat." Adam reached for the light on the nightstand and sat up against the headboard. Owlishly, Josy blinked up at him.

"How did Wilson know we were alone in the house tonight?" she asked.

"Brug knew. He must have told him. Maybe that's why he came back. Though I doubt if Wilson cared who was inside the house."

"That's what I thought."

"Josy," he warned, "don't go there."

"What do you mean?"

"You're getting ready to tell me you have to leave for the girls' sake."

"Adam—"

"You aren't going anywhere."

"He'll send someone else, Adam."

"We'll be ready for him."

Josy sat up, too, ignoring her nudity. "We can't put the girls at risk anymore."

"We aren't going to." Adam got out of bed.

"Where are you going?"

"To call Calvin Milton."

"At six-thirty in the morning?"

"He's a rancher. He'll be up. I'm going to have him bring the girls out to the air park. How'd you like to go meet my sister and her husband?"

"We're going to fly to San Diego?"

Adam began dialing the familiar number. "Just as soon as you get dressed."

JOSY'S RELIEF AT SEEING the girls brought a lump to her throat. They were fine. Scared but fine. Calvin had told them about the fire at the house.

"Aunt Josy? Are you okay?" Suzie ran over to greet her, Killer barking happily at her feet.

"I'm fine, kiddo. Just fine."

Suzie stared at the small fire holes that dotted her sweat suit, then down at her sock-clad feet.

"Here you go, ma'am," Calvin Milton said, handing her a plastic sack. "Deborah had me bring you some clothing. She said these will be a mite big, but she added a belt and said she thought you could make do."

Josy hugged the man fiercely and took the clean clothing with gratitude. She used the ladies' room to slip into the woman's skirt, blouse and sweater. The clothing hung on her skinny frame, but the belt cinched the skirt to her waist and the outfit was far better than her fire-riddled clothing. Deborah had even included a pair of new-looking tennis shoes that tied so they would stay on Josy's feet. And, bless her, there was a shoulder purse with toilet articles. The tube of fresh lipstick brought tears to Josy's eyes. The woman didn't even know her.

Josy had always hated taking charity, but that didn't keep

her from being eternally grateful to those who offered it in times of need.

Tilly ran over to her as soon as she stepped outside. "You look pretty, Aunt Josy."

"Thank you, Tilly."

"Is it true? Uncle Adam said the house is gone."

Josy laid a hand on her slender shoulder. "I'm afraid so, sweetie."

"There's nothing left?"

"Not much."

"But," Adam's gruff voice said from behind her, "we're going to build a new house. And you ladies are going to have to sit down and help me plan it."

Adam was flanked by the other two girls. He had also changed, she noticed, and Calvin Milton's clothing fit him a lot better than Deborah's fit her. But then, Adam would look good in a plastic grocery sack.

"A big house like the other one?" Suzie asked.

Adam frowned. "If that's what you want."

"Uh-uh. I want a house like we used to have when Mommy and Daddy were alive."

"What kind of house was that?" Josy asked.

"Big, with lots of color."

"A rambler," Adam explained.

"Ah. I like ramblers best myself. No stairs."

A grin slid across his face. Warm, sexy, devastating to her senses. She forced back memories of their wild love-making.

"Sounds good to me," Adam said. "While I fly, you ladies can plan your new rooms right down to the colors. And," he added, "you'll all need new wardrobes."

"What's a wardrobe?" Bitsy asked.

"Clothes," Tilly informed her. "We get to buy all new clothes."

"Okay. I want blue."

Adam laughed and herded them out to the plane. Josy came to a stop, staring at the machine for the first time. "*That* is supposed to fly us all the way to San Diego?"

"It's a six-seater Cessna. Top of the line. I fly it all the time, Josy."

"It's a toy! Where's the string the man on the ground holds while it goes around and around? And what do you mean, *you* fly it?"

"You were expecting a pilot and a 747?" Adam asked.

She rounded on him. "Yes! I drove an old minivan bigger than this. Besides, you're too tired to be piloting a plane."

He came over to her, all masculine arrogance and good-humored teasing. "Trust me."

"Ha."

He tilted her chin with the tip of his finger. "Get in the plane, Josy."

There was hint of steel beneath his order, and she knew the girls could hear them. "Okay, but I don't have to like it."

She was startled when he drew her forward and kissed her soundly. She wrapped her arms around his neck, glad for the feel of his body warm against hers. Her borrowed sweater was no match for the cold wind nipping at them, but together, they produced enough heat to ignore Mother Nature.

Adam released her slowly, a satisfied grin on his face. How she loved that face. She touched his cheek in wonder and saw three pairs of eyes staring at them from the windows inside the plane.

"Adam, the girls," she admonished.

"They'll have to get used to watching me kiss you. I plan to do it a lot."

Hope soared in her heart, but she couldn't think of a reply to that. They'd made love this morning, but he hadn't said the words again. Of course, neither had she. Josy shelved the questions for a more private moment and changed the subject. "Where's Killer?"

"Calvin's going to keep him until we get back. He'll have Pete keep an eye on things for us, but I don't want anyone to know where we are. Now, get in the plane. Please."

Josy got, but she prayed all the way to San Diego.

Josy liked Adam's sister and brother-in-law immediately. Their four children fit age-wise right between the girls, so there was a playmate for everyone except the baby, a two-year-old toddler.

Josy was glad Adam's wallet had been in his pant pocket because they certainly gave his credit card a workout buying clothing for everyone.

Questions waited until the children were down for the night and the four adults were sitting outside on the deck overlooking his sister's backyard pool.

Carlene shook her head. "How are you going to prove Pandergarten is behind everything?"

"Ned Pohl's working on it," Adam told his sister.

Bill nodded. "Good man. Something wrong, Josy?"

"Bringing me here might have put your whole family in jeopardy," Josy fretted.

Bill tipped his head as he looked at Adam. "She doesn't know?"

"Know what?" Josy asked.

"Bill's the chief of police here in San Diego," Adam explained.

Josy swallowed her surprise. After all, Bill Durbin was a large solid man with an air of authority. "That doesn't make him invincible, you know."

"No," Bill said with a kindly smile, "but it does give me a lot of manpower to call on. I promise. You and the girls are perfectly safe here."

Josy didn't voice her doubts in the face of the three smug faces, but she remembered all too clearly when Adam had told her the very same thing. She hoped that this time they were right.

Chapter Twelve

"Where do you think you're going?"

Tensing, Adam turned around in the darkened bedroom. He'd been sure Josy would sleep soundly enough for him to get away without a scene. He should have known better.

"Go back to sleep," he whispered.

"Like heck." She flung back the covers and stood. "I'm going with you."

Adam found himself staring at the shadowy body he had just loved so thoroughly, and rational thought flew right out the open window. She'd become so precious to him.

Adam dragged his gaze upward. Her soft-kissed lips were set in a hard, firm line right now. Eyes that had gazed at him in loving pleasure only a few hours ago were narrowed in determination. Adam sighed.

"You aren't going to let me do this the easy way, are you?"

"I'm not going to let you do it at all," she stated calmly. "I'm going with you."

"No."

"Fine. You fly the toy plane, and I'll take a real plane and meet you back home."

She had come to think of his place as home. Enormously pleased, he watched her bend and reach for the pool of silk puddled on the floor. He'd had a lot of fun removing that nightgown last night and he felt a decided stirring at the memory.

"Josy, I want you to stay here with the girls."

"No." She held the gown, but didn't put it on, probably to keep him distracted. It only worked partially.

"You're safe here," he told her.

"So are you."

"I have to go back."

"So do I. Either you take me with you or I fly there in a real plane. Your choice." She headed for the hall bathroom but paused to toss over her shoulder, "I told the girls last night we might be leaving before they got up this morning, so you don't need to wake them to say goodbye."

Stunned, Adam watched her close the bedroom door. How the devil had she known what he planned? He hadn't said a word to her.

Well, she wasn't going, and that was final. Adam threw his meager clothing into the bag he'd borrowed from his brother-in-law, cursing under his breath. Josy wasn't safe in Wyoming. He and Bill had discussed this. That's why Adam had planned to leave her here with his family. He'd hoped to be out of the house before she even woke up. Maybe if he hurried...

Adam opened the bedroom door and stole down the hall like a thief. He stopped dead at the sight of Josy standing by the front door, tapping her foot imperiously, a small suitcase at her feet.

"What took you so long?" she demanded.

"How did you...?"

"I took my shower last night, remember? And I left clothing in the bathroom, so all I had to do was brush my teeth."

"Josy—"

"Save your breath, Adam. I'm going with you. Hit men don't grow on trees. I doubt if Pandergarten has found a new one already. He probably doesn't even know his cousin is dead yet."

She'd worn that same determined look the night they'd met when she was facing down Pandergarten's two goons.

"Look," he said, knowing it was pointless to argue with her. "If you're going with me, then you're going to do exactly what I tell you, is that understood?"

"Sure," she replied, opening the front door. "As long as I agree with what you say."

Irritation gave way to a rueful smile. The woman was irrepressible. "Will you at least take reasonable orders?" he asked as he started the rental car.

"No, but I'll consider reasonable requests. I like your family, Adam."

Adam gave up. "So do I, most of the time."

She grinned. "Carlene didn't tell me a thing, if that's what you're thinking. You're easier to read than the girls. I won't get in your way, but I want to be there when you talk to Hank."

"See?" He slammed the heel of his hand against the steering wheel. "That's exactly what I'm talking about. You aren't getting within a hundred yards of Hank. I don't know what his connection is to all this, but Mark Wilson worked for him. I'll be the only one talking to Hank."

"Get it through that thick skull of yours that we are in this together. What did Ned Pohl tell you when you called him?"

"How did you know—?"

"You were gone for the duration of the movie the kids were watching. Either you hate home movies or you were on the phone. No human bladder takes that long to empty."

"The CIA could use you," he grumbled.

"How do you know they didn't?"

Adam nearly sideswiped a sedan, staring at her smug features. He quickly adjusted back into his own lane, gave an apologetic wave to the other driver and tried not to grit his teeth. "Is this your subtle way of telling me you remember something?"

"Nope. It's just one of a billion possibilities. Adam, my memory is gone for good. Accept it. I have. The doctors tell me there was too much damage for it to suddenly come back."

"You've been having flashes."

"Yes, and sometimes I remember them and sometimes I don't. The flashes are just that—tiny snatches of memory that have no context for the most part."

"Do you remember telling me the other day that you'd driven a minivan?"

"No." She looked surprised. "I wonder if I really did. Drive a minivan, I mean. My memory plays tricks. I can't trust it, Adam. That's what makes it so ludicrous to think someone wants to kill me for what I know."

He patted her hand as he pulled into the rental lot. "After I turn the car in, we'll catch the shuttle to the airport."

JOSY WATCHED ADAM CHECK the toy plane from front to back. She was afraid to ask what he was looking for. At least this time she didn't have to hide her fear. Adam already knew she was scared. His small, frequent touches did little to soothe her dislike of small planes, but they went a long way to making her feel special. How she was coming to love this man.

He handed her a headset.

"Put that on. We're going to have to keep an eye on the weather. It could get a little bumpy. There's snow moving into Wyoming later today."

"Snow?"

"Relax. As long as we stay ahead of things, we'll be fine."

"Comforting."

Adam smiled. They flew in companionable silence for a long time. The noisy engine was lulling, but Josy was too keyed up to sleep. She kept wanting to ask Adam if he'd meant what he'd said on the roof of the house. She wanted to believe his declaration came from more than a shared moment of crises. Would he still think he loved her once this was over?

"Are you okay over there?" Adam asked.

"Fine."

"You were frowning."

"I was thinking."

"Uh-oh."

She couldn't ask him something so vital in a plane where she wouldn't have his full attention.

"It still bothers me that Pandergarten waited so long to come after me," she said instead.

"Obviously, he either didn't know you were still alive or he didn't know where you were until I found you."

"Or," she suggested cautiously, "I wasn't a threat until you found me."

Adam frowned.

"If you assume Pandergarten had something to do with my disappearance and subsequent fall down the mountain, why didn't he make sure I was dead? And why did he bring me all the way out to Colorado in the first place?"

"You're assuming Pandergarten is the reason you came to Colorado."

"What other reason would I have?"

"Your mother?" he suggested.

"Then why can't Mr. Pohl find her now?"

"Josy, if I had answers—"

"I know, but I've been thinking. Could we be looking at things from the wrong end?"

"What do you mean?"

"Mark Wilson worked for Hank, not Pandergarten, and Hank wants custody of his granddaughters."

Adam frowned.

"Forget about Eleanor and her snooty friends for a minute. What does Hank get out of raising three little girls that he obviously doesn't feel paternal toward?"

"Peace at home?"

"I'm serious, Adam. You bought me because having a wife made it more likely the judge would award you custody."

Adam scowled. "Josy, I didn't *buy* you. I know I called it that earlier, but—"

She waved his words aside, not wanting to be distracted. "Never mind the semantics—your case is stronger with a wife. Isn't that why you wanted me back?"

"Josy, Hank's not a murderer. The man's a state senator. He's got money and power—"

"His wife has the money," she reminded him. "Or so you told me. What if he needs money for some reason? What if that ranch the girls own has gold or uranium or some value we don't know about?"

Adam chuckled. "Not a chance. I read the reports as soon as Hank became insistent that I sell."

"Insistent. That's exactly what I'm talking about. Why is he insistent? Who inherits if the girls die right now?"

The words hung in the air like an explosion.

"I do," he said softly.

"But only as long as you're their legal guardian, right? Let's take this one step at a time. With me out of the picture, Hank may believe he has a stronger chance to get the girls legally. He tries to scare me away, but it doesn't work. He sends Wilson to kill me, but the bullet hits Martha instead. Now if we both die, the girls go to Hank by default, don't they? And what's theirs is his.''

''Josy—''

''Take it a step further, Adam. If all of us die, who inherits that ranch? You said Wilson didn't care who died in that fire. It's possible you're more right than even you knew.''

Adam swore.

''It fits, doesn't it? And it makes a lot more sense than this mysterious Pandergarten wanting me dead for reasons unknown.''

''Josy, I've known Hank Claussen for years. We don't share the same politics and I don't like him on a personal level. But I honestly don't believe he would kill his only granddaughters.''

''I don't like to think so, either, but Brug did know the girls were gone the night of the fire. I'd like to believe Hank knew they were gone that night, too.''

Adam rubbed his knuckles across his chin. He'd shaved, she suddenly realized. He must have been up longer than she'd thought before she woke and heard him moving around this morning. Had he gotten any sleep at all last night?

''Ned said Pandergarten, not Hank, wants the property,'' Adam continued cautiously. ''And let's not forget Wilson is Pandergarten's cousin.''

''What if Hank and Pandergarten are friends?''

Adam snorted. ''Wyoming State senators don't have casino owners for friends.'' He stopped abruptly and began to curse.

''What?''

His fingers balled in a fist. "Hank's sponsoring that bill to legalize gambling in Wyoming."

"So they are friends?"

"I don't know, but even if they are, we don't have a shred of proof. The only connection is Wilson, who's wanted for murder, according to Ned."

"You think anyone will believe Wilson coincidentally picked Hank's ranch to hide from the law?" she scoffed.

Adam shrugged. "No. But there's lots of possibilities, Josy. We need proof. If—and it's still a huge *if*—Hank and Pandergarten are in bed together, finding proof is going to be close to impossible. Hank has a million connections, and Eleanor has more. Her family won't stand by and see their name smeared, even by association. Hank will bury any traces so deep they'll never be found."

He reached for her hand, and the plane gave a sudden lurch like some giant had just swatted them.

"Adam?" Dread ripped his name from her throat, just short of a scream. The clouds weren't below them anymore. They surrounded the plane like an evil cocoon. Adam turned to his controls.

"Hang on. This is going to be a bit choppy until I can get us out of this weather."

Choppy. A serious euphemism. The plane bounced across the sky while her heart headed up her throat for a firsthand look. Josy gripped her hands together, feeling the nails pierce the skin with each jolt. She didn't need Adam's expression to know this wasn't normal.

"We're going to have to set down," he told her.

There was nothing around them but clouds. "Where?"

"Would you like to see the girls' ranch for yourself?"

"If it means bringing this plane down, I'm all for it."

The tiny lines around his eyes crinkled. "Down it is."

Josy stared at the clouds anxiously while Adam spoke

on the radio and did incomprehensible things to the controls. Her fear increased when she saw snowflakes drifting past her window. Snow wasn't good. She was sure it wasn't good. Adam wanted to stay ahead of the snow. He looked as grim as on the night of the fire.

"You okay?" he asked suddenly.

"Marvelous."

Adam spared her a small smile. "You might want to close your eyes. Chad's ranch has its own airstrip, but to be honest, I'm not sure it's long enough for this plane under these conditions."

Not at all what she wanted to hear. Josy shut her eyes.

They came in hard and fast. The plane touched down and bounced back into the air again. Josy barely bit back a scream before they repeated the process. They bounced several more times, but finally stayed down. She didn't open her eyes until the plane came to a lurching stop.

"There," Adam said, sounding strained, "that wasn't so bad."

Josy peeked between her fingers. "Compared to what?" The world was still white. "Where are we?" She was proud that her voice didn't crack.

"At the moment, we're in the north pasture. Welcome to the Double C. Chad's legacy to his daughters."

"We made it?"

"You doubted me? I'm crushed."

"No. Fortunately, that fate didn't await us this time."

Adam had the nerve to laugh. "Come on. I radioed ahead. Don Grommet's coming to meet us. He's the foreman here. The hangar's back over there, behind us."

Josy followed the direction of his pointing finger and made out what appeared to be a large gray shed, partially hidden in the snow. Adam taxied closer to the building, and Josy saw a much smaller plane tucked inside the open doors.

She shivered with cold as she waited inside the open doors while Adam secured his plane. A blue pickup truck appeared out of the snow. The driver was a big rugged man with a homely, friendly face. Adam went out to meet him.

"Josy, meet Don Grommet."

"Ma'am." He nodded. "Where's your coat?"

That was one purchase she hadn't thought to make in sunny California. Josy pulled Deborah's sweater more tightly around her and let the men hustle her into the warm cab of the truck.

"I hate to drop you at the door and run," Don told them, "but this snow came in earlier than we expected."

"Don't apologize, Don. I should be back at my own spread right now."

The men talked ranching while Josy tried to see the passing terrain hidden by the falling snow. Was there something valuable about this land?

"Thanks, Don," Adam said as the truck slowed in front of a low frame rambler she could barely discern in the blowing snow. "Come on, Josy."

Snow flogged them toward the front door, which Don assured them he'd left unlocked so they could get inside. Adam pushed it open, letting Josy precede him into the warmth.

"'Bout time you got here," a gravelly masculine voice greeted. A man strode from the hall to the foyer, where he came to an abrupt halt as his startled gaze swept the two of them.

A burly man of average height in his midfifties, he wasn't dressed like a ranch hand. The neatly pressed dress slacks and monogrammed white dress shirt would look more appropriate in an office than a barn. He also wore jewelry, including a thick gold chain at his throat and a gaudy gold ring from which an obscenely large cluster of diamonds winked even in this dim light. Definitely not a ranch hand.

Shock gave way to calculation as he studied them in return. "Well, well, well. Now, this is an unexpected surprise."

Adam shouldered her aside, his body taut. "Who are you?"

A tiny smile played at the corners of that hard mouth. "Enrique Pandergarten."

Josy sucked in a gasp.

"Come in, Mr. Ryser. I wasn't expecting you."

Adam reached for the zipper on his duffel bag, but Pandergarten suddenly held a large black gun in one fist.

"I don't generally shoot people, but I won't hesitate to make an exception. Drop the bag and step into the living room."

Adam dropped the bag in tight-lipped silence. Josy didn't take her eyes from the man as he urged them into a homey, warm room that she would have found comfortable under other circumstances.

Adam had been right after all. Pandergarten had been behind everything. Anger found her voice. "You don't generally shoot people, you just have them shot—is that it?"

The smile widened. It was not a friendly sight. "Precisely. Sit on the couch. You've been a real thorn in my side, lady."

"Glad to hear it."

Adam squeezed her arm in warning as they sat, but she ignored him as her anger mounted.

"You should have stayed dead," he groused.

"You should have done a better job when you threw me down that mountain."

"Still mouthy, I see. No one pitched you off that cliff. You did that all by yourself, running from Vince. All he did was set the scene so it looked like an accident."

"He should have made sure I was dead first."

Pandergarten snorted. "You were so busted up he didn't think that was going to be a problem. You're tougher than you look."

"Is that why you waited so long to finish the job?"

Enrique Pandergarten stared at her from cold dark eyes— a stare just like Mark Wilson's. "If I'd known you were still alive, I'd have seen to the matter a long time ago."

"You don't watch the news?"

Pandergarten looked angry. "You should learn to watch that mouth of yours. It's gonna get you killed. I shoulda had you shot and buried with your mother. People who get shot dead tend to stay that way."

"You killed my mother?" Pain blossomed for the mother she couldn't remember knowing and now never would know. She barely felt Adam's hand on her arm. Rage threatened to choke her.

"Your mother was stupid. She thought being a mistress gave her rights."

Josy trembled. She would have come off the couch if Adam hadn't restrained her.

"What do you want, Pandergarten?" Adam demanded.

The man eyed Adam coldly. "This ranch, for starters."

"Not a chance."

His lips curled. "The property belongs to your god-daughters. Once you're dead, Claussen will sell."

Adam forced himself to remain still. Pandergarten regarded him without emotion, which was more scary than the gun.

"What's so important about this ranch?"

"It's going to be the next Las Vegas," he announced.

"You're crazy." Josy told him.

Pandergarten's eyes narrowed dangerously. "That's what they said when the first casino was built in Vegas, and look how that turned out."

"Except that gambling is illegal in Wyoming," Adam reminded him.

"Temporarily."

"People have tried to legalize it here before."

"Yes, but I've paid a great deal of money to see that this time the bill passes."

"You *paid* Hank?" Adam asked, wondering why Hank would take a bribe. Eleanor's family was old money.

Pandergarten bared his teeth. "I didn't need to pay the good senator and his influential wife. There were other ways. Those two are my ace in the hole. Josy could tell you all about our deal—if she could remember her past." He regarded them with a hard, unwinking stare. "Unfortunately, she doesn't recall our meeting outside her mother's apartment, do you, Josy?"

Tension vibrated from her. Adam wondered how long he could keep her from flying across the room, gun or no gun.

"You don't even remember your mother approaching you outside that hotel in San Diego, do you? She wanted to go to the press with her sad little story. We couldn't have that, so we waited for her to turn up. We knew she'd run to you." His expression tightened. "But you were very uncooperative that morning. Vince still has the scar where you bit him."

"Good."

Adam nearly came off the couch himself, but the gun and the hard expression on Pandergarten's features held him in place. He couldn't figure out why the man hadn't killed them already.

Josy surprised Adam by relaxing slightly. "Don't worry,

he won't shoot, Adam. He still uses his cousin to do all his dirty work.''

Adam laid a warning hand on her shoulder, too late.

"My cousin?" The words were clipped.

"Surely you remember Vince, or should I call him Mark Wilson?"

New alertness charged Pandergarten's expression. "How do you know he's my cousin?"

"I had you investigated," Adam intervened quickly, pressing his fingers painfully into Josy's arm to keep her quiet. He suspected if Pandergarten knew his cousin was dead, he'd pull that trigger without any more talk.

"Why?"

"Because someone had a hand in my disappearance," Josy said, jerking free of Adam's hold. "And you were the only pond scum in sight." She moved to the edge of her seat, practically thrumming with suppressed energy.

"I thought you had amnesia."

"She does," Adam responded quickly. "But you sent that pair of thugs after her in Reno. Remembering that, I wondered if you might still be after her for some other reason."

"You know, Ryser, you're almost as nosy as Josy and her mother."

"If I'm such a threat, why did you wait to come after me?" Josy demanded.

"Claussen neglected to inform me or Vince you were still alive. Vince got a nasty shock when he walked in and found you sitting in the senator's house waiting to have dinner. He called me, and I dropped everything to pay the senator a little visit the next day."

The white Mercedes with the tinted windows, Adam realized. No wonder Hank wouldn't see him after that.

"We agreed it was time to remove you permanently,"

Pandergarten continued. "Claussen *does* watch the news. He's known for some time you were alive. He decided as long as you had amnesia, it didn't matter, but he wasn't totally stupid. He had someone keeping an eye on Ryser. Then he panicked when Ryser *did* find you. The fool tried scaring you off." Pandergarten smiled coldly. "I could have told him it was a waste of time. Me, I'm not that subtle. You should have left her in Hayes," Pandergarten told Adam.

Adam was thinking much the same thing.

"Claussen was afraid she'd recognize him and remember everything. I suspect he sent Vince to the house that night as a sort of test case, to see if her memory would return."

Adam suddenly realized Hank had avoided meeting Josy at every opportunity. He should have caught on to that faster. He moved to the edge of the couch with Josy, wondering if he could rush Pandergarten before the man could pull the trigger.

"So you told your cousin to kill Josy even though her amnesia made her no threat at all," Adam said to keep him talking.

"*If* she really had amnesia. And *if* her memory never returned. Big *ifs,* wouldn't you say, Ryser? Why take chances with a mouthy broad like this one?"

The front door opened on a gust of wind. Pandergarten lifted his head and the gun just slightly. Adam surged off the couch in a low dive. The gun roared as Pandergarten jerked out of the way. Something hot seared Adam's shoulder. He fell to the floor, blood flowing down his back. Josy had come off the couch when he did, but she'd gone to one side. Now she stood poised above him, the fireplace poker in her hands.

"What the hell's going on here?" Hank Claussen demanded.

"Get in and shut the door," Pandergarten said. "Where's Vince? We need to dispose of two more bodies. Put the poker down, Josy."

Adam saw the horrified expression on Hank's face. The man had aged tremendously in the past few days, although for someone who was supposed to be suffering from a back injury, he walked across the room without a trace of a limp or a wince of pain. Another ploy to keep from facing Josy?

"Vince is dead," he told Pandergarten.

Pandergarten swung his gaze back to Adam. He didn't so much as hesitate. He brought the gun into line, and Adam knew he was dead.

The explosive sound of the shot seemed to echo. A bullet plowed into the chair mere inches from Adam's head. But it was Enrique Pandergarten who fell to the floor.

Adam stared in confusion at the small revolver in Hank's hand. Then he realized there had been two shots, nearly simultaneous. His neighbor had gotten off the first shot, saving his life.

"You really know how to make an entrance, Hank," he said shakily, getting to his feet and trying not to be sick to his stomach as fire licked down his arm and back.

"Is he dead?" Hank asked.

Josy crossed to the fallen man, the poker still in her hand. "No. His chest is moving, but he's losing a lot of blood. I'll call 911."

"Stay where you are." The gun swung toward Adam. "It wasn't supposed to happen like this."

Adam kept his voice low and level, battling new fear. "What *was* supposed to happen, Hank?"

"If you'd just left Josy in Hayes, everything would have been fine."

Adam realized Hank was gearing himself up to shoot them.

"I tried scaring her off. I even borrowed a truck off a friend's lot so I could follow you without being noticed."

"You were the one who tried to run us down?" Josy asked in surprise.

"I was trying to scare you into staying put. I went to your apartment first, but you weren't home and a neighbor nearly caught me. When I saw the two of you just standing there on the sidewalk, I gave in to impulse. But you nearly killed me with that rifle!" He sounded outraged.

"Sorry I missed," Josy snapped.

Hank didn't seem to hear. He was staring at her face. "You know, despite all the surgery, you still remind me of your mother," Hank told her wistfully. "She was beautiful."

Josy inhaled sharply. "You were my mother's lover. It was never Pandergarten."

Surprised by her intuitive leap, Adam realized that made sense. If Hank had been supporting a mistress, it gave Pandergarten the perfect leverage to use against him. Eleanor wouldn't have stood for another woman in Hank's life.

"I knew you'd remember eventually," Hank said.

"I didn't remember anything," Josy replied in annoyance. "It's the way you're looking at me."

She took a step closer to him. Adam tried to distract Hank, afraid he'd pull the trigger. "Is that why you tried to kill Josy in the barn that day?"

Hank looked pained. "It just happened—I didn't plan it. I was supposed to meet Brug, but she walked in. I figured that mean-tempered stallion would kill her and it would look like an accident. Only that damn dog got in the way, and then Brug came in."

"Wasn't Brug working for you?" Josy asked, inching closer still.

"He just kept me informed. I was always afraid Adam

would find you. He wouldn't stop looking. Brug and Martha tried to make sure he never saw any of the articles on you, but we missed that one.''

"And I didn't," Adam said. "How much were you paying them to help you?''

"Nothing. Brug wanted to help once I explained Josy was an opportunist. I told him I had proof she intended to take you for a worse ride than Alyssa did. He thought he was protecting you."

And Martha had been protecting Brug, Adam realized.

Josy took another step closer. "You were the one who broke into the house that night, weren't you?''

Hank wasn't wearing gloves today, but if Josy hadn't said something, Adam wouldn't have noticed the telltale scab on the man's bare wrist.

Hank sighed. "I wanted a look at the papers you had on the ranch. Pandergarten was putting all this pressure on me to get you to sell it to him that I thought there must be something valuable here I didn't know about. I was leaving when that damn dog came sniffing around the door and I realized I'd left the key to my friend's truck on your desk. I had to get it back so I waited. When the lights went out, I took a chance, but I ran into her."

He moved the gun in Josy's direction, and Adam's heart nearly stopped. At that range, she'd be dead before she hit the floor.

"So you came back the next day for the key," Adam said quickly to divert him.

"That wasn't me. By then, Vince had seen Josy. I had to tell him what I'd done, and he told me he'd get the key and handle things."

"You mean kill her, don't you."

Hank wouldn't meet his eyes. "I got Brug to take her into town, but I knew he'd just go back. I didn't have any 'choice, Adam. Then the hotshot killer missed and got Martha instead.''

"He could have hit Bitsy,'' Josy said angrily, taking another step toward him.

Again, Adam tried to distract him. "You were willing to let him burn your own granddaughters alive?"

"No! I didn't know about that! I knew he liked setting fires, but I didn't know he was going to do that. The girls weren't in the house, were they?" His features went gray. "Brug said they were spending the night at the Miltons'.''

Brug, who'd wanted to talk to Adam. Who'd probably recognized Wilson when Martha was shot. Who'd come back in time to save their lives.

"I didn't have any choice, Adam,'' Hank repeated sadly.

"You do now. Put the gun down, Hank. We can work this out."

Hank shook his head. Adam saw Josy take another step toward Hank. She was almost in striking range.

"A good lawyer—" he began.

"Don't be stupid. When I realized you'd married Kathy's kid, I knew it was only a matter of time before everything unraveled. Did you know Pandergarten brought them here? Right here to this ranch. That's kidnapping, Adam.''

"Why would he do that? Why didn't he just kill them and dump them in California, or even Mexico?"

"He wanted a better hold on me,'' Hank said wearily. "And I gave it to him. I agreed to meet them here. I offered Kathy and Josy anything for their silence, but Kathy wanted me to divorce Eleanor. She didn't understand my career would have been over.''

"So instead you let Mark Wilson kill her mother?"

"It was an accident! Kathy was furious. She came at me and we struggled. I didn't mean for the gun to go off! Josy broke away and stole my car. She made it into Colorado before Vince caught up. If the car hadn't run out of gas, she might have even gotten away. Vince had to go after her on foot, but she panicked and started climbing Rock Ridge. He said she fell. I was in shock. I didn't know what to do.''

There was a decided tremor in Hank's gun hand.

''Pandergarten said he'd take care of everything. I should just go home and pretend nothing had happened.''

Beads of sweat dotted Hank's forehead. Josy inched into striking distance. Adam wanted to shout to her to stay still. Hank was right on the ragged edge.

''He had the gun. It would tie me to Kathy's murder. I couldn't let her daughter ruin me. You can see that, can't you, Adam?''

Josy swung the poker. Hank raised his arm to deflect the blow, and the gun went off. Adam rushed forward before he could bring it around to fire again. He tried compensating for the numbness in his left arm, but Hank was a big man, and smart enough to capitalize on Adam's injury. Hank brought the gun down in a bone-jarring blow against the wound. Adam collapsed as another shot rent the air.

Hank toppled onto the sofa and didn't move.

Adam strove to push back the black, pain-filled fog rippling at the edges of his mind. He saw Pandergarten through a closing tunnel. The man had half-risen to shoot Hank. As if in slow motion, he saw Pandergarten bring the gun around to point it at him. And he saw Josy raise the poker, smashing it down on Pandergarten's gun hand. Then he saw nothing at all.

Chapter Thirteen

Four months later

Killer jumped to his feet and dashed to the front door. Josy lifted her head from the sample book as a key entered the lock and the apartment door suddenly opened. The dining-room table was spread with wallpaper samples, fabrics and paint chips while a nearby chair held the rolled-up house plans.

Adam entered, pausing to greet Killer while melting snow fell from his coat and hat. Josy spared the patio window a glance and saw a snow shower in progress. Spring-time in Wyoming could bring just about any type of weather, she'd learned.

"What are you doing home? It's only one o'clock," she said, nodding at the wall clock over the table.

He dropped his hat on the chair with the plans and hung his coat in the closet as Josy got to her feet.

"Making any headway?" he asked, indicating the mess on the table.

"Some. The girls are going to decide on their color schemes this afternoon. What's happened?" Josy stared at his ruddy face and the guarded expression it bore. She braced herself for bad news.

Adam rubbed absently at his shoulder, which she knew still ached occasionally from the bullet wound four months ago. The other, internal scars would take more time to heal.

"Do you want some lunch?" she asked.

"I grabbed something at the hospital."

"The hospital?" Fear jabbed her, and her gaze rapidly traveled his body, seeking injuries.

"I'm fine, Josy. Hank died this morning."

"Oh."

She didn't know how to feel about that. The man had tried to kill them. By his own admission, he had killed her mother. Still, part of her mourned his death since he was the only connection she'd had to her mother and the past that was lost to her.

"A blood clot traveled to his heart," Adam continued. "It's for the best. The trial would have been a media circus, and Hank wasn't coping well with the idea of being paralyzed."

Josy shuddered. She hadn't seen Hank since they airlifted him to the hospital in Hayes that day, but Adam had talked to Eleanor several times. They were both amazed that Eleanor had stood by her husband's side. Then again, he'd covered his trail pretty well. Investigators could show that Hank and Pandergarten knew each other, but so far they'd found no evidence to prove he'd been taking bribes, or even that he had been Kathy Smith's lover. Hank refused to say a word.

While investigators searched for her mother's body, Josy accepted the fact that they might never find her. Only Pandergarten could have told them where to look, but he had died en route to the hospital that day.

"Eleanor is moving to Cheyenne to be near her brother. She offered us the use of the big house until the new one is finished," Adam told Josy.

"Are you going to take her up on it?" The two-bedroom furnished apartment they were renting was cramped for the five of them, but she still hoped Adam would choose it over Eleanor's formal house.

"How do you feel?" Adam asked.

"Her house would be closer to the ranch," she said cautiously. "You wouldn't have to commute every day."

Adam sighed. "C'mere and sit down."

Her heart began thumping as she joined him on the ugly tweed couch. For months, they'd put off any personal discussion, having so many other, more urgent matters to take care of. But that was about to change, she realized.

"Brug and Martha are getting married."

Josy blinked at the sudden change in topic. Martha had moved in with Brug after her release from the hospital, but Josy hadn't seen or talked with either one of them. They'd apologized through Adam for their part in the events, and Josy felt no animosity toward them. They were truly remorseful, and they'd had Adam's best interests at heart. She could understand that better than anyone.

"Brug's taking a job with a friend of mine outside Gillette."

"Who's going to run your spread?"

"I'm going to make Pete foreman. He and Tim can hire more hands."

"Oh."

"The house won't be done until this summer," he continued, "but we should finalize our plans."

Her mouth felt dry, and she resisted an urge to rub her hands together nervously.

"Funny. I've never known you to be a coward about anything before."

She jumped at his perception. "Nothing else ever mattered this much before," she told him honestly.

His expression gave away nothing. "Are you planning to stay once the house is done?"

"That was the deal," she began uncomfortably. "I promised Suzie—"

"Forget the deal!"

If only she could.

"You know," he went on more calmly, "my sister once told a friend that getting married was a memory a woman would cherish for the rest of her life."

Where was he going with this?

"Since you don't remember our wedding, I thought we'd do it right this time. A church, the girls, my family—" he reached into his pocket and pulled out a small box "—even a ring. You interested in making a new deal?"

Josy thought her heart might break free its confines and push its way out of her chest and into his waiting hands.

"That depends on what sort of a deal you want to make this time."

He stood so close she inhaled the faint scent of his aftershave.

"I want a permanent contract without loopholes."

A tear slipped down her cheek.

"I love you, Josy. I told you that once before, but you never said anything."

"The house was on fire at our backs. I thought your words were just spoken in the heat of the moment."

"No pun intended?"

More tears leaked from her eyes. "You never said it again."

"I was waiting for you to tell me how you felt."

"I showed you. Every night. In every way I could."

"But you never said the words, Josy. I needed to hear them, too."

"Fool." Her voice was thick with tears and emotion. "I love you so much, Adam."

"Good." His smile wove itself around her soul. "For a minute there, I was worried."

"You're crazy."

"About you, I am. Will you marry me?"

"We're already married." She looked at the wedding set he held and saw there was a man's ring, as well.

"Do you remember our wedding?"

"You know I don't."

"Then we have to do it all over again." He wiped away her tears, but more continued to fall. "This time, I want to make sure you'll always remember me."

Amnesia...
an unknown danger...
a burning desire.
With

HARLEQUIN®

I N T R I G U E®

you're just

A MEMORY AWAY

from passion, danger...
and love!

Look for all the books in this exciting new miniseries:

Missing: One temporary wife
#507 THE MAN SHE MARRIED
by Dani Sinclair in March 1999

Mission: Find a lost identity
#511 LOVER, STRANGER
by Amanda Stevens in April 1999

Seeking: An amnesiac's daughter
#515 A WOMAN OF MYSTERY
by Charlotte Douglas in May 1999

A MEMORY AWAY—where remembering
the truth becomes a matter of life,
death...and love!

Available wherever Harlequin books are sold.

HARLEQUIN®
Makes any time special ™

Look for a new and exciting series from Harlequin!

HARLEQUIN *Duets* ™

Two __new__ full-length novels in one book, from some of your favorite authors!

Starting in May, each month we'll be bringing you two new books, each book containing two brand-new stories about the lighter side of love! Double the pleasure, double the romance, for less than the cost of two regular romance titles!

Look for these two new Harlequin Duets™ titles in May 1999:

Book 1:
WITH A STETSON AND A SMILE
by Vicki Lewis Thompson
THE BRIDESMAID'S BET
by Christie Ridgway

Book 2:
KIDNAPPED? by Jacqueline Diamond
I GOT YOU, BABE by Bonnie Tucker

2 GREAT STORIES BY 2 GREAT AUTHORS FOR 1 LOW PRICE!

Don't miss it! Available May 1999 at your favorite retail outlet.

HARLEQUIN®
Makes any time special.™

Look us up on-line at: http://www.romance.net   HDGENR

HARLEQUIN®

I N T R I G U E ®

COMING NEXT MONTH

#509 THE BRIDE'S PROTECTOR by Gayle Wilson
Men of Mystery

When CIA agent Lucas Hawkins rescues a bride-to-be from assassins, his only thought is to get the beautiful Tyler Stewart to safety. Now Tyler is the only person who can clear his name, but only if he can keep her alive....

#510 REDHAWK'S RETURN by Aimée Thurlo
The Brothers of Rock Ridge

Travis Redhawk had sworn a blood oath that he'd always be there for Katrina Johnson in times of need. Now that danger surrounds Katrina at every turn, is Travis strong enough to be the man Katrina needs—and wants?

#511 LOVER, STRANGER by Amanda Stevens
A Memory Away...

Who was Dr. Ethan Hunter? The greedy, selfish man others described, or the strong, honorable doctor standing before FBI agent Grace Donovan? Grace's investigation—and her life—depended on Ethan regaining his memory. But if he did, would she lose the only man she could ever love?

#512 HIS SECRET SON by Jacqueline Diamond

Joni Peterson woke up next to the body of her ex-husband, with no memory of killing him, although the evidence against her was damning. She turned to the only man she could trust, Dirk Peterson, her husband's estranged brother—and her son's secret father....